M000042324

Heatherfield

Heatherfield

M. Jean Pike

Black Lyon Publishing, LLC

HEATHERFIELD
Copyright © 2008 by M. Jean Pike

All rights reserved. No part of this book may be used or reproduced in any way by any means without the written permission of the publisher, except in the case of brief quotations embodied in critical articles and reviews.

Please note that if you have purchased this book without a cover or in any way marked as an advance reading copy, you have purchased a stolen item, and neither the author nor the publisher has been compensated for their work.

Our books may be ordered through your local bookstore or by visiting:

www.BlackLyonPublishing.com

Black Lyon Publishing, LLC
PO Box 567
Baker City, OR 97814

This is a work of fiction. All of the characters, names, events, organizations and conversations in this novel are either the products of the author's vivid imagination or are used in a fictitious way for the purposes of this story.

ISBN-10:   0-9793252-8-5
ISBN-13:   978-0-9793252-8-1
Library of Congress Control Number: 2007937933

Written, published and printed in
the United States of America.

Black Lyon Paranormal Romance

For Noah,
who is and will always be
my greatest accomplishment.

Acknowledgments:

The writing of this novel was a two-year process, a twenty-four month roller coaster ride of despair and euphoria during which I would have given up at least a hundred times if not for the support and encouragement of many: Marilyn Meredith, who gently guided my footsteps throughout the plotting of this story. Elizabeth Parsons, who lent her expertise as a poet, and her ear as a friend. Loretta Proctor, who believed in Tory and Jake even when I didn't. Todd, who never stopped believing in me, and who never allowed me to stop believing in myself. Kerry Jones at Black Lyon Publishing, whose support, vision and energy brought the dream full circle. From the bottom of my heart, thanks!   -M. Jean Pike.

Prologue
Heatherfield
1949

It had no business growing there, or so the old-timers said. The soil was rich and fertile, the drainage generally good. It was western New York state, where rain and snow could be counted on for at least thirty-four inches of precipitation each year and the average growing season lasted 130 days. It was potato country, for God's sake, not the British Islands.

It grew all the same, growing with a vengeance in the fields below the softly sloping hillsides, with thick carpets of purplish red bells that trilled silently from the first spring breezes until October, when the snow came again.

It was heather.

Legend told that a band of gentle fairies, wishing to escape the wrath of angry Thor, fled across the seas. Finding open country on the other side, they scattered the seeds of joy bells to mark their safe passage. Where the seeds took root and grew, the fairies remained, calling that land blessed.

In all of North America, it grew only there.

That was the kind of place Heatherfield was—magical, a place where anything might happen.

At least, that's how the old-timers would've told it had anyone cared to listen. Most of Heatherfield's 18,000 residents were newcomers who didn't care.

The old-timers said things changed after the war. A flood of GIs streamed back to the home front, took wives and made babies. They multiplied like mice until the cities split at the seams with the weight of them. They spilled over the boundaries of Rochester, fifty miles north, desperate for places with clean air, shady parks and good schools for their children—places like Heatherfield.

It was '47 or thereabouts, when the ruthless hands of progress came in the form of snorting bulldozers and big yellow earthmovers, with the words Matthews Developing printed crisply on their sides. They dug up the heather until it was no more. In its place, they planted rows of tiny look-alike houses, all white, which the newcomers bought up like boxes of Cracker Jacks and called Victory Park.

The old-timers called it a sin.

The last of the heather bells wept quietly in a fifty-acre filed at the base of a densely wooded hillside known to old-timers as Zed Benjamin's place. The fact Zed had been dead since '22 was beside the point. When he passed on of polio, the land went to Jedediah. A logging accident ended his life in '44, and the property passed by rights to his only son, known to the old-timers as young Jake. To the newcomers, he was Sir.

It was whispered in town, on the rare occasions when he went down from the mountain, that the scars inside Jake Benjamin went deeper than the ones the war left on the outside. Newcomers knew nothing of the starry-eyed boy who left Heatherfield in '42. They knew only that the mountain of a mountain man, whose haunted eyes stared from a lacerated face, was rumored to tramp the forest at night, communing with the spirits of the dead. Other vets assumed he was shell-shocked, that he wasn't right and was probably dangerous.

At that, the old-timers scoffed. Sure, he came home different, but he'd come home! If he preferred to hole up on his land like a hermit, what of it? It was his land, by God, land he staunchly refused to sacrifice on the altar of progress. That, even more than the Bronze Star or Purple Heart he won, made Jake Benjamin a hero to the old-timers, who frowned on progress.

What business they had, they did on Old Main Street, the block of tired, red-brick buildings that once comprised Heatherfield's entire business district. Most were abandoned, their dusty windows staring like vacant, glassy eyes at the sidewalk that was empty of all but a handful of old-timers who still patronized Milady's Salon, Old Main

Smoke Shop, and Parker's Drugstore.

The newcomers preferred it that way. Who wanted a bunch of dinosaurs puttering about the plaza, pushing Bible verses and cautious advice? It was all superstitious nonsense.

The newcomers were superstitious in the way only young people were of anything that might threaten their carefree lives. They went about their business, ignoring such unpleasantness as the Cold War and the distant rumble of racial unrest. Life was good in Heatherfield, filled with modern wonders like Tupperware, Frank Sinatra and cake mixes that came in a box.

Most of the men worked at the buckwheat mill, just south of town. Others commuted to Rochester where they were stockbrokers, lawyers and dentists. The women never left Heatherfield at all. Why return to the city? They had everything they needed right there.

Pierce Matthews saw to that. He appeared in the plaza every day, a handsome man with startlingly blue eyes that continually moved over his creation, never quite getting their fill. He stopped to talk to the shopkeepers about business or baseball, depending on his mood. They altered theirs accordingly, as would the waitresses at the Stardust Diner where he ate his lunch just like an ordinary man.

To the newcomers, Pierce Matthews was no ordinary man.

He was a man of vision.

On a huge expanse of wasted potential that had been the Heatherfield Hotel, the tumble-down remains of a 1920s speakeasy, he saw a park, a shady plot with fountains, benches and cobbled paths where salesgirls could go on their lunch hour to stretch their lovely legs.

In the horseshoe of tarpaper shanties that encircled the park, he saw a bustling plaza. The first block he dedicated solely to the newcomer's entertainment. He put in bowling alleys, restaurants, dance halls and a movie house where the sparkling marquis announced *Movies Shown Every Saturday Night!*

In the second block facing the park, he soldiered a row of trim white shops with perky green awnings that happily sold the newcomers everything they needed or wanted, from toilet seats to toilet water, or so the advertisements read. The shops marched around the corner and stopped abruptly, though, where Pierce Matthews' vision was shattered.

Between Newman's Haberdashery and Bonner's Department Store, like a middle finger thrown from a dainty white-gloved hand, a weathered, two-story building squatted in a ragweed plot as if a strong wind lifted it from John Steinbeck's Cannery Row and carelessly set it there among the broken soda bottles and tattered newspapers.

Three crooked steps, jutting from a broken sidewalk, led to a porch where summer and winter a screen door yawned open on rusting hinges. Above the door, like a belligerent child, a jaunty red sign shouted its name.

Penny Candy's.

To newcomers, Penny Candy's was a firetrap and a disgrace.

To the handful of tourists who straggled through town each summer on their way to the lake, it was a quaint oddity.

To Pierce Matthews, president of Matthews' Developing, it was a continual source of vexation, a gray-shingled blot on the face of his love child.

Like it or not, it seemed the aged variety store, which squatted on its crumbling foundation through two World Wars and the Great Depression, was charmed.

It was there to stay, as much a part of Heatherfield as the unseen forces that governed it.

PART ONE
CORNING, NEW YORK
1999

Chapter One

"Will you come and get me?" The small, terrified voice echoed in Tory's head as she sped out State Route 415 past the sleeping city and deeper into the night. It was the voice of a child in trouble—her child. No, that wasn't quite right.

Please, Tory. Hurry.

"I will," she whispered.

She couldn't. It was like one of those awful dreams in which the pursued dreamer was rooted to the ground, wanting to run but unable to move. Tory wasn't running away from danger. She was moving straight toward it. Though the needle on the speedometer climbed to eighty, her destination seemed farther away every minute.

Hurry!

She felt the car fishtail and eased off the accelerator. Her slick hands gripped the steering wheel. It was snowing, but that wasn't quite right, either. She never saw snow like that before. It was as if her car was shrouded in a thick, white veil, but the road reflected in her headlights was dry.

She hugged the steering wheel, squinting through the windshield. She mustn't miss the turnoff. Her child was in trouble.

Will you come and get me?

Despite her mounting sense of urgency, she eased off the gas even more. Her instincts told her what her eyes couldn't see—the curve was just ahead. Fear clawed at her insides. She must be very careful.

She eased into the turn, barely breathing. *So far, so good,* she thought, slowing to forty, praying. *Please, God, let it be all right.*

Please hurry!

"I can't," she whispered. "Not just now."

She rounded a sharp bend and was almost across the bridge when the truck appeared. Two white lights like wide, startled eyes sliced a path through the snow directly toward her.

"No!" She jerked the wheel to the left, clipped the side of the bridge, and slammed back into her own lane. The truck struck her car's rear, sending her spinning into a guardrail.

With a mind-shattering crash, she tore through it—and then she was airborne, floating through the clouds. The whiteness that seemed to have swallowed her was broken only by the taillights of the departing truck. They blinked twice, then disappeared around the bend.

When she opened her eyes, she stood shivering in a forest.

The whiteness clung to her like a cold wet blanket. She peered into a grove of trees where her blood-spattered car was twisted like a big, red question mark around the base of an evergreen. Beside the broken car, a woman lay facedown on a blanket of pine needles. Her hand was raised, beckoning.

Don't look! a voice warned.

Tory recognized the body as hers. She walked closer to the small hand and saw a thin silver band, her mother's wedding ring, on the index finger. She took another, uncertain step. "Mama?"

No! Don't!

She dropped to her knees and touched a pale braid matted with blood. "Mama?"

No voice answered except the wind whispering in the trees. She gently rolled the body over. The quiet white face was hers, and she screamed.

When her screams tapered off into faint, choked sobs, Tory lay wide-eyed in the half-light. Her raw throat needed water, though her face and hands were drenched ...

That much had been true, anyway. Drumming rain beat against her window. She took a deep breath and slowly released it.

Relax.

The light of a street lamp spilled through her window, casting shadows against her bedroom walls. Her glance crept across the room, caressing objects that never looked more dear—her bureau, bookcase, and messy computer desk, strewn with folders, photographs and the stumps of spent candles.

Relax.

The digital clock beside her bed read four o'clock AM. Swinging her legs over the side, she pulled on a terrycloth robe. There would be no more sleep that night. She walked down the hall to her kitchen where she measured three generous scoops of Maxwell House into her coffee maker instead of her usual two.

It would be a long day.

Moments later, she stood under the hot shower spray, still shivering.

She'd been having the dream for as long as she could remember. Once or twice a year when she was a child, her blood-curdling screams sent her mother racing to her bedroom in the middle of the night.

She pulled Tory into her pillow-soft middle, stroking her hair. "It's all right, Victoria. Honey, it was only a dream." Her gentle murmur chased away the nightmare.

When Tory reached her teens, the dream came more frequently. By then, her mother was dead, so she faced the terror alone. She remembered lying in bed, screaming into her pillow, as afraid of disturbing her father as of the nightmare.

By the time she reached her twenties, she had the dream every month. During the past month, it came every night. Most of the dream didn't make sense, but she supposed nightmares rarely did. The only realities were the terror and confusion it brought to her otherwise-healthy psyche.

She worked a handful of jasmine-scented shampoo into her unruly blonde curls, wondering again whether the dream was a warning. That was an unpleasant thought, so she firmly pushed it from her mind.

By five o'clock, she was sitting over her second cup of coffee, dressed in a short, white skirt and her favorite pale-blue blouse. It was the same shade as her eyes, she'd often been told. Her curls, now plaited into submission, hung damply between her shoulder blades. The scents of lavender and eucalyptus candles filled the kitchen, where she sat with her head bent over a file labeled *Gibson, Alison*.

"Well, Counselor," she said, sighing, "you wanted a challenging career. I'd say you got it."

She hadn't doubled up on her classes and finished high school at the age of sixteen just to work for Women, Incorporated. She applied to the University of Rochester as much to escape home, where she felt unwanted, as to earn her bachelor's degree in human services.

She met Kate while interning at an East Rochester safe house. Kate, a fellow Corningite, was a bulldog of a boss with a heart of gold. She dreamed of starting an agency back home and making a difference. Over the space of one year, one hundred bottles of Chablis and as many debates over feminism and social injustice, she convinced Tory to come with her.

Tory flipped through Alison Gibson's file, reviewing her earlier notes, twisting the end of her braid as she read. *I must be a masochist to be this much in love with a job that as often as not breaks my heart*, she thought.

Initially, she recommended four hours' counseling per week for the young rape victim, along with weekly support group and monthly reevaluation. Despite Tory's strong recommendation, Alison resisted the idea of putting up her unborn child for adoption.

One year later, it was clear she wasn't adjusting to her infant son. A frown creased Tory's brow as she read her notes from the previous day. *Client seems agitated and displays hostility toward this counselor. Episodes of weepiness ...*

Stressed young mothers made Tory nervous.

She made a note to bump the counseling up to six hours a week. She'd fit it in somehow, and recommended the eighteen-year-old receive bi-weekly in-home visitation.

She printed the word "advise" in bold, red letters across the file, underlined it twice and set it aside, then reached for a file labeled *Reeves, Francesca.*

Flipping through the file, her earlier notes made her smile. Tory hadn't thought the girl would make it. Frankie was her biggest success story, and God knew in four years spent working with battered women, she hadn't seen nearly enough stories with happy endings.

She smiled again. In her best scrolling hand, she made the recommendation for Frankie to be relocated from the battered women's shelter to one of their support apartments. Her arguments listed in favor of the move were merely a formality. Kate trusted her judgment implicitly.

At seven o'clock, her paperwork done, she slid open the oversized window in her living room to let in the cool morning breeze. The rain had stopped, but sparkling beads of wetness clung to the city, making it live up to its name as the Crystal City.

Pressing her forehead against the glass, she hungrily inhaled the spring morning. Lights flickered on across the bridge as the city awoke.

By afternoon, the quiet streets would be a confusion of tourists come to view the ancient art and Steuben glass for which the city was famous.

Her gaze went to the parking lot under her window, where a faint prism enveloped the metallic silver coat of her Mitsubishi Eclipse, loaded with safety features. A horrible drain on the budget, she thought, but worth its weight in peace of mind.

She glanced gratefully into the brightening sky. It was April. Months away from snow.

•

Eighty miles north, Roy Ramsey was having the same thought. March went out like a lion. The insurance adjuster told him it was El Niño, that problem child of Mother Nature who dumped six feet of snow on his East Rochester warehouse and collapsed the roof.

"The pillow fight of the century," the adjuster joked.

To Roy, it was no laughing matter. Losing his two best trucks put him weeks behind schedule.

He sniffed appreciatively at the crisp morning air, gulped the last dregs of coffee from his styrofoam cup and climbed behind the wheel of his extended van. He no sooner turned on the two-way radio than Rosemary's voice crackled through it.

"Roy? Are we copacetic here?"

He gritted his teeth and reminded himself she worked for minimum wage.

"I'm here, Rosie."

"Can you squeeze in a last-minute run to Canandaigua this afternoon?" She popped her gum in the background. "Or should I throw it to Slim?"

He shook his head. She didn't get it. It was Friday. An extra run meant paying Slim overtime. There was no point to that. He could load up, drop the junk off in Savona, shoot over to Corning with the books and be back by one if he didn't stop for lunch.

"No. I'm good, Rosie. I'll take it."

"Ten-four."

He heard one last pop of her gum before the radio was silent. He pulled onto the boulevard, narrowly missing the front end of a champagne-colored Cadillac. The driver blared his horn, and Roy waved Italian style. Lead, follow or get the hell out of the way was his motto. He hadn't gotten where he was by being cautious.

After only three years in business, Ramsey Express was the biggest of the little guys, employing six drivers and Rosemary. He made a name for himself by being twice as fast and half the cost of the larger companies. Now he pulled in contracts from all over western New York and northern Pennsylvania and could charge whatever he liked.

He maneuvered his way across the city and pulled into the driveway of the Lyle Avenue address on his work order, cursing a Ryder truck that blocked his way. Before he could get out and curse it up close and personal, a woman barged up to his window.

"You with the trucking company?" she barked.

He jerked his thumb at the side of the van, which bore the bold red, white and blue words *Ramsey Express—We Deliver.*

"What tipped you off?"

"The movers are unloading in front," she said through thin lips. "You're to load up in back." She turned and marched toward a large outbuilding behind the house.

He ground his gears and eased past the Ryder, his eyes on the woman's small, tight butt. She was just the sort of woman he hated, rich and wearing nice clothes.

"Probably had everything she ever wanted passed to her on a silver plate," he muttered.

When he stepped from the van, she said, "Everything's here in the garage. I moved it here to avoid confusion. The new owners want to take possession of the house immediately, as you can see."

Roy squinted into the dusty barn, calculating and ignoring Miss Rich and her platoon-sergeant voice.

"I held an estate sale last week. I was fortunate to unload these leftovers. I couldn't bear the thought of grandmother's things on display at the Goodwill Center. She was such a proud woman."

Roy saw six small pieces of furniture and about a dozen boxes. It would be tight, but he should have enough room left over for the pallet of books waiting in Henrietta.

"She was a famous novelist, you know. The antique dealer in Savona contacted me right out of the blue, saying he'd buy all that was left, sight unseen."

Roy grunted. A carryover from his six years as a bartender seemed to be an aura he was cursed with that made people want to tell him things. He couldn't go to the supermarket without some poor slob pouring out his life story to him, complete with pictures—as if he gave a damn.

The woman hovered at his side as he loaded the boxes into his van.

"This house has been in my family for generations," she sniveled. "My sister inherited it in 1972 when Grandmother died. Now she's marrying. It's been a dreadful ordeal all the way around."

His eyes darted from her sagging breasts to her unadorned left hand. Everything about the woman screamed desperate! He grunted and slammed shut the doors. Standing beside her in the driveway, he shifted his weight from foot to foot as she sniffled into a soggy tissue. If there was one thing Roy Ramsey couldn't bear, it was a woman in tears. He laid a meaty hand on her shoulder, patted it clumsily and withdrew it.

"I'm sorry," she said, wiping her eyes. "Here. For your trouble." Producing a twenty from her sleeve, she pressed it into his hand, a gesture Roy took as the ultimate insult. She treated him like the hired help, not the owner of a thriving business.

He stuffed the money into his pocket.

At 7:35, he pulled into the parking lot of the Henrietta warehouse right on time. A young kid in baggy jeans and a Red Dog baseball cap checked the papers and waved Roy toward the second bay. After a fruitless five-minute search for the pallet labeled Hardback's/Corning, Red Dog redirected Roy to bay three.

"Sorry," he mumbled. "My mind's not on it today."

Roy grunted and checked his watch. He'd lost six minutes. Cursing silently, he opened the van's rear doors then stood aside, impatiently tapping his foot as Red Dog mounted a forklift. He set the pallet crookedly into the van, tearing one of the boxes from the estate sale.

Roy cursed loudly, but the kid merely shrugged.

"Sorry," he said. "My girlfriend moved out last night. We've been together two years."

Roy pulled out his utility knife and sliced through the tape sealing the box, imagining crushed crystal or shattered Depression glass.

He braced himself as he tore back the flaps.

With a sigh of relief, he whistled. "Just some old paperbacks." He laughed and kicked the box to one side of the van. "Mildewed, anyway."

"Two whole years we were together," Red Dog said mournfully. "Wanna see her picture?"

Ten minutes later, Roy maneuvered into the swell of traffic on Route 390, whistling. The morning was clear, and the traffic, relatively light. He could make up the lost sixteen minutes once he got past Mt. Morris. From there, the drive would be easy.

•

Clyde Hardback opened his bookstore at precisely eight o'clock, just as he'd done every weekday morning since 1948. Leaning on a hand-carved walking stick, he moved to the coffee bar, putting three shining silver coffeepots to work for Cappuccino, French vanilla and, for his health-conscious customers, a weak pot of decaf.

He restocked a display of gourmet coffees that sat at the end of the bar like a no-pressure salesman, just like Clyde. Humming cheerfully, he retrieved a dust cloth from behind the counter and began wiping down the display case he had reserved at the front of the store. He shook his head at the empty space. He hoped the books he ordered would arrive that day. He was hosting a reading the following night, something that always generated interest in dead poets and blank journals.

His old heart skipped a beat as he thought about the upcoming event. More than the stepped-up sales and the interest the monthly readings generated in his fifty-year-old store, Clyde Hardback delight-ed in doing his part to keep culture alive. Literature was the one love left in his seventy-six-year-old life. There were few pleasures to equal seeing the spark of knowledge ignite in a young person's eyes and to know he played a role in passing on that love.

He resumed dusting.

The grandfather clock in the corner chimed eight-fifteen. He put away his cloth. It was time for his daily reading session. He shuffled down the aisle labeled *Poetry* and stood for a moment.

Byron? he wondered. Yeats? Tennyson? So many books, so little time left.

He sighed.

He pulled a leather-bound copy of *Book of Major Poets* from the shelf and settled into his favorite wingback chair when the phone rang. He set down the book and hobbled back across the room.

"Good morning. Clyde Hardback's."

"Clyde? It's Sonya."

"Sonya, my dear. How are you this beautiful morning?"

"Not well, I'm afraid." She coughed into the phone as if to prove it. "I seem to have come down with a touch of the flu."

"I'm sorry to hear that."

"I hate to let you down, but I'm afraid I won't be able to make the trip out tomorrow night after all." She coughed again. "Doctor's orders."

"Oh, dear. Well, that's perfectly understandable." He forced disappointment from his voice. The New York City poet had recently published her third volume, so she would've been his biggest drawing card.

"I feel terrible to let you down like this."

"Think nothing of it, my dear."

"I've Fed Exed a few dozen signed copies of my new book. Can you get someone to stand in for me?"

"I'm sure any one of the ladies in the poetry society would jump at the chance," he said, grimacing. "Get well, my dear."

Moments later, he hung up, his mind running over the possibilities. It had to be someone with the voice of a seraph to do justice to Sonya Spaulding's work. Who could he find at such a late date?

•

Twenty minutes outside Savona, Roy Ramsey felt ill. *There must be a flu bug going around*, he thought.

He pressed the back of his hand to his forehead. He was burning up with fever. He rolled the window down, but the cool air didn't dispel the fire inside his brain. Beginning to hallucinate, he thought he heard the distant rumble of gunfire.

"Hell, Ramsey, get a grip," he told himself. "You're coming unglued, Old Man."

It must've been a semi running over the rumble strips along the side of the highway. He glanced in the rearview mirror and saw only an Escort heading westbound on the other side of the median.

"Funny. I could've sworn ..."

The rest of the sentence was drowned out by the sound of grenades. A putrid odor assaulted his senses, taking him back twenty years to his twelfth summer.

He spent that July at his cousin's farm in Lancaster, Pennsylvania. He and Al were goofing around in the barn when Al suggested they play bank robbers. They filled squirt guns with water from Aunt Ruth's rain barrel. When that ran out, they graduated to a can of gasoline Uncle Gus kept in the barn for his John Deere tractor.

Tired of the game, they went to the loft to smoke the Lucky Strike cigarette they'd boosted from Uncle Gus' pack. Al lit a match, and the loft was instantly filled with flames and shrieks of pain—and the most horrid stench Roy ever knew, one he would remember the rest of his life. It was the stench of burning flesh.

He pulled to the shoulder, bolted from the van and vomited beside the highway.

Somehow, he made it to Savona. He pulled into the parking lot of the Antique Place and honked the horn, too weak to get out, then he sat there, moaning and mopping his forehead while the dealer and his son unloaded the van.

"Are these ours?" The dealer indicated the pallet of books.

"No," Roy wheezed. "All the books go to Corning, a place called Hardback's."

"Sure you can make it that far? You don't look so good."

"I never felt better," he growled, grinding gears as he drove off toward Corning. The world spun crazily around him.

He drove for six miles with his head out the window, his lungs grabbing for air. Without warning, the sky erupted in a bloody mushroom cloud. Hot, searing pain tore through the left side of his face. He screamed, then slowly pulled over to the shoulder again.

He sat for a moment, moaning and clasping his cheek.

What more? he wondered.

It wasn't bad enough to be running a fever. He had to be stung by a damn bee, too? When the pain subsided to a faint tingle, he jerked the rearview mirror to one side and pulled his hand away, expecting to see the angry knot of a hornet's sting.

There was nothing.

Sheer force of will propelled him the last five miles to Corning. He swung into an alley behind the Market Street bookstore and leaned on the horn. An old man with a long, gray ponytail and cane appeared at the back door and shuffled across the alley until he reached Roy's window.

"May I help you?"

"I've got a load of books for a dude named Clyde Hardback."

"Wonderful. I've been expecting you."

"You Hardback?"

"In the flesh."

Roy groaned and dragged himself from the van. The man had to be eighty years old.

"Why don't you sit tight, Son?" Hardback asked. "I'll get them.

You're not looking well."

Roy cursed under his breath. *Why do these old dudes think they're all twenty years old?* he wondered. *All I need is to have an old fart keel over on my tab.*

"Naw. I'll get 'em."

He stepped into the back of the van, cursing again when he saw the damaged box still sitting beside the pallet. Why hadn't he checked the order after the dealer and his son were through unloading?

He stared at the box, indecision swirling through his brain. Getting back off the highway would cost him another fifteen minutes and the dealer had checked the ODC box, for Order Delivered Complete.

Roy shrugged. What was the big deal? They'd never miss one stinking box of books.

He hefted the box of paperbacks from the van as he heard more distant gunfire. He shook his head. God, he was sick. He couldn't remember being that sick before.

He carried the last box into the store and set it on the floor. The old man pointed a bony finger at the junk-sale box.

"That one seems damaged," he said.

"It's a freebie," Roy said quickly. "The warehouse threw it in. No charge."

The old man frowned as he sifted through the box. "Why would they send me a box of used books?"

Roy shrugged. "No telling."

"Would you mind taking it over there, to the aisle marked Bargain Row?"

"Sure thing." Roy carried the hated box across the store and dumped it in the aisle, glad to be rid of it.

Moments later, the old man followed Roy to his van, scrawled his name on the paperwork, and handed it through the window.

"It's a long drive back to Rochester. Sure you'll make it all right?"

"I'll be great." Roy stuffed the work order into his shirt. "Right as rain."

Oddly enough, by the time he exited Denison Parkway and crawled into the westbound lane that led to Rochester, he was.

Chapter Two

Later that morning, while the Ramsey Express van barreled back toward Rochester, Tory nudged her Mitsubishi into what appeared to be the last available parking place in the city of Corning.

Market Street was bustling, beautifully chaotic with lost tourists, truant teens, and hustling office girls. She shrugged out of her jacket, tossed it onto the back seat, and stepped from the car. After she pressed the autolock button on her key ring, the car gave two soft beeps that sent a pair of flustered mourning doves fluttering to the roof of a nearby shop.

Tory walked down the block, exchanging a smile with a shopkeeper who wheeled his racks of T-shirts onto the sidewalk. It was one of those winter-is-over-at-last smiles only upstate New Yorkers in April understood.

She breezed past the work crew who affixed bright baskets of geraniums to the street lamps, forgiving their Neanderthal grunts of appreciation. It was spring and she was healthy and twenty-seven. It was great to be alive.

Across the river, a factory whistle mourned the coming hour. As if on cue, the perky rhythms of Jewel and Natalie Merchant spilled from open café doors. She and Frankie would eat in the square that day, under sunshine and striped table umbrellas.

She stopped at her bank to cash her paycheck, then ducked into the florist's to buy Frankie a sunny bouquet of daffodils.

The young man behind the counter eyed her legs as he wrapped the bouquet with a cheery red ribbon. Tory handed him a twenty-dollar bill, which he held up to the light.

"Crisp," he said. "Just printed today?"

Even the tired old joke seemed fresh on that first-of-spring morning. Tory rewarded him with a smile then stepped back onto the street, her nose pressed into the bouquet. The agency frowned on counselors giving gifts to clients, but Tory Sasser wasn't averse to bending a few arbitrary rules. If ever flowers were in order, she thought, patting the other gift tucked in her skirt pocket, it was that day.

She slowed as she passed Clyde Hardback's Books of Distinction. *No*, she thought. *I'd better not stop.*

She was pressed for time and Clyde's was a dangerous place for her. In there, minutes became hours, and a newly cashed paycheck was reduced to nothing but a handful of change. She took a moment to read a poster in the window, which boldly advertised a poetry reading.

Express Yourself! it demanded.

She hurried on, making a mental note to stop later.

When she entered the square at twelve-fifteen, Frankie sipped lemonade at a glass-topped table, looking lovely in a sage-colored jacket and skirt that was a discount store rip-off of the designer clothing Tory often wore.

Frankie's olive skin was radiant. Her hair was pulled back into a dark, glossy version of Tory's own trademark plait. *That's a far cry from the smartass punk with the kicked-puppy eyes who was added to my case load six months ago*, Tory thought with a smile.

When Frankie noticed her, she grinned hard enough to almost erase twelve of her nineteen years. "Over here, Tory!" She waved.

Tory slid into the opposite chair.

"It ain't like you to be late," Frankie scolded. "I was starting to worry that you wouldn't show."

"And miss lunch with my favorite banker? Not a chance."

"Bank teller."

"Head teller." She handed Frankie the bouquet. "I'm really proud of you, Frankie."

Frankie beamed and set the bouquet in her drinking glass. Then her brows furrowed. "Tory, I got something to …"

"How are you ladies doing today?" A waiter, cute in a Ricky Martin way, set two menus on the table, accidentally brushing Frankie's hand. She blushed, pulling her hands to her lap.

"Our specials today are pretty amazing." He stared into Tory's eyes. "California Medley, Cajun Chicken, and egg and olive croissant. Your choice of side. Six and a quarter each."

The golden thread of his voice seemed to tie Frankie's tongue into knots. She blushed, tried to speak, but failed.

"We'll need a few minutes," Tory said.

"Take your time." He winked. "You two are great advertising."

Frankie watched him walk back into the café. "He was nice."

Tory chuckled. "That's one adjective."

"Get anything you want," Frankie said, flipping open her menu. "It's on me."

Tory smiled behind her menu, feeling like a mother on her kid's first day of school.

As Frankie bubbled about her new promotion, Tory's thoughts drifted to the lovely weekend ahead. Like a hard-won hundred-dollar bill, she was free to spend it as she wished. She promised herself an extra-long run in Denison Park, then an equally long soak in the tub with a bottle of bubble bath and a new book.

"... a dozen sweetheart roses. That's a lot, don't you think?"

Her attention snapped back to the present. "I'm sorry, Frankie. What did you say?"

"I asked how much a guy would pay for a dozen roses."

"I don't know. Why?"

Frankie shrugged. "No reason."

A smile tugged at the corners of Tory's lips. "Did some guy buy you flowers?"

She shrugged again.

When they finished their lunch, the waiter returned to clear the table. Once he was safely out of earshot, Tory slipped the other gift from her pocket and set it on the table.

Frankie reached for the small, silver key. "What's this?"

"I've talked to Kate," Tory said. "She agrees you're ready to move out of the shelter. One of our north side apartments just became available last week. It's small, but the rent's low. You can move in as soon as you like."

She sat back and waited for Frankie's face to light up. Instead, she tapped the key back toward Tory. "Hang onto that, Tory. I might not need it."

Tory watched her carefully, trying to read her.

"I might be moving back in with Zach."

Tory's club sandwich cart wheeled in her stomach. She took a soft breath and slowly released it. "Do you think that's wise, Frankie?"

"He's sorry for what he did. He's changed."

Tory tapped her finger against her lips to check the rash words that threatened to tumble out. "He's been through rehab?"

"No." Frankie lowered her eyes.

"He has given up the drinking and drugs, though?"

"He's going to."

Tory slapped the table in exasperation. "Get your head out of the clouds, Frankie."

"I believe in him, Tory. He says I'm the only one who ever has. Please don't be mad. He needs me," she added meekly.

"He broke your nose, Francesca. What makes you think he won't do it again?"

"He said he wouldn't." Frankie stared miserably at her hands while Tory struggled to detach herself.

"I'd advise you to start slowly," she said crisply. "Short dates in public places."

"I'm going home for the weekend."

Tory heard an alarm shriek in her head. She thought of an isolated farm in Savona, fifteen lonely miles outside the city and the day she took a battered, trembling Frankie escorted by a State Trooper there to retrieve her clothes. Mostly, she thought of Zach's junkyard-dog eyes and how they followed Frankie's every move.

"God help you," Tory whispered.

Suddenly, the sun seemed glaringly bright on the sidewalk. Tory felt a headache creeping up the back of her neck. She pulled a scrap of paper from her purse, scribbled down a number and handed it to Frankie.

"That's my pager. I want you to promise you'll call if you have any trouble this weekend."

"Don't worry." Frankie gave her a quick hug and slipped the scrap of paper into her purse. "I know what you're thinking, and you're wrong. He loves me, Tory."

Tory watched until the double doors of Key Bank swallowed up Frankie, a sense of foreboding choking out her earlier joy. She doubted even an hour at Hardback's could revive her spirits. She made a fist and lightly struck her thigh, fighting back tears.

He loves me.

Four years of battered women coming and going through her life like it was a revolving door had shown Tory what a man's so-called love could do to women like Frankie. They were so starved for human touch they were willing to believe broken bones somehow translated into love.

Tory knew better. She didn't need love. Men were like evil spirits. Her credo was, if she didn't believe in them, they couldn't hurt her.

Chapter Three

Clyde Hardback's was a smaller, cozier version of Barnes and Noble. The free self-serve coffee bar offered only three selections. When the occasional tourist commented on how charmingly Clyde reproduced his big-name competitor, Clyde gently but firmly pointed out he'd been there for over fifty years. The larger store had copied him.

The three-story, turn-of-the-century building had served humbly as a lunch counter and drugstore from the twenties until a fire forced Clyde's parents to board it up in 1939. When he reopened it as a bookstore in '48, Clyde repaired the melted tin ceiling and restored, as best he could, the original woodwork. He added oriental rugs, a sound system and richly upholstered chairs. By way of tribute, he kept his father's signs taped in the corners of the oversized windows, quaintly advertising cod liver oil, waxed paper and the county fair.

Tory found the signs charming.

Opening the front door, she was instantly soothed by strains of classical music and the sweetly masculine scent of cherry pipe tobacco and old leather.

Clyde sat in a wingback chair, his gray ponytail bent over a book. He glanced up when he heard the chimes, then smiled.

"Victoria. How lovely to see you again."

She'd always thought Victoria was an outdated name, given by out-of-date parents who cherished their late-life daughter's femininity. She spent her early teens rebelling against her mother's absolute adoration. She cut her hair, traded her ballet slippers for track shoes, and shortened Victoria to a simple, straightforward Tory.

Clyde's use of her former name always brought a brief pang of regret. She'd cut school to get high the day her mother died. Someone found Tory at a friend's house at two o'clock that afternoon and told her about the accident. Tory rushed across town to the hospital, arriving two hours too late to say goodbye.

"How are you, Clyde?"

He set aside the book. "Very well, thank you. To what do I owe this unexpected pleasure?"

"I was hoping you might have a book on dreams."

"Let's see what we can find." He hobbled to his computer and clicked through several screens. "Hmm. Yes, here we are. *Your Dreams and What They Mean.* Oh, dear. Looks like I've sold all six copies. Shall I order it for you, or are you in a hurry?"

"No hurry."

"It'll arrive by the middle of next week. Shall I call you when it comes in?"

She gave him her phone number, then, lured by the neat rows of books, walked down the aisle labeled *Suspense.* As long as she was there, she might as well look around, but only for a minute.

"Got anything new by Stephen King?" she asked.

He grimaced. "I'm afraid not. Perhaps you'd like to try his forerunner." He handed her a book from the shelf.

The Masque of the Red Death by Edgar Allan Poe. The title called to mind her blood-spattered dream car, so she quickly returned the book. "Come to think of it, Clyde, maybe I'd better go with something a bit more ..."

"Those dreams we were talking about?"

"Yeah. Maybe I'll peek at the romance section."

She wandered the aisles, pulling down books at random and replacing them. She'd looked forward to one of her monthly reading weekends, when she lay around the apartment in sweat pants, armed with a good book, a jar of Peter Pan crunchy peanut butter and a box of Saltines. The disastrous meeting with Frankie put her decidedly out of the mood.

She glanced at her watch. It was getting late. She'd look through Bargain Row then return to work.

As she walked down the aisle, she stumbled against a box sitting on the floor. "Ouch." She rubbed her ankle. "What's in the box, Clyde? Cement blocks?"

"Books, of course," came his muffled reply. "A freebie from the distributor. Nothing very exciting, I imagine."

An unaccountable thrill passed over her. "Do you mind if I look?" She was already on her knees, her long plait falling over her shoulder.

"Be my guest."

She pulled back the flaps. She had to look. She couldn't imagine not looking.

She sifted through the box and set aside mildewed westerns, a handful of dog-eared paperbacks with no covers. At the bottom, beneath a pile of moldering romance novels, she found a metal box. Tucked inside, under a layer of yellowed tissue, was a book entitled *Heatherfield*. In contrast to the damp paperbacks, the hardcover book was warm. She pulled it from the box, sat back on crossed legs and studied it.

The cover was worn and tattered, but the picture in the center was exquisite, depicting a cabin nestled in the woods. Tory could almost hear the calls of sparrows in the evergreens and the babble of the river that wound its way through the center of them. Lace curtains, real enough to touch, seemed to flutter in the cabin's open windows despite the approaching storm clouds. Curious, she turned the book over to check the author's name.

"Destiny Paige," she said softly.

Glancing through the yellowed pages, Tory's eyes were drawn to a passage.

•

> It's worse than your worst nightmare, Louise. I've seen things no man should see. Done things I never thought a Christian man would do.
>
> War changes everything. I can't explain what it's like, that burst of adrenalin that pumps through a man's veins, that taste of copper and blood. A demon rages in his head, shouting, "Kill! Kill! Kill! Kill those damn enemy bastards!" But at night, I lay in the dark and can't stop seeing their faces. The people I'm supposed to hate—what if they're just ordinary guys like us? This is the hard part. Some are only boys.
>
> I'm killing children, Lou, eleven- and twelve-years-old. They tell us not to think of them as human, and some of the things they do aren't human, but neither are some of the things we do. God help us.
>
> Every hour of every day, my prayer is this nightmare will end. I'll make it back to Heatherfield in one piece and take you for my wife. That's the day I live for, Lou. Every hour I live is one hour closer. If I live, it'll be to cherish this freedom bought

with blood, and you and every minute we spend together until the end of time.

But if I die here, Louise—if I die here, I'll go to my grave knowing my life counted for something, because you loved me.

Yours always,
Jake

•

The book trembled in Tory's hands. In her mind, she saw him, a young soldier writing by flickering candlelight. His sandy head was bent over a sheet of paper, his brow knit in concentration as he scratched out words, chewed his pencil in thought and added others.

Then he looked at Tory, or through her. In his warm, brown eyes were unspeakable sorrow, pain and anger.

Shaken, she closed the book and the image vanished.

A war novel, she told herself. Such things didn't interest her. It was probably written fifty years earlier.

She flipped to the title page but there was no copyright date. She turned another page, and a chill like an icicle dripping down her spine shivered down her back. The handwritten inscription read, *For Victoria, With Love.*

She snapped shut the cover. "Get over yourself, Tory. It's not as if you're the only Victoria in the world."

"Find something of interest?"

She jumped at the sound of Clyde's voice. "Maybe." She handed him the book. "Have you ever heard of this author?"

The old man squinted at the spine and smiled. "Ah. Destiny Paige."

"You've heard of her?"

"She was a local celebrity of sorts. From Rochester, I believe. She wrote a handful of romance novels in the forties. Mild by today's standards, but quite steamy for their time."

"Why haven't I heard of her?"

"Poor Destiny wasn't all that respected in the literary world, I'm afraid. She had a nasty habit of tooting her own horn. She liked to write herself into her stories, which were rather insipid to begin with, as I recall."

"Did you know her?"

"I did, in fact." He pulled out his reading glasses and leafed through the book. Tory watched over his shoulder.

"This seems incomplete," he said. "You see?"

The book's last sentence ran across the page and came to an abrupt halt in mid-sentence.

"By night, he walked the land," Tory read aloud, glancing at Clyde in surprise. "The ending's been taken out."

"Not taken out, just never put in. It's obviously been bound incomplete." He snapped it shut.

"What'll you do with it?"

"It's not saleable as it is, though it has a pretty cover. You may keep it, if you like."

When she walked from the bookstore moments later, Tory saw the morning sun was swallowed by the temperamental spring clouds. Tucking the book into her handbag, she hurried to the last block of Market Street where her Mitsubishi gleamed despite the gray day.

An ominous feeling crept over her as she sat behind the wheel. She shrugged it off, attributing it to concern for Frankie's safety.

Back at the office, she retrieved her pager from the top drawer of her desk, clipped it to her purse and went to tell Kate the news.

"We're pushing for child and spousal support," Kate said, a telephone receiver cradled against her ear as she furiously scribbled notes. "Given the circumstances, it doesn't seem too much to ask."

She motioned Tory in with a jerk of her head. Tory, moving a stack of folders from the only other chair, sat down to wait. Her eyes swept over Kate's office. It was a bigger version of Tory's but essentially the same airless compartment with gray cinderblock walls. Equal-opportunity claustrophobia, Kate often joked.

Tory stared at Kate's flamboyant red jumpsuit and winced inwardly. Rather than try to hide her large size, Kate seemed determined to accentuate it despite Tory's tactful suggestions.

"You're damned right I do!" Kate said. "If you think I'm kidding, try me." She slammed down the receiver. "Bureaucrats!"

"If it's any consolation, you're beautiful when you're angry."

Kate smiled. "How'd it go? Was she ecstatic?"

"Less than."

"You're kidding."

Tory tossed the key onto Kate's desk. "She's spending the weekend with Zach."

Kate's eyebrows shot up. "Zach the ripper?"

"Afraid so."

Kate closed her eyes, pinched the bridge of her nose between her thumb and index finger and shook her head. "Damn."

"How do we stop her?"

"We don't."

"We don't? Six months of rehab down the drain, just like that?" She snapped her fingers. "We build her back together piece-by-piece, just so that bastard can tear her apart again? Is that it?"

Kate sighed. "Tory ..."

Tory jumped to her feet, struggling to control her temper. "Sometimes I wonder what I'm even here for."

"To keep me sane, for one."

"I'm serious, Kate."

"You did what you could, Kiddo. The agency can't hold their hands forever."

"I wish I felt like any of this made a difference."

"It does make a difference. Six months ago, she didn't know she had any options. She's stronger and smarter now." Kate walked to the coffee maker in the corner of her office. After measuring half a cup of thick, brown sludge into her mug, she returned to her chair. "They're like kids learning to walk. They fall down and scrape their knees. When they do, it's our job to patch them up and send them back out again. I know it sucks. That's the way it is."

Tory sighed. "Let's just hope she's still got legs to walk on after a weekend with that animal."

Kate eyed her speculatively. "You're too close to this one, Kiddo. You know that."

"I know."

"You can't keep taking your job home with you. You'll never make it if you do."

After a brief silence, Kate eyed the book sticking out of Tory's bag. "I'm guessing this will be a Peter Pan weekend."

"Yeah." Tory snorted. "But even that won't prove satisfying. True to form, I seem to have fallen in love with another misfit." She pulled Heatherfield from her bag, flipped it open to the last page and showed it to her boss. "A book that has no end. Perfect, huh?"

"By night, he walked the land," Kate read, handing it back. "Spooky. What is he, a werewolf?"

"No, a soldier," Tory snapped, snatching the book from Kate's hand. Her tantrum surprised both of them. What was wrong with her? "I'm sorry, Kate. I didn't sleep well last night."

Kate waved the apology aside. "Go start your weekend. I'll cover your calls. We'll talk on Monday."

As Tory turned to leave, Kate asked, "Tory? It is an important job and you're damned good at it, okay?"

"If I'm so good at it, then why do I ... ?"

The jingling of Kate's phone interrupted Tory. Kate signaled her to wait. "Women Incorporated, Kathleen Hager speaking. What?"

The alarm in Kate's voice sent a wave of uneasiness rippling through Tory's stomach. She caught Kate's eye and mouthed, *What?*

"Oh, dear God. No." The color drained from Kate's face. "All right. Yes, we'll come right down."

"My God, Kate," Tory said as Kate hung up. "You're as white as paper. What's going on?"

"Tory." She pressed a trembling hand to her lips. "The police want us to come to the station and answer some questions."

"About what?" Tory felt herself growing numb.

"Oh, God." Kate buried her face in her hands.

"Kate, what?" Tory demanded.

"Alison Gibson strangled her baby this morning."

•

Her training, degrees and the work to which Tory had dedicated her life were all for nothing.

That thought permeated her mind as she walked from the police station an hour and a half after Kate received the call. As Tory turned toward her car, Kate gently touched her shoulder.

"You all right, Kid?"

Tory nodded, unable to force words past the lump in her throat.

"Do you want to get a cup of coffee somewhere and talk?"

"I don't think so, Kate."

"Okay." She patted Tory's arm. "This wasn't your fault. No one could've known."

Tory nodded again.

"I'll walk back to the office. You go home. We'll talk tomorrow."

As Tory crossed the parking lot, her eyes filled with the tears she'd stoically held back during the police questioning.

"Your name?"

"Victoria Sasser."

"What's your status regarding Miss Gibson?"

"I'm her counselor."

"You're a psychiatrist?"

"No, Sir. I'm a certified counselor."

"I see. When did you last counsel Alison Gibson?"

"Yesterday."

"You didn't see any signs that might indicate a problem?"

"She seemed stressed. I noted undue aggression toward me. I was working to modify her plan."

"You noted aggression but didn't think it necessary to take action in the child's protection. Is that it?"

"Yes, Sir."

"Excuse me?"

"Yes, Sir. That's correct."

Kate said it wasn't her fault, but Tory wasn't so sure. She climbed behind the wheel of her car, staring blankly across the parking lot. She went over the previous day's session with Allison, wondering if there was something she should've noticed.

Her thoughts lingered on Allison's baby—his smile, his chubby fist curled around her thumb and his little bare feet. Her heart didn't break. It shattered. She laid her head against the steering wheel and sobbed.

A pair of doves circled above the car. A breeze blew the scent of impending rain through the open window. It started as a gentle pit-pat against the roof and built to a persistent drumming, drowning out her sobs as Tory, like the heavens, emptied herself of tears.

She didn't know her actions were being closely monitored.

•

Behold. The Beloved.

She's lovely.

She's the essence of beauty and innocence, pure and undefiled.

That's rare in this realm. Why does she cry?

She's tenderhearted. That's why she's been selected.

Of course.

Is everything in place?

Yes, Sir.

Good.

Will she read it, do you think?

She must.

Will she come?

She must. You must see to it.
Yes, Sir.
The time is at hand. What was started must be finished.
Yes, Sir. It will be finished. We'll see to it.

Chapter Four

After a long, mindless drive, Tory returned home. She shook three Ibuprofen tablets from a bottle and swallowed them without water, then walked into the living room and lit the twelve votive candles that littered her coffee and end tables. She massaged the screaming knot of muscles at the base of her neck, breathing deeply as the candles perfumed the air.

Relax, she told herself.

Sifting through the day's accumulation of junk mail, she tossed the unopened stack on the sofa. Lord, it had been a hellish day. She needed to run long and hard to pound her anger and frustration into the earth and feel the cleansing power of the rain.

She walked down the hall to her bedroom where her answering machine blinked cheerfully from its table beside the bed. She absently punched the play button, half-listening as she stepped out of her skirt.

The machine recorded two hang-ups and a message from Floyd, an instructor she met at the college where she attended a lecture the previous month, who invited her out for a drink.

"I guess I'm asking for another chance," Floyd said. "Could you please call me tonight?"

"No, Floyd, I can't," she muttered, pulling off her blouse.

Which sucks, she thought, remembering his warm, hot-cocoa eyes. Floyd was cute, charming and intelligent—traits she greatly admired in a man. But he made a fatal mistake when he wasn't honest with her.

Had he really thought tacking a phony PHD onto his name would impress her? She threw her blouse onto a pile of dirty clothes in the corner. A guy who'd lie about something like that would lie about bigger things, too. If there was one thing Tory Sasser couldn't abide, it was a liar.

After a short beep ended Floyd's message, the machine recorded a series of pops and crackles as if the caller was using an out-of-range cell phone. She pressed the On/Off button, and the crackling continued.

Odd, she thought, ready to press it again, and then she heard a faint sigh. Her hand hovered over the blinking red light, then pressed more firmly.

The sigh was louder next time. A long, shuddering breath that made the hair on the nape of her neck prickle.

"That's cute, Floyd. Real cute."

"Victoria," the voice whispered.

It sounded ageless, not old. She yanked her hand back from the button as though burned.

"Victoria."

She thought briefly of Clyde Hardback, the only one who ever used her real name, then rejected the thought. Obscene phone calls weren't Clyde's style.

"Vic—"

She pounded the button with her fist.

"—toria."

The whispering was more intense, like the sound of a wailing wind as the voice was joined by a chorus of other whispering voices. Frozen in horror, she listened, able to pick out only fragments of sentences.

"Please ... come ... Waiting so ... Waiting ... so ... long, Victoria."

She yelped in fear and yanked the phone cord from the jack, silencing the machine.

"Real cute," she said shakily. She stared at the phone a moment longer, her heart pounding, and then pulled a clean jogging suit from the closet as she backed out of the room.

•

She would be the perfect choice.

The girl had the voice of an angel and a face to match. Lord, how could any woman's eyes be so clear and blue?

•

Clyde locked the front door of his bookstore, emptied his cash drawer into a bank bag and set about rinsing his coffeepots. It occurred to him when he heard her read. Although it was only one small sentence, he knew. She would be the perfect stand-in for Sonya

Spaulding. He should've asked her right then. The poetry reading was scheduled for the next night. Why hadn't he asked her?

He shook his head, chuckling to himself. Eyes that clear and blue had the power to incite shyness. Even an old, used-up codger like himself wasn't immune.

He wiped down the coffee bar, then resolutely straightened his shoulders. The poetry reading was tomorrow night. Though he was sure any of the five women in the poetry society would be thrilled to stand behind the podium, it would be a sin to entrust the words of Sonya Spaulding to any of their old, cackling-hen voices.

Only an angel would do.

He marched behind the counter to leaf through a stack of purchase orders, looking for the one he wrote that afternoon.

"Here we are," he said in triumph. "Victoria Sasser, 107 Overland Drive."

He carried the order to the phone and carefully dialed the number. No answer. He let it ring twelve times before he hung up.

•

When she returned from her run nearly two hours later, Tory's muscles were taut, her tendons screaming. The candles burned to stumps while she was out. Instead of their usual calming effect, the heady aromas of patchouli and vanilla spice filling her apartment only reignited her anger.

She always thought of her apartment as a safe haven, an emotional safe place where she could rejuvenate at the end of the day. She picked up a scorched votive cup, frowned at it and slammed it back down on the table.

This was her home! She'd be damned if some pervert would whisper to her over the phone lines and chase her out. She walked briskly to her bedroom and plugged in the answering machine, glaring at it as if daring it to speak.

It didn't.

She would call the phone company first thing Monday morning and have her number changed. Problem solved.

She made a tossed salad, took three bites, realized her appetite was spoiled and threw it into the garbage. She turned the radio to the classical music station and rummaged in the cupboard for a bottle of Chablis.

Probably not a wise decision, she thought, but it was the most direct route to oblivion she knew.

"Next stop, I-don't-want-to-know Street," she said, popping the cork on the bottle.

She carried the bottle and her favorite long-stemmed wineglass to the bathroom and filled the tub. As she pulled off her jogging suit, her thoughts went to Frankie. God, she'd left the apartment so fast, she forgot her pager.

She hurried back into the kitchen and dumped out her bag on the table, grabbing the pager from the heap to check its tiny window.

There were no messages.

Heatherfield stared up at her from the table, the cover open.

For Victoria, With Love, the inscription read.

Somehow, the words seemed comforting. Picking up the book, she carried it to the bathroom. With a wry smile, she added a capful of jasmine bubbles to the running water. She had a bottle of wine and a book without an ending. If there was a better way to end a hellish day, she didn't know what it might be.

With a groan, she sank into the tub and flexed each knotted muscle from toes to neck. When she felt herself reach a state of complete relaxation, she poured a glass of wine and opened the book.

It was a typical forties read—pleasant and meandering. She sipped her wine and let herself be pulled into the world of Jedediah Benjamin. Having, in the same year, lost his father to polio and his young wife to scarlet fever, Jed married himself to his land, entrusting his only son's upbringing to his late wife's gentle German mother.

"How sad," Tory murmured.

She turned to the second chapter and read of young Jake Benjamin, a ragamuffin boy who spent his lonely childhood exploring the 300 wooded acres around his home. Reading of his unrequited yearning for his father's approval, she felt a kinship with him.

As she read, she was only vaguely aware of a change taking place. The words in the book began forming a series of pictures in her mind. At some point, she stopped reading and began watching.

The pictures rolled and changed.

Before her eyes, Jake Benjamin metamorphosed from a pale lad with dirt-smudged cheeks into a sturdy, handsome young man who burned with passion.

•

He sat beside a river under the sheltering branches of a

red maple while a pretty girl with auburn hair lay on a pink blanket beside him, a blanket the same shade as her dress.

The sun rained down around her, turning her hair the color of autumn leaves. He couldn't bear the beauty of her, reaching across the blanket for her hand.

"Jake? Why are you staring at me like that?"

"Do you love me, Louise?"

"Silly. I've told you a hundred times or more."

"Tell me again."

"Silly." She sighed. "All right, Jake. I love you. Now stop looking so morose."

He pulled a silver band from the pocket of his dungarees, his heart beating so hard his chest ached. Sliding it onto her finger, he saw afternoon sunlight reflecting in the small diamond in the center.

"Jake! Are you asking me to ...?"

"Yes."

"I don't know what to say."

"Say yes."

She lowered her smoky, gray eyes.

His heart almost stopped beating. Then she smiled. "Yes."

•

Tory dabbed a tear from her eye and laughed at herself for crying over a silly love story. What in heaven's name was the matter with ...?

She inhaled sharply. He kissed Louise, and she felt the pressure of his lips and the heat of his hands as if they touched her own skin.

•

"We aren't married yet, Jake."

"How can that matter when a fellow loves a girl as much as I love you?"

"Oh, Jake, you say the sweetest—"

He cut her off with a kiss. His hands slowly unbuttoned her dress.

•

Tory shivered, unable to stop feeling the heat of his hands, the sweetness of his kiss.

•

"Some day all of this will be yours, right?" Louise murmured, her hand sweeping to include all the forest.

"Ours, Darling." Jake kissed her again. "Ours."

•

Tory watched as summer became breathtaking autumn. The forest pulsed with color. Infused with the energy born of love, Jake bought one acre of land from his father and began building a cabin as a labor of love, wrought by his own hands. It would be a home for his bride-to-be. He, the dashing hero, won the hand of his love.

The story should've ended there. It didn't.

News of war whispered through the village, etching deep creases into the men's faces and stealing the smiles from the women's. Jake's grandmother grew thin and somber as war raged in her beloved Germany.

Autumn became winter. On a frosty December day, while Jake and Louise happily planned their future, the unthinkable happened. The Japanese bombed a naval base in a faraway place called Pearl Harbor.

America was at war.

Abruptly, the pictures changed again. Tory watched in horror, staring into hell.

•

It was as if the whole world was burning. Even the sky was on fire. Jake's eyes and lungs burned with the smoke of ruined aircraft and the pungent odor of bloated bodies, decaying under the South Pacific sun. The battle had been fierce and costly.

"Take his feet, Private. I'll take his head. What's left of it."

Jake fought back nausea as he and the corporal loaded the corpses into the waiting ship. Burial at sea was kinder than leaving the dead for the enemy to find and mutilate. Come nightfall, the company had to move on. Marines never left their dead behind.

•

The bathwater was cold. The wine bottle was empty, but still, Tory read.

•

He carried her pictures, one ragged and torn, in the pocket of his fatigues. The other was emblazoned in his mind. They alone blocked out the horror.

It was her letters that kept him alive more than his grandmother's benevolent German God, more than the dehydrated rations of food and the scarce, bitter water. The letters were his link to himself and a world that seemed as far from Guadalcanal as the moon. It was a long time since he heard from her. Time had no meaning on that godforsaken island.

Jake nearly trembled with anticipation as he opened the small, thin envelope carefully so he wouldn't tear a single precious word. He pulled out the letter and his face turned the color of ashes as he read, then reread, the words she wrote:

Dear Jake,

I didn't want to write you like this and add to your suffering, but I couldn't let you hear it from someone else. I got married last week and am now Mrs. Pierce Matthews, and so very happy! I'm sorry.

Yours,
Louise.

P.S. I hope we can still be friends.

•

Tory thought she'd spent her last tear earlier that afternoon in the parking lot of the police station, but she found herself crying like she hadn't cried in years. Tears spilled over her cheeks and into Heatherfield's pages, making the ink run.

She set the book on the floor beside her empty wine bottle and reached for a tissue, weeping like a lovesick teenager for the broken heart of a man who didn't exist. It didn't get much worse than that.

When she composed herself, she reached for the book and continued reading.

•

He'd been on watch most of the night, standing guard over a shipment of badly needed supplies that arrived that evening, mostly ammunition. He watched the darkness intently, with only the murky, green half-light to aid his red eyes.

He was hungry. For the past six hours, that thought dominated his sleep-starved brain, but that wasn't what bothered Jake Benjamin the most. His years of hunting in the silent forest and tracking wild animals by the scent of their fear told him someone was out there—and he was scared.

Though his ears heard only the raging thunder of his own pulse, his gut told him an enemy was near. Jake trusted his instincts. He slowed his breathing and willed himself to become one with the dank atmosphere.

Yards away, he caught a flicker of movement and squinted. Two enemy soldiers crawled as silently as the night toward the supply tent. He crouched, his weapon trained on the moving figures. He licked salty bead of sweat from his upper lip.

"All right, Sweetheart," he whispered to his rifle. "It's just you and me." As though they heard him, the two enemy soldiers stopped and peered in his direction, then scrambled for their guns. Jake didn't flinch. The bastards could kill him for all he cared. He had nothing to go home to anymore.

With a last steadying breath, he aimed, prayed for forgiveness and fired. He heard the angry hiss of a grenade. Then the world exploded.

•

The bathroom lights flickered and died. Tory sat in the darkness, clutching the book until the lights flickered on again. A chill that had little to do with the coolness of the bathwater shivered over her.

She climbed from the tub and hurriedly toweled off. Pulling on a nightshirt, she carried the book to her bedroom and sat on the bed, nervously wetting her lips and opening to where she left off.

•

He told Louise war changed everything. It would be four years before the truth of that statement hit home. He left for war at twenty-two, his whole life ahead of him, but he returned an emotionally bankrupt man. His girl married someone else, his father was dead and his grandmother was old and sick, struggling to hold onto their land.

Heatherfield was changing, too. The small, neighborly village had sprung tracts of look-alike houses, military in their sameness, each with a small patch of yard and a barbecue grill. It was the new American dream.

Crescent Street was unrecognizable to him with its shopping centers and dance halls. It was a prefab town, prosperous and heartless—and it was owned by Matthews Developing. It was a town Jake Benjamin wanted no part of. In his absence, his grandmother contracted the hardwood off one hundred acres, sacrificed the Douglas fir and pine for the beams and flooring that built the new American dream. The documents, signed and dated, were legal so the lawyers said. Jake had no other choice.

He let those acres go to save his birthright. The centuries-old trees were severed from their roots, like a man who amputated a limb to save his body. That he'd grown wealthy in the process didn't interest Jake.

•

Tory reluctantly turned to the last page, feeling as if she were saying good-bye to a dear friend or leaving a cherished lover.

•

Three years later, at thirty, Jake lowered his grandmother into a grave in the family cemetery. He was utterly alone. From high on his mountain, he watched the town evolve into a city while he remained a wealthy, lonely man with deep scars. He no longer took pleasure in hunting the deer and the fox that shared his solitary world. By day, he worked like a man driven by demons to religiously clear the forest of brush and standing dead. By night, he walked the land—

•

Tory began to shiver uncontrollably. She closed her eyes as if to erase what she saw, then opened them only to find the vision still there. Words tumbled across the page, like that afternoon, but amazingly there were more.

—looking for someone to blame, looking for a reason for his existence and finding none.

This night, rain was coming. He smelled it in the distance and saw it in the way the leaves drooped on the trees. Surely, it would rain. Something else was there, too. He felt it in the wind and heard it in the stillness of the forest. Something ... someone was coming.

•

"It's not possible," she whispered. "Books don't add to themselves." She snapped shut the cover and opened it again with trembling hands. The new words were still there staring at her, oblivious to her distress.

Relax, she told herself. *All right. I was mistaken. I missed it the first time, that's all. I must have. Because books do not add to themselves!*

What about Clyde and Kate? a small voice nagged. *Did they miss them, too?*

She shut the book again. As her eyes fell on the cover, her breath cut a jagged path to her throat.

The picture was different.

Two wicker rocking chairs appeared on the porch of the cabin. Worse than that, the forest was on fire and the little cabin was almost completely engulfed. The storm clouds became smoke while the waning sunlight changed into flames that licked the treetops.

Horrified, she threw the book across the room where it landed in a pile of dirty clothes with a soft thud. It stared back, the cover open, and the words *For Victoria, With Love* plainly visible.

The shrill ringing of the phone sent her bolting from bed. She stared at it wide-eyed, afraid to answer. After three rings, the answering machine took over.

"Hi, Tory," Kate said. "I guess you're not home. Listen, I—"

Tory grabbed the phone. "I'm here, Kate."

"Were you busy?"

"No. I was just … reading."

"Oh. How'd the werewolf story come out?"

"Um." Tory drew a shaky breath and glanced at the book. "It didn't, remember?"

"Oh, right. The book has no ending."

"Hey, Kate?"

"What?"

"Never mind."

"Are you all right, Tory? You sound pretty shook up."

"No. I'm okay. I think."

"Any word from Frankie?"

"Not a peep."

"Good." Tory heard the forced cheer in Kate's laughter. "What do you want to bet tomorrow, we'll be moving her into that new apartment?"

"I hope so."

"Are you sure you're all right, Kiddo?"

"Yeah. Maybe a little hammered. That's all."

"It's been that kind of day."

"Yeah, it sure has."

Tory's gaze wandered back to the book. If anyone could help her put the situation into perspective, it was Kate. But what could Tory say?

She imagined herself asking, "Hey, Kate, remember that book I got today? The thing is, it's finishing itself before my eyes. It also repainted its cover and knocked out my electricity. Some crazy book, eh?"

Kate would laugh and agree, and then she'd call the psych center.

"Do you feel up to stopping at the jail to see Alison tomorrow?" Kate asked. "If not, no biggie. I'll go alone."

"I'll go, then I think I'll take you up on that cup of coffee."

"Why? What's going on?"

"I'm not sure. It might be something totally weird, or I might be totally crocked. Maybe you can help me make sense of it."

"Sounds serious. Should I come over right now?"

Wind howled outside and rain splatted against the window. "No. It can wait until morning."

After she hung up, Tory carried the book to the kitchen and resolutely slid it into a drawer. She returned to the bedroom and sat at her computer. It took half an hour of searching before she found what she wanted.

Destiny Paige, nee Dierdra Pratt, was born and raised in Rochester, just like Clyde said. She penned eight romance novels in the forties. Tory read the list twice, but there was no mention of a book called *Heatherfield*.

She scrolled down the screen, reading through the brief biography. When she reached the last line, she stifled a cry.

Destiny Paige died of liver sclerosis on June 10, 1972—the same day Tory was born.

"So what?" she asked. "It's just a coincidence. That's all."

Her words didn't ring true. The corresponding dates were another eerie ingredient to add to the witch's brew of weirdness that had been simmering since Clyde gave her that damned book.

She pondered all that as she stared at the screen. It was more than she could handle, at least that night.

She turned off the computer and climbed into bed, lying there for a few moments to stare at the ceiling. Then she padded back into the kitchen and slid open the drawer. Removing *Heatherfield* from its place among the dishcloths, she studied the cover.

Heat from the flaming hillside seemed to pulse under her fingers. She threw the book back into the drawer and slammed it shut, obviously too drunk to make sense of it all that night.

Brain weary and bone tired, she climbed back into bed, turned off the light and buried her head in her pillow. She wouldn't mention the book to Kate after all. She'd give the damn thing back to Clyde and forget she ever saw it. Problem solved.

That was her last thought before she tumbled off to sleep.

Chapter Five

She'd been asleep for what seemed like minutes when the urgent beeping of her pager pulled Tory from a dream. As she groped beside the bed, her wine-and-sleep-fogged brain registered the pounding of rain on the window. It had stormed heavily while she slept and had knocked out the power. The digital clock beside her bed flashed, stubbornly insisting it was midnight, midnight, midnight.

She turned on her bedside lamp and fumbled for her pager. Before she saw the number in the little window, she knew it was Frankie.

Frankie answered after only half a ring.

"Is that you, Tory?"

The terror in her voice made Tory instantly sober.

"It's me, Frankie. What's going on?"

"Tory, he ..." She choked on a sob. "He beat me up. He don't want me to be strong."

Tory cursed under her breath. "Where is he now?"

"He's gone. I don't know where. He's been smoking crack. Oh God, Tory. I hurt. Will you come get me?"

"Frankie, listen to me. Lock the doors and call the police. Don't open up for anyone without a badge. I'll be there in twenty minutes."

"Please hurry."

"I will, Frankie. Just try to calm down, okay?"

After Frankie promised to call the police, Tory scrambled from bed, pulled on a pair of jeans and a sweater and yanked open her night stand drawer to pull out the .22-caliber Derringer Kate bought her for a birthday present the previous year.

"A girl's best friend," Kate said, only half-joking. "You never know, Kiddo."

"You never know," Tory said as she calmly loaded the gun. Slipping it into her purse, she sprinted out into the night.

She sped down Overland Drive and onto I-86. After half a mile, she screeched to a halt. She rubbed a circle in her rain-fogged windshield and peered out. A tractor-trailer had jackknifed in the road, blocking both lanes of traffic. The police weren't even on the scene yet.

"Move, damn it!" She slammed her fist on the steering wheel.

After a quick glance in her rearview mirror told her the coast was clear, she threw the wheel sideways and drove across the median. She'd have to take back roads, which would cost valuable time.

She began praying as she steered through the rain-slicked streets, past the sleeping city, over lonely country roads that stretched beyond the reach of the street lamps.

Please, God, let him stay away until I get there. Please don't let him hurt her anymore.

She cast worried glances into her rearview mirror as she drove, hoping Frankie remembered to call the police. Her windshield wipers worked furiously against the pouring rain. When her rear tires lost traction for a second, she eased off the gas.

"Slow down, Tory," she muttered.

The advice came two seconds too late.

She slid through a turn and collided with a thick wall of fog. Tires grabbed at pavement, overcorrected, then slid sideways and back. She squinted into the dim beam of her headlights, wondering if she was still on the road. She'd never seen such thick fog before. It was almost like driving through clouds—or heavy snow.

"Oh, God," she whispered. "No."

Her hands shook. She crawled across a bridge, barely breathing. When she saw approaching headlights, she glanced left and right but there was nowhere to go.

"Please, God. I don't want to die," she whispered.

Her prayer was cut short by a sickening crash. Over her own hoarse screams, she heard the sound of metal grinding against metal, and seventy pounds of windshield shattering, and then there was only darkness.

I'm in shock. This is what it feels like to be in shock.

She couldn't shake the thought. It formed a singsong in her head, blocking out another, more terrifying thought.

I'm dead. This is what it feels like to be dead.

She didn't remember leaving her car, but she found herself stumbling through a thick forest, dazed and disoriented. Icy sheets of rain plastered her sweater against her skin. She barely noticed, so lulled by the sound of the wind and the patter of rain on the carpet of pine needles underfoot.

She stopped walking and steadied herself against a tree. If only she could find a place to lie down and sleep for a few minutes, she could get her bearings.

Snap out of it, Kiddo! a voice warned. *Get hold of yourself before you become some bobcat's borscht.*

"There are no bobcats," she said, but the thought was enough to get her moving again. She stumbled on, trying to find her way back to the road. Intermittent lightning broke the darkness that seemed to have swallowed her.

"Which way?" she whispered.

Around her, towering trees swayed in the wind, their long black branches like fingers pointing in all directions, mocking her.

"Which way?" she shouted.

Wailing wind answered her. She trudged a few steps forward, and then stopped, frozen with fear, because it wasn't the wind she heard. It was voices.

She heard them clearly, the same whispering voices that were on her answering machine hours earlier. Instead of talking to her, though, she felt they were talking about her—or someone they called the be-loved.

"It's only the wind," she said.

"Victoria."

She ran, desperate to escape the voices, but the faster she ran the louder they were. They came from around her and inside her head. She felt their icy breath against her cheek, raging at her back.

"Victoria. Welcome, Victoria."

"No!" she shouted.

She ran on, concentrating on the sound of her ragged breathing and the crash of her footsteps on the earth, not certain if she ran toward the road or away from it. Not that it mattered. She ran until the woods thinned and she came to a clearing.

She bolted into the open. The rain-sodden ground was too spongy to support her sudden weight. As she turned to throw a terrified glance over her shoulder, she pitched forward. Her knee struck a stone and she was thrown to the ground.

The pain was like a bolt of lightning searing her leg. She screamed in agony, and the voices moaned in response. She clutched her knee with one hand, the other grasping the object over which she stumbled. Pulling herself to her feet, she took a succession of ragged breaths and peered into the darkness.

A flash of lightning exposed a dozen headstones leaning in drunken rows across the clearing.

"Oh, God," she moaned. "Please don't let this be happening!"

"Victoria," the voices moaned. "Vic—"

She pressed her hands over her ears.

"It's not happening!" she shouted. "I'm in my bed! I'm dreaming this!"

Ignoring the throbbing in her leg, she darted back into the forest, welcoming the comparative safety of the trees. Her foot snagged a tree root and she fell again.

Her breath came in short, sharp gasps. It hurt to breathe. Everything hurt. The pain in her knee was nothing compared to the one raging behind her temples. She struggled to free herself but couldn't, and a wail of fear was torn from her throat.

She counted slowly, matching the number with each jagged breath until her galloping pulse slowed to a canter.

"All right, Counselor," she whispered. "Take it easy. Relax."

Her eyes searched the relentless darkness for a clue, any sliver of light that might indicate her proximity to the road. She couldn't have come more than a mile, two at most. Had she run in a straight path or had she been going in circles?

Her train of thought screeched to a halt as a shadow emerged from the other shadows around her. Her breath lodged in her throat, strangling a scream.

It was a man.

She clamped one hand over her mouth to prevent a scream from giving her away as she peered into the shadows. To her horror, the man peered back. Her mind shouted at her to pull free and run, but she felt as if she were made of lead. She couldn't run or move. All she did was sit and stare.

He stepped toward her.

Two terrifying thoughts came to her simultaneously. The approaching figure was the devil, or it was Frankie's boyfriend, Zach.

Either way, she was dead.

He was so close, another bolt of lightning would show her his face, and it would certainly reveal hers. She backed up to a tree and fanned out her hands, feeling for her handbag, keeping her eyes firmly on the patch of darkness where he'd been. The Derringer held two bullets. If she were careful, she'd only need one.

He stood near her feet. She groped wildly, willing her hand to connect with the strap of her bag. She would aim for his leg, but she wouldn't shoot unless he forced her.

He came closer. When lightning finally came, she didn't see his face, just the item in his hands. It was a black leather handbag with silver buckles just like hers.

Murphy's law! she heard Frankie say. *If anything bad can happen … I hate to say it, Girlfriend, but it looks like you're toast.*

"No, I'm not," she whispered, moistening her lips as her hands continued groping.

She touched the end of a broken branch. It wouldn't be as effective as her Derringer, but anything was better than nothing.

He took another step. He was big and he definitely wasn't Zach. She sensed him watching her in the darkness, deciding.

All right, she thought. Okay.

She braced herself against the tree, the branch held tightly behind her back. "What do you want?" she shouted.

The wind whipped away her words. He dropped to a squat beside her and extended his hands, and they looked big enough to snap her in two. She closed her eyes and swung the branch with all her might.

A hush fell over the hillside. The voices fell silent, as if the entire forest held its breath, waiting.

PART TWO
HEATHERFIELD
1949

Chapter One

Even in sleep, he couldn't escape the horror of the war and the destruction and death he saw. Mornings when the sun shone through the trees, the mountain echoed with bird song and his hands were busy, he could almost forget. At the end of the day, when he closed his eyes, it all flooded back.

As a soldier, he learned a man could survive on two or three hours' sleep per night. Four years later, his body stubbornly clung to that concept. He filled his days with harsh physical labor. His nights were filled with walking.

One night, dreams of war pulled him from his bed at one o'clock. Following his usual path, he walked past the old sawmill and through the graveyard. He felt restless. He might've walked for another hour or until dawn if it hadn't started raining. Icy drizzle poured from his hat and into his jacket collar, soaking the back of his shirt. Even his socks were wet.

That wasn't what bothered him, though.

He looked up at the raging sky, clear and moonlit when he left the house an hour earlier, and wondered where the hell the lightning came from.

He cut through the woods, thinking to take the shortcut down the old logging trail. Wind slammed against his back as he walked. It tore off his hat and plunged icy fingers through his hair, whispering urgently in his ear. Thunder crashed in the trees.

He pulled up his collar and kept walking. As thunder rolled off the hillside, the wind shifted and he thought he heard something. He stopped, ears straining against the wind until he heard it again.

It was a faint moan.

He closed his eyes. Ignoring the rain that pummeled his face, he concentrated on the heavy scents in the air, noting rain and wind, cedar and pine, and something else—fear.

Common sense told him it was an animal, but his gut said otherwise. He turned and slogged through the trees toward the sound his instincts said was human. Above all, he knew to trust his instincts.

A series of quick white flashes like camera bulbs lit the forest enough to give him a clear picture before darkness fell again. He stood stock still, peering into the trees where, for a moment, he thought he saw a woman's face.

He took an uncertain step forward, waiting for the lightning. He was right. It was a woman. He stared at her, speechless with surprise.

"What do you want?" she shouted.

That surprised him even more. What did he want? She acted like he was a peddler who came to her front porch with a suitcase full of goods. It occurred to him maybe he was scaring her standing there like a statue staring at her.

"Are you in trouble?" he shouted.

She didn't answer. Another flash of lightning showed her problem. Her foot was caught up in some tree roots. He hooked the handbag he carried over his shoulder and went to her, hands extended to free her.

It happened fast.

Another man would've been caught off guard, but four years in battle left him with finely honed reflexes. He sensed rather than saw her swing at him. His forearm snapped forward, neatly blocking the attack. The tree limb she'd intended to hit him with broke in two and skittered into the trees.

He was a man slow to anger, but sudden moves made him nervous. He held her shoulders and pushed her back until she was pinned against the ground.

"I'm trying to help you," he rumbled. "You can let me or you can take your chances out here. Your choice."

Another flash of lightning revealed the face of an angel. The sight knocked the breath from his lungs, but his hold on her shoulders remained firm.

She lifted her chin in defiance, but her eyes showed defeat.

He worked quickly. Within moments, she was free. He took her hand and helped her to her feet, shouting to be heard over the storm.

"Can you walk?"

She said, "Yes." But after one step, her knees gave out and she buckled against him. His arm went around her waist.

"Go ahead," she shouted, wrenching free. "I'll be all right."

He lifted wary eyes to the sky. The lightning was a couple miles away, coming dangerously closer with each second. With a muttered oath, he swung her into his arms and carried her. Though prepared for a fight, he felt her crumple against him, her face pressed into the folds of his jacket.

She was deceptively small, weighing 130 pounds or less, but most of it was muscle judging by the sturdy legs under her slacks.

He trudged through the forest trying to reason it out. She was dressed like a college girl in dungarees and a sloppy joe sweater, but the nearest college was fifty miles away. She couldn't be a high-school kid. She was at least twenty years old.

Lord, what a strange night.

Rain came out of nowhere and the wind whispered in the trees. It spoke to him, not in words but in feelings, and he'd known something was coming, but a woman?

He hadn't been prepared for that. When he found the handbag, he assumed it was from the teenagers who came to the graveyard on Friday nights to drink beer and make love. He saw them there more than once on his nightly treks, though he never made his presence known. He had his own reasons for going.

Marines never left their dead behind.

He hitched the woman closer and found she reeked of alcohol. She must be a college girl home on spring break that'd gone out joy-riding and wrecked her car. She'd wake up in the morning hung over and embarrassed, then he'd offer dry toast and coffee before driving her back to town.

He hugged her closer to shelter her from the wind as he plodded up the hill, spurred on by the light that glowed softly from his porch. Moments later, he maneuvered the front door open, pushed through into his dimly lit living room and deposited her on the couch. He straightened, rubbing his arms and she took the gesture as an affront.

"You didn't have to carry me," she snapped. "I would have been fine."

He laughed softly in irritation. "There are three hundred acres of woods out there, Sis. You should be glad I came along and not a pack of wild dogs."

She thrust her chin in the air, eyeing him with suspicion. "Can I have my purse, please?"

"I found it on my grandmother's grave." He handed it to her and waited for an explanation. Instead of giving him one, she hugged the bag to her chest.

"Thank you."

Her lips were purple, her teeth chattering. He turned away from her eyes, which were a pale shade of blue that were almost entirely iris. He'd never seen such beautiful eyes.

"You're soaked through," he growled. "I'll see about something dry you can put on."

Walking to the stairs, he turned for another glance as if she were an apparition that might vanish. "I'll be right back," he told her.

When searching through his dresser didn't produce anything suitable, he walked down the hall to the room that had been his grandmother's. Rummaging through her closet, he was glad he hadn't packed up her things. Three threadbare flannel nightgowns hung side-by-side. He chose the least ragged and carried it to the living room. The girl sat there looking around in the dim light.

"My grandmother wasn't what you'd call a fashion plate." He offered the pale pink gown. "I hope this will do."

"Thank you." She took it from him without looking at him.

He retreated to the bathroom and pulled on a dry pair of dungarees and white thermal top. After toweling his hair dry, he chose another clean, white towel for her.

After giving her ample time to dress, he ventured back downstairs, letting his feet pound heavily on the wooden planks to announce his arrival. She was lost in the folds of the nightgown, half-standing, gingerly testing her weight on one leg. With a wince, she fell back onto the couch.

"Your leg?" he asked.

"The knee. Just bruised, I think."

He handed her the towel. "For your hair."

When she released it from its plait, her hair cascaded down her back in a profusion of damp, honey-colored curls. Her beauty took away his breath. She eyed him warily as she ran the towel over her curls, her expression a mixture of curiosity and anger.

He saw her notice his scars and self-consciously turned away his face.

"Have you got a name?" he asked gruffly.

She continued drying her hair. "You can call me Tory."

Hostility dripped from her voice and he wondered at the reason.

"All right. You can call me Jake."

Something like fear registered in her eyes before she closed them. She ran her fingertips along the angry, purple bruise on her forehead and winced again.

He noticed the bruise. "You're hurt."

"I'm fine." She sighed. Once again, her bottomless blue eyes fixed on his scar. "I'm not so sure about my Mitsubishi, though."

He gave her a hard stare that was part amusement, part annoyance. In his mind, he saw a Mitsubishi A6M3 Zero, code-named Zeke—one of the sleek, deadly bombers the Japanese turned out cookie-cutter style throughout the war. She must be further gone than he guessed.

"You … you came in a Mitsubishi?"

"Yes, an Eclipse." She made a last swipe at her hair with the towel. "I'm not sure I'll be leaving in one, though. I don't suppose there's anyone in Savona who handles imports?"

"Savona?"

"This is Savona, isn't it?" Irritation tinged her voice. "That's where I was headed when I crashed."

He shook his head at her nonsense. "You must've gotten off the track somewhere, Sis. This is Heatherfield."

The look in her eyes was unmistakable. It wasn't fear or irritation, it was terror. She moaned softly, her body trembling.

Jake pulled a blanket from the back of the couch and tucked it around her. "You're in rough shape, Sis. Sit tight. I'll make you something warm to drink."

He went to the kitchen to fill the coffeepot, then set it on the stove to boil. Retrieving a mug from the cupboard, he considered adding some brandy, then thought better of it. *Poor kid*, he thought. He'd seen men tougher than her fight off the DTs.

When he returned to her with a steaming cup of coffee, she was asleep or pretending to be. He set the coffee on an end table and tucked the blanket closer around her. She smelled fresh, like wind and rain—and something else.

He moved closer and inhaled, catching the scent of jasmine. When he whispered her name, there was no response other than the flickering of her eyelids.

That was just as well. Living alone on a mountain, a man's social skills tended to atrophy.

She clutched the bag and stroked it in her sleep like a talisman. His eyes were drawn to the small, silvery band on the index finger of her left hand. He felt a sharp pang but refused to acknowledge it as disappointment. Instead, he wondered at the ring's significance.

That girl was a whole lot of unusual.

He gathered her wet clothes and hung them over the back of a chair, carefully avoiding the silky, white brassiere. He examined the faded dungarees, dirt-caked and torn, and her miniature combat boots. He'd heard it said that imitation was the highest form of flattery.

There might be something to that, but still, he couldn't get used to the new breed of woman the war had birthed. They preferred a man's work and a man's clothing. He wiped the mud from the boots and set them side-by-side on the floor. Women weren't men, damn it. He'd been raised to believe women should be cherished and protected.

His gaze crept to the sleeping beauty on his couch. Obviously, some man hadn't been doing his job.

He cracked open the door to the stairway to let in a sliver of light, turned off the living room lamp and sank into the chair across from her. As he watched her sleep, a million questions fought for dominance in his mind.

Who is she?

He first thought her a college girl, but it was clear she was closer to his own age of thirty, maybe a little younger. He recalled the trek through the woods and how nice it felt to hold her. Then he took a mental sledgehammer to the thought. He stopped entertaining notions like that a long, long time ago.

Light played softly on the wedding band on her finger. He shook his head. Some poor bastard would be sorry as hell come morning.

He stood and carried the cup of coffee to the kitchen and dumped it down the drain, then quietly climbed the stairs.

In his bedroom, he stripped off his clothes, sank into bed and lay staring at the ceiling. Tomorrow, he'd find her car, fix it up if he could and send her on her way. His life would continue as planned, without surprises and without beautiful women on the other side of the wall.

He lay awake for the rest of the night listening to the rain, carefully avoiding the thought that refused to let him sleep—he wanted her.

Chapter Two

Tory lay with her eyes closed long after the first rays of morning sun warmed her face. Her neck was cramped. Her head throbbed. She'd had a terrible dream, but not the car dream. It was worse.

She'd open her eyes sometime soon and find herself in her own bed, just like the previous day.

She must've left the window open last night. A breeze drifted into the room, carrying with it the sound of twittering robins and babbling water.

Strange, she thought. *It's Saturday.*

She should be hearing weekend sounds—the rumble of garbage trucks, the shrieks of children playing in the park across the street, the howl of tomcats in the alley separating Overland Apartments from Catillo's Market next door. She shouldn't be hearing birds and streams.

She cautiously opened one eye. Sunlight filtered through white tab curtains, spilling onto unfamiliar green walls and a clutter of well-worn furniture. A scratchy blanket under her chin had the letters USMC stamped on the hem. Oh, God.

She closed her eye and took a deep breath.

The accident was real, then. Judging from the dull pain in her leg, so was her encounter with the tombstone.

That meant the man was real, too.

She slowly relived last night's events, trying to piece together what happened. The man found her in the woods and brought her there.

He gave her a pink nightgown and went to change his clothes while she slipped into the gown. He returned, tucked that god awful blanket around her, but by then she was deep in a wine-induced nightmare. She dreamed she was rescued by Jake Benjamin, the man in the book. Dreamed that she, herself, was in the book.

Of course, that was just a dream.

She placed her feet squarely on the floor and took a moment to massage the lameness from her leg before attempting to stand. When she finally felt able to walk, she wandered around the man's living room, seeing sturdy no-nonsense furniture, wooden lamps and books, though none of those were penned more recently than 1945. A bulky vacuum cleaner poked its head from a closet. There was a phonograph and a case full of 78 rpm records.

A small voice chattered in the back of her mind, telling her something wasn't right, but she ignored it.

So he likes antiques, she thought. So what?

He'd put her clothes over the back of a chair. Her Levi's were split up the back and caked with mud. Beside them lay a frock and a pair of white ankle socks. She unfolded the dress and studied it. The hem was frayed and the red fabric had long since faded to pale rose.

Total Hausfrau, she thought, smiling at the memory of what the man said about his grandmother not being a fashion plate. That was for sure.

She wandered to the foot of the stairs and peered up.

"Hello?"

There was no answer. She padded to the kitchen where the faint smell of burned toast lingered, then stared in fascination at the wooden cupboards that stretched from the ceiling to the painted plank floor. A scrubbed pine table sat on sturdy, thick legs in the middle of the room. An array of dishes dried on the drain board beside an old metal sink.

It looked like a set for an old movie.

No!

She focused her attention on the enamel coffeepot on the stove. Beside it, the man set out a clean coffee cup and pitcher of cream with a note propped against the sugar bowl that read, *Help yourself.*

She poured a cup of lukewarm coffee and carried it back to the living room, sinking into a chair beside the softly playing radio as she tried to form a plan. Her car would definitely not be drivable. She'd have to call a few garages to see if she could arrange for a tow.

She tipped the coffee to her lips, drank deeply and heard the big-band music on the radio fade away.

"You've been listening to the sounds of Al Jolson on WNNY," the smooth-tongued announcer said. "The time is seven o'clock. In the news today, President Truman has approved a fifteen-percent wage increase ..."

Her hands shook violently, making her coffee spill over the rim of her cup. She stared at the radio in disbelief.

"In other news, nearly thirty-three years to the day after the bloody Eastern Rebellion, the twenty-six counties that make up the Free Irish State have extricated them—"

Tory, snapping off the radio, pressed trembling fingers to her lips. It had to be a joke. Someone was playing a colossal joke on her.

She raced to the phone in the kitchen and fumbled with the clumsy rotary dial. With hands that refused to stop shaking, she dialed Kate's number. After several moments of static, an operator said, "Hello, this is central. What party are you trying to reach?"

"I'm dialing Kathleen Hager on Strutt Street in Corning." She gave the operator Kate's number.

"I'll connect you. One moment, please."

Tory clutched the receiver with white knuckles as she waited.

"Ma'am, I'm having trouble making this connection. What city did you say your party is listed in?"

"Corning."

"What state is that, Ma'am?"

"New York!"

"Would you spell it for me, please?"

"C-O-R-N-I-N-G."

"One moment, please."

"Oh, please," Tory whispered. "Please."

"I'm sorry, Ma'am. There's no such city listed in my directory."

"There has to be!" she pleaded. "Corning, New York. It's only fifteen miles down the road!"

"I'm sorry. Would you like to try another party?"

She tried her favorite cousin in Buffalo with the same result and then hung up the phone, fighting panic. Maybe she was still dreaming. Maybe the other life was a dream and the present one was reality.

Maybe she was losing her mind.

She hurried back to the living room and dumped the contents of her bag onto the coffee table. Shoving aside gum wrappers and half-spent tubes of Chapstick, she grabbed her wallet and rifled through it frantically. She tore her driver's license from its slot and scanned it, devouring the information with her eyes.

Her name was Victoria Sasser. She lived at 107 Overland Drive, Corning, New York. Her date of birth was June 10, 1972.

She kissed the license. She wasn't dreaming, nor was she crazy. However, she was definitely in trouble.

"All right, Counselor." She took a deep breath and released it slowly. "Slow down. Take it one step at a time."

She carefully placed the items back in her purse. "Step one. Put on some clothes."

A hot bath helped ease the knots from her muscles, and it quieted the churning in her stomach, too. More than that, she found the simple act of doing something normal therapeutic.

She lay back in the tub, taking deep breaths and trying to think rationally. If there was a way in, there had to be a way out. If she somehow drove through a time warp, all she had to do was drive back out. All she had to do was get in the car and go.

First, she had to find her car. Someone must've found it by then, and reported it to the authorities. She stepped from the bathtub and toweled herself dry.

"Step two. Call the police," she said, pulling on the frock Jake set out for her and returning to the kitchen.

She picked up the receiver and dialed O.

"Central. How may I help you?"

"Yes, Operator. Would you please connect me with the police?"

"What city?"

A lump came to her throat.

"Heatherfield," she croaked.

"One moment. I'll connect you."

Seconds later, a brusque male voice said, "Heatherfield Police. Hopewell, here."

"Yes, Officer. I wonder if you can help me. My car seems to have been stolen and I was wondering whether—"

"Stolen?"

She heard him shuffling papers.

"Yes. That's what I said."

"I'll need some specifics. Let's start with the make and model."

"It's a ..." Tory had a sudden sinking feeling in the pit of her stomach. A Mitsubishi Eclipse made in 1999.

"Ma'am? Are you there?"

What did they do with the psychotic in 1949? she wondered. Send them for counseling? Probably not. They'd be more likely to lock them in a padded room and throw away the key.

"Hello? Ma'am?"

She hung up feeling more alone than she'd ever been in her life, more alone than when her mother died even. At least she had friends then. She was completely on her own here.

She forced down a slice of toast, pulled her hair into a plait, and left the house, choosing the wide rutted path leading through the woods.

The hillside was steeped in sunshine. As she walked, she breathed deeply the pine-scented air and glimpsed patches of sailor-blue sky between the sheltering branches above.

Chipmunks and rabbits scampered across her path, unmindful of her. The calls of sparrows and chickadees volleyed in the trees as if to announce her arrival.

Despite herself, she was charmed. The forest, which had seemed so terrifying last night, wrapped her in a warm embrace.

She followed the road until it tapered to a footpath. A truck was parked across the widest point, a chunky black Model A, old even for 1949. She heard muffled sounds in the distance of someone chopping wood. She followed them to a small clearing where Jake was hard at work. Staying well hidden, she watched.

He was beautiful as he worked among the trees. He fit, as much a part of the forest as the sturdy pines and towering cedars. He wasn't wearing a shirt and even from where she stood, Tory saw muscles in his back and arms rippling as he leveled a series of short, clean blows against the base of a tree.

He stood back as the tree crashed to the ground, opened a canteen and swallowed. He poured water into his hands and ran them through his sandy-brown curls. After another long drink, he spoke without turning.

"Good morning," he said.

"Good morning." She stepped out from the trees, embarrassed he'd caught her spying. "I thought I might try to find my car."

He nodded and took another swallow of water.

"I'm not sure I know where to start," she added.

"You'll want to stay on the skid road." He gestured toward a well-worn path winding through the trees. "It's easy to get lost out here if you don't know the way."

"Yeah. I know."

He capped the canteen, set it down and faced her. She fought to hide her surprise. Last night in the shadows, his scars weren't that pronounced. They extended down his neck and across his chest like bolts of lightning splitting a perfect summer sky.

She lowered her eyes. "Well, then."

"I'm almost finished here. If you want to wait, I'll help you look."

"No," she said quickly. "I'm sure I'll be fine."

He picked up his ax and cleanly sliced through a limb on the fallen tree. "Mind you, stay on the path," he said gruffly. "I wasn't kidding about those dogs."

She clutched her purse.

"How many dogs run in a pack like that?"

He shrugged. "Depends on the pack. Four, five, maybe eight."

"Oh."

Her Derringer held two bullets.

Jake lopped off another branch, pulled a bandanna from his jeans pocket and wiped sweat from his forehead. "I'll be glad to go with you if you want to wait."

"I don't want to be a nuisance."

He shrugged and resumed chopping. She watched in silence as he effortlessly severed branches as thick as her thigh. Her eyes moved over the strong line of his jaw and the cleft chin under his curving lower lip. She was partial to brown eyes. His looked as if they'd seen a million sorrows. Eyes like that made sensible women do stupid things.

Only the scars made his heartbreakingly good looks bearable. They splintered the left side of his face like shattered quartz on the face of a priceless grandfather clock. If not for those, he would've been as perfect as a hero from a romance novel.

In the wake of the realization he wasn't real, the sound of his voice startled her.

"We should probably start with the main road. There are bound to be skid marks where you went off." He buried his ax head in the tree trunk. "What kind of car did you say it was?"

She was ready for that and knew the only way to protect herself was to plead ignorance. She wasn't accustomed to lying, and she desperately hoped her naiveté wouldn't betray her. "I don't know. It's funny. I can't seem to remember much of anything." She wet her lips. "I don't even remember my name."

"It's Tory."

"What?"

"That's what you said last night. You said I could call you Tory."

"I did?"

"Yep."

"Oh. Well, that's a start, I guess."

His eyes went to her handbag. "You must be carrying some identification, maybe a driver's license or a checkbook."

"I spilled my purse last night in the graveyard." She was amazed at how easily the lies came. "I'm afraid I must've lost my wallet."

"You don't remember anything?"

"Nothing."

His brow furrowed. "Don't worry. We'll figure it out."

He retrieved a blue work shirt from a nearby branch and pulled it on, buttoning it up the front. "You said you were headed toward a town called Savona. Does that ring any bells?"

She shook her head.

"Hmm."

"How far is Savona?" she asked.

He shrugged. "Never heard of it."

Her heart sank. Corning and Savona didn't exist. Neither, for that matter, did Buffalo. She had no idea what did exist in that world. Living there would be more difficult than she'd guessed. She had to be very careful what she said.

Jake, sensing her despair, extended his hand as if to touch her and then let it fall to his side.

"I can finish up here later," he said. "We'll start with the main road."

Moments later, they rumbled down the rutted path in his Model A truck. She stared out the window as they passed his house, a large cabin devoid of a woman's touch. It looked more like a lodge than a private dwelling. A riot of wildflowers sprang up in haphazard patches all over the yard. As they passed, a plot of daffodils waved their yellow skirts in the breeze, like a hundred ladies dancing.

Just beyond the house, she saw an abandoned sawmill and looked at him questioningly.

"My father was a logger," Jake explained. "All of the Benjamin's were."

"You, too?"

He shook his head. "Not anymore."

She waited for him to elaborate, but he didn't. *He uses words sparingly,* she thought, *like they're small pieces of himself he can't bear to give away.*

At the end of the path, they turned onto a wide, paved road that went in either direction as far as she could see.

"Do you own all this land?" she asked.

"All but this road. My grandfather sold this stretch to the county in the twenties." In a voice tinged with anger, he added, "Not that he had much choice in the matter."

She glanced at him in surprise. "Why not?"

"Because all at once, everyone had a Model T and nowhere to drive it." He shrugged. "The price of progress, I suppose." He slowed to a crawl. "It was probably somewhere along here that you went off. Does anything look familiar?"

Her hopeless feeling returned. "No. Nothing."

He continued up the hill until the road dipped into a valley. Abruptly, the forest stopped.

"This is the county line. I doubt you'd have tackled the woods if you broke down past this point." He gestured out the window. "There's a village not far past that last grove of trees. You'd have probably gone that way."

She sighed.

"Don't worry." He lifted his hand again and let it drop. "We'll find it."

He turned around and drove back, checking his side of the road while Tory checked hers. There was nothing disturbed and no evidence a car had gone down the steep incline. They crawled along the road that cut through the forest until the terrain flattened again. At the bottom of the hill, the road split in a T. Flanking it on either side were rolling fields of purple. Almost surreal in its beauty, it reminded Tory of pictures she'd seen of Scotland.

"What are those beautiful flowers?" she asked.

"You mean the heather?"

"Heather? I didn't think heather grew in New York state." She turned to him wide-eyed. "I'm still in New York state, aren't I?"

He faced her with an unreadable expression. "Yes, Darlin'. You're still in New York state."

Not even fifteen minutes from home, she thought, yet I'm light-years away. She faced the window, stared at scenery too perfect to be real, and realized it wasn't.

Jake pointed left. "That road leads to the highway. The other goes to Heatherfield city. I doubt you could've made the hill in your condition."

She looked at him in surprise. "What do you mean?"

"You were drunk."

"I was not."

"Yes, you were."

"Jake, I wasn't drunk."

"Call it what you want," he said angrily. "You shouldn't have been driving."

"I had one glass of wine, maybe two."

"I thought you didn't remember anything."

"I don't." She turned away, flustered. "I'm sure I'm not the kind of woman who operates a motor vehicle while under the influence of alcohol. Can we turn back now, please?"

He made a U-turn and drove back up the hill.

"We'll start on foot. Shouldn't take more than a few hours to cover the perimeter. If we don't find it by this afternoon, we'll call the police. It must've turned up somewhere."

"No," she blurted. "I—I'd rather not involve the police."

"Why not?"

"Because—" She groped for a reason. The fewer involved, the better. The last thing she needed was the police asking a lot of questions she couldn't answer.

She hoped it wouldn't come to that. If they could find her car, and Jake could make the necessary repairs, then what?

She'd think about that when the time came.

Meanwhile, he was watching, waiting for an answer. "You were right. I was drinking last night. At least, I woke up feeling like I had been. I probably shouldn't have been driving. A person can get into trouble for that, I imagine."

"I imagine," he said softly.

He turned his gaze back to the road, but not before she saw a shadow of doubt move across his face.

Chapter Three

While Jake and Tory tramped through the forest in search of the missing car, Penny Candy made her slow journey down the steep back stairway leading from her apartment to her store.

"La la la … la la la la la laaaa, and la la la la la, la la, oh, la la la de daaaaah," she sang. "La, de, da, dedadedadada … Oh! Good morning, Thomas. Come for breakfast, have we?"

She stooped to scratch the ears of the old, gray tomcat that waited at the bottom of the stairs, a gesture that made her arthritic knees scream in protest.

"Gracious!" She righted herself with a creaking of bones and gripped the handrail until the pain subsided. She felt as if she'd slept for fifty years. Her eyes wandered the length of the plaza where baskets of red and gold tulips glistened with leftover raindrops. Glory, but it was a pretty morning.

She thought, as she'd thought every morning since the shops came to share her little corner of the world, how gay it would be to set baskets of such flowers about her porch. Her grand idea was always forgotten before the church bells tolled noon. Prettying up her property was something Penny never quite got around to.

Not that she didn't love the old place. She thought of her store as an extension of herself, as essential to her being as her built-up shoes and silver spectacles. Both were a wee bit past their prime, but still in remarkable shape given their mutual age of seventy-two.

Her gaze shifted to the park across the street where a pair of young lovers exchanged a morning kiss. She sighed, remembering days of stolen kisses behind the old hotel. She'd been such a pretty girl then, and Dwight—

"Meow!"

"Goodness, Thomas. Here I am woolgathering, and you're still waiting for your breakfast. Come along, then."

She hobbled across the yard to the front of the store, as the stray trailed eagerly behind. Climbing the three steps leading to the porch, Penny jammed her key into the lock and jiggled open the door. She savored the soothing, slightly musty smell that had greeted her every morning for almost fifty years.

She moved through the dust-scattered shadows, not wanting to turn on the lights yet. Smiling like a mother gazing at her sleeping children, she studied the case of bright candies, displays of greeting cards and holiday decorations, and racks of scrumptious romance novels, wondering which, if any, would find their way into the world that day.

Thomas slunk past and leaped to his spot in the window where he always spent the morning licking his fur until the patch of yellow sunlight shifted to the back of the store.

"Meow!"

"All right. Don't get your tail in a knot, Old Son." She glanced out the window. The couple was still embracing, as if unable to tear themselves apart. Penny smiled. It was a pity the way the other old-timers went about with sour faces, begrudging the young their youth.

Personally, she adored them for it.

She loved the children who came in after school and stood with their dirty faces pressed against her candy case. As often as not, when an occasional butterscotch or licorice drop found its way into a grubby pocket, Penny looked the other way.

She loved the teenagers with their grand dresses that flared fetchingly at the hip, ankle socks and dungarees cleverly rolled to the knee. She loved their Marlon Brando and Lone Ranger, their Frank Sinatra, and—

"Meoooow!"

"All right, Thomas. All right."

She gave his ears a final scratching and retreated to the back of the store. In the small kitchenette, she took a tin saucer from the cupboard and rummaged for her bottle of cod liver oil.

The cat turned up his nose at the three drops she added to his morning cream, but she did it anyway. It was for his own good, putting a shine in his coat and a sparkle in his eyes.

She pulled the bottle from its place and shook it. Seeing it empty, she frowned, thinking of the unopened bottle in her upstairs apartment in the cupboard above her sink. Penny sighed. The thought of another trip up and down those stairs was enough to make her bones ache.

"He'll have his way this morning for once," she told the bottle. "Only this once," she added sternly.

"Fools rush in, where ..." she sang. As she fumbled with the lid, the bottle of cream slipped from her knotted hands and crashed to the floor, the contents pooling in a thick white puddle at her feet.

"Oh, no!"

She bent to retrieve the bottle, her knees shrieking in protest. She straightened with a creak. Lord, she hated being old. She squandered a brief moment lamenting the fact it happened so quickly, and then squared her shoulders. There was no sense crying about spilled milk or spent youth. She'd just take some petty cash from the drawer and pop over to Grimley's for another bottle, or had she spent the last of that cash yesterday on soda crackers and tuna?

Penny sighed again. She never bothered keeping a ledger, but if she had she supposed it would be filled with a startling shade of red. It wasn't like years earlier when hotel guests came over for a book or a postcard. Back then there were also the railroad wives who lived in the houses where the shops now stood. They were such lovely women, always stopping by to ...

Another mournful howl came from the outer room, reminding Penny what she came for. She poured the last of the cream into her saucer and went to find the cat.

Out front, she found the screen door wide open and squinted into the pale morning sunlight.

"Thomas? Don't tell me you left without your breakfast."

When no answering howl came, she moved closer to the window, still squinting. "Thom ...?"

The word died on her lips when she saw the dark figure silhouetted in the doorway. It was too dark to make out his face, but before she stepped close enough to see his eyes, as blue as the devil's britches, she knew it could be only one man.

Penny frowned. "What do you want?"

He closed the front door and turned to face her, arms folded on his chest. His lips smiled, but the eyes remained cold.

"Why so hostile, Old Gal? I've only come to talk a little business."

"I have no business with you, Pierce Matthews."

"Come now, Penny." He stepped close enough that she smelled his coffee and cigarette breath. "Why do you persist in being stubborn?"

The saucer of cream shook in her hands, belying the firmness in her voice. "This property is not for sale."

"And if I doubled my offer?"

"No, Sir."

"I'm prepared to pay you four times what this old tinderbox is worth."

"This old tinderbox happens to be my home." She raised her voice. "I'll thank you to take leave of it this instant."

"Home," he sneered. "A drafty old box held together with crumbling mortar. I'm offering you the opportunity to live in comfort. You can have your choice of houses in Victory Park, free and clear, just as soon as you sign the papers."

"I'll do no such thing." She barely heard her words over the pounding of her heart. "I've told you before. This property is not for sale."

Pierce gave up the pretense of a smile. His hand snaked to her wrist, and the saucer clattered to the floor.

"Do you have any idea of the time and money I've invested in this plaza? Do you?"

"This store isn't hurting your old plaza." She bit her lip, fighting tears as his fingers sank deeper into the fragile bones under her flesh.

"This store is an embarrassment!" he bellowed. "It makes a mockery of everything I've tried to do." His eyes glittered with hatred.

Penny had never seen pure, unmasked hatred before.

"I don't take kindly to being made a fool of, so listen to me, Old Gal, and listen good. I have plans. Big plans. And you're sitting square in the middle of them."

He twisted her arm behind her back.

She groaned, certain her brittle old bones would snap like matchsticks. "Please," she whimpered. "You're hurting me."

He didn't seem to hear.

"You're a stupid old woman living in the past. Look around you. Times have changed. Get out of the way or take the consequences."

The room spun crazily. Penny lost her balance and pitched forward, her free hand groping for something to hold onto.

"When I think of what I've accomplished," he rasped, "single-handedly, how I've built this town from nothing. You people owe me."

In fact, he built his plaza on a loan with money borrowed against his wife's trust fund, but that wasn't the time to quibble over details. White lights danced before Penny's eyes.

"Now they want a roller rink for their brats to skate on. You see how it is?" He shook her arm, making pained breath hiss through her teeth. "They're like ungrateful children. No matter what I give them, they aren't satisfied."

Penny gasped in horror as her bladder emptied.

"Enough," she cried. "I'll do as you ask. Only, please ... let me go."

He loosened his grip slightly.

"Having a change of heart, are we?"

She nodded the affirmation her lips refused to speak. Mercifully, he freed her.

"That's fine. I'll have the papers drawn up this afternoon. With any luck, we'll be able to wrap things up by the end of today."

The words struck like a bucket of ice water to the face, making her forget her throbbing wrist. She fought to clear the cobwebs from her mind, desperate to find the words that would stall him.

"T—today? But I—I can't possibly make all of the arrangements today. I—I need time to select a house and sort through my things. It's fifty years' worth of clutter. I'm not a young woman. You said so yourself. I don't move as quickly as I once did."

His eyes, gleaming with triumph and suspicion, swept over her.

"Perfectly understandable. I'm a reasonable man. I'll give you until Monday evening."

Her heart sank. That was only two days away.

"But—I—"

"If you're thinking of double-crossing me, I wouldn't recommend it. I've been patient with you, Penny, but every man's patience has a limit. The next time I come here, it'll be to do more than talk. That's a promise."

She nodded miserably.

"I'm glad we understand each other." He walked to the door, turned and tipped his derby. "Until Monday."

Penny stared after him as he strolled across the park. Tears stung her eyes. She rubbed her wrist. Already, and angry, red cuff was forming. He meant every word. She had no doubt of that. She'd been dancing a dangerous tango with a madman, but her dance card was full.

The next time, he would kill her.

She sank into a nearby rocking chair and wiped away her tears with a tattered handkerchief. Thomas reappeared, daintily sidestepping the puddle of urine and jumping into her lap. She absently stroked his fur.

Pierce would kill her next time, but so what? What was the point in living if not in her dear, wretched citadel that sheltered her for over fifty years? How could she possibly move into one of Pierce Matthews' miserable white boxes when all of her memories were here? How could she bear it?

As she sat in the chair, sniffling and wiping her eyes, the shadows of ghosts flitted across the walls—a pretty girl of twenty-two, twirling in the arms of a merry-eyed man of forty.

She shouldn't let herself watch them, she knew. It was dangerous. The longer she dwelt on the past, the more difficult it was to keep her mind in the present, but her ghosts were so lovely. Would they follow if she left, or would they stay and be lost in the rubble once Pierce Matthews and his wrecking ball were through, lost to her forever?

"Don't leave me," she pleaded. "I couldn't bear it. I couldn't." Fresh tears sprouted. Penny buried her face in her hands and sobbed.

When someone spoke her name softly and tenderly, she glanced up. "Who is it? Who's there?"

She squinted into the sunlight and smiled. It was Dwight, dancing with her long-lost self.

He waltzed her across the dusty floor, a makeshift dance floor, flanked on either side by display cases draped in white linen. When the song on the old Victrola came to a scratchy, off-key ending, he dipped her low and kissed her.

"Is it really ours, Dwight?" She asked breathlessly. "Really and truly?"

"Yours, Darling." He gazed tenderly into her eyes. "A sweet little store for a sweet little girl."

"I can't hardly make myself believe it. So many good things all at once." Her hand crept to her abdomen. "What shall we call it?"

He placed his big, gentle hand over her small one. "The little one will bear my name. The store, yours. We'll call it Penny Candy's."

She smiled sadly as the ghosts faded.

The morning after they danced, Dwight made a big, red sign for the store. That afternoon, he kissed her and set out for the rail yard, whistling and swinging his black lunch pail.

She never saw him alive again.

That the child in her womb died the same day, the townspeople said, was Penny's just desserts. She conceived in sin, in a den of iniquity called the Heatherfield Hotel. A wedding ring after the fact didn't change what she was. She should go away and hide herself in shame.

She hadn't, by God!

A shunned, shattered Penny Candy thrust out her chin. With the insurance settlement from the railroad accident, she made her store a success. Through good times and bad, and more strongly than ever in the past few weeks, she felt a loving presence lingering nearby. The fairies were smiling on her, or so her grandmother would have said.

She felt it washing over her now, in the form of golden sunlight.

She stood, abruptly spilling the cat to the floor.

"Mind the store, won't you, Thomas, while I pop upstairs and make myself presentable? I can't very well greet the day with water in my eyes." She frowned at the soggy stain spreading across the front of her dress. "Not to mention my bloomers."

With an optimism she thought remarkable, given her set of circumstances, she hobbled across the store and out the front door.

Stepping from the porch, she glanced at the sun that blazed like a fairy wand above her store. A smile spread across her face.

Oh, yes, indeed.

Unless she missed her guess, a miracle was on its way.

She propelled herself across the lot, a rusty but undeniable spring in her step. She felt it in her bones, as sure as she stood there.

A miracle was on its way.

Chapter Four

Pierce Matthews strode across the park, whistling, glad it was over at last. It was a pity he hadn't used force from the start. He could've had the roller rink built and been recouping his investment in the time he'd been pussyfooting around.

"No more Mister Nice Guy," he murmured with a smile, liking the sound of it. Mister Nice Guy didn't get the job done. He just hoped the old bird wouldn't call the police.

As though summoned by the thought, Tom Hopewell, the chief of police, cut across the park directly toward Pierce. Pierce tensed when he called out to him.

"Morning, Pierce." Tom tipped his hat brim.

"Morning, Tom."

"Got a minute? I'd like to ask a couple questions."

"Of course." Pierce's easy smile belied the rigid cords tightening in his neck. He wondered what the going rate was for assault and battery. One hundred dollars? Two hundred?

"The thing is," Tom said, "Nancy and I have started another baby."

"Congratulations," Pierce said dryly.

"Thanks. Anyway, you know how women are when they're in a family way."

"I'm afraid Mrs. Matthews and I haven't been blessed. You'll have to clue me in."

"Oh. Right. Sorry." Tom shifted his considerable bulk, glancing up and down the park before lowering his voice. "She's got a bee in her bonnet about putting an addition on the house. I don't think I can swing it. Could you maybe stop by sometime and take a look? Maybe you could tell her the old place isn't sturdy enough or something like that?"

The cords in Pierce's neck loosened. Tom didn't know a thing.

Pierce promised to do what he could and continued walking across the park. He never liked Tom in the past, and he'd come to dislike him even more. Tom had been a decent ballplayer once, but that was history. He'd become fat and lazy.

Pierce shook his head. It was pathetic a lawman was afraid to lay down the law to his own wife. Still, it never hurt to do a cop a favor.

He smiled as he recalled the look of terror on Penny Candy's face. His fears were groundless, the product of an overactive imagination fueled by too many sleepless nights. Penny's expression was as good as a signed deed.

He hated old people. He hoped she didn't try to double-cross him like James Conswell, the old gopher who'd owned the Heatherfield Hotel. He would hate for things to get messy again.

He crossed Crescent Street and paused as he did every morning to admire the handsome gold lettering on the door of his office building: *Matthews Developing: Pierce Matthews, President.*

Once inside, he thought of Mae, his pretty new secretary. He'd call her into his office around eleven to take a letter, then he'd suggest an early lunch. He hung his derby on the hat rack inside the door and carefully smoothed his hair. After lunch, if his luck held …

"Mr. Matthews, Lord am I glad to see you." Mae shot him a frantic look from behind the mountain of paperwork scattered across her desk. When the phone rang, she groaned.

"Matthews Developing, Mae Davenport speaking."

His gaze lingered on her neatly pressed blouse for a moment, before moving to her pretty, flushed cheeks.

"I'm not sure. One moment, please."

He raised an eyebrow as Mae covered the mouthpiece with her hand and mouthed, *Wes Tanner*?

He shook his head violently.

"He's not in at the moment, Mr. Tanner. May I take a message?" She winced as she scribbled on her memo pad. "All right, Sir. Yes, Sir. I'll be sure to tell him." She hung up.

"Problem, Mae?"

"They've been calling all morning." She flipped through her tablet. "Mr. Peters, Mr. Slade and Mr. Brothers. They all want to know when the work will be started on their new houses." She raised her hands in a gesture of helplessness. "I don't know what to tell them."

His good mood evaporated, making him glare at her.

"Do you have any idea the kind of pressure I'm under, Miss Davenport?"

"I ... yes, Sir."

"Do you appreciate the tremendous amount of work that's involved in building a house?"

"Yes, Sir." She lowered her gaze.

"Good, because none of those people do. I'm a busy man. I would've hoped you'd be capable of seeing to some of the details, such as pacifying impossible clients. That is what I'm paying you for, isn't it?"

"Yes, Sir," she said meekly.

"If they call again, kindly explain to them I'm moving as fast as I can. I'll get back to them when I have something worthwhile to tell them. Until then, they must be patient."

"Okay, Mr. Matthews."

When the phone rang again, he gave her a withering look and retreated to his office, slamming the door behind him. He kicked his chair back from his desk, threw himself into it and swiveled to face the window. As he lit a cigarette, he eyed the ramshackle variety store with hatred, his earlier victory forgotten.

Blowing thick rings of smoke at the yellowed ceiling, he grimaced at the sound of the ringing phone. They wanted the houses they'd been promised—houses they'd paid for in advance. It was spring. The ground had thawed. There'd be no more putting them off.

The cigarette burned to his fingers. He crushed it out in an overflowing ashtray and lit another. Yanking open his file cabinet, he took out a folder labeled *Victory Park* and spread the contents across his desk.

He went over the figures for the millionth time. Why in the devil hadn't he left well enough alone? He could've lived more than comfortably off the interest from the houses that were already finished. He had no idea how well the properties would sell. People literally stood in line to buy the nasty, 800-square-foot boxes, and he eventually got carried away, selling two hundred too many.

He pulled a map of the city from its place on the shelf and studied it. There had to be something he overlooked. An ash fell onto the map, and he impatiently brushed it to the floor. He took a red pencil from the pencil holder on his desk and outlined the block of Victory Park, a useless potato field he converted into a gold mine surrounded on three sides by county roads he'd come as close to as he dared. There was no place else to go, except ...

He circled in black the fifty prime acres that butted against his property and crushed out his cigarette before lighting another. Damn it all to hell, he had counted on that land! Without it, he had to renege on two hundred sales and give back two hundred deposits.

"What should I do?" He rested his head in his hands, listening intently. There was a force, a power inside him that had guided him his entire life, but now when he needed it most, it was silent.

He closed his eyes and strained uselessly. The voice spoke only in its own time, not before.

"Tell me what to do," he hissed. "For God's sake!"

"Pierce? What are you doing?"

He snapped to attention at the sound of his wife's voice. Louise stood in the doorway, her red lips pulled back in an amused half-smile. He realized how he must've looked, palms spread open, face straining, weak. He detested weakness.

"What is it, Louise?" he snapped.

"I got a call from Dorene Watson this morning. She and Les have invited us for dinner and cocktails. I said we'd be there at seven. Is that all right?"

He sighed and rubbed his eyes. He couldn't possibly have felt less like socializing, but Les was one of his biggest backers. "I suppose so."

"We don't have to go." She crossed the room and rested her hands on his shoulders. "If you're tired, I'll call her back."

"I'm not tired." Gathering his papers, he stuffed them into the folder. "I'm extremely busy, though, so if you don't mind ..."

"I'm off to my shop, anyway. Shall I meet you at the diner for lunch?"

"I haven't got time today."

Though she'd clearly been dismissed, Louise hovered over him like a small, gray cloud. "You have to eat, Darling. The break might do you good."

He plucked a new pencil from the pencil holder and snapped it in two. "Unlike some people, my work doesn't always allow for personal comfort. I'm not selling dresses here, Louise. I'm planning futures. Try to remember that, won't you?"

"I wish you wouldn't belittle my work." She bit her lower lip, looking ready to cry. Her tears had no effect on him. He once found her child-like quality enchanting, but it eventually became a constant source of irritation. She had outlasted her usefulness. He was sorry he married her.

"Run along to your dress shop, Louise. I'll see you after work, probably close to six. Have my white shirt pressed by then, won't you?"

She threw herself through the door without another word.

Sighing, he turned his attention back to his file. She could have her little tantrum. He had bigger problems.

He skimmed through the figures again, tracing the fifty acres in black. If only Jedediah Benjamin had lived. A man who knew the value of a dollar, Jed would've seen the opportunity to unload fifty dormant acres as the lucrative business move it was. Pierce would've made him see it.

Things were never that simple.

Jed died in a logging accident, forcing Pierce to contend with Jed's mother-in-law, a stubborn old Kraut. He persuaded her to sell him one hundred acres of timber, offering twice what he planned. If Jake hadn't come marching home from the war, Pierce would've gotten the fifty acres at the bottom of the hill out of her, too.

His lip curled. It was unthinkable the wheels of progress were mired in the mud over the likes of Jake Benjamin.

It was all because of Louise. Pierce laughed—a small, bitter sound. For half a dollar, he'd swap Jake a useless wife who couldn't even manage to produce an heir for a useless piece of land overgrown with weeds.

In the next room, the phone rang incessantly, making it impossible to concentrate. He heard Mae doing her best to keep the wolves at bay. He would make it up to her in her pay envelope—or in another way.

For a moment, he entertained a host of pleasant possibilities.

They were driven from his head when a surge of energy, as strong as an electrical current, shot through him. Without understanding why or how, he knew the force had returned, the one that gave him the image of Victory Park and drove him to succeed.

It gave him another picture at the moment, one he wasn't sure he wanted to see.

"Are you sure?" he whispered.

The picture came more vividly and beads of sweat broke out on his forehead. It would be risky. He had always relied solely on himself, but for the next step he needed a professional. If he failed, he'd lose everything.

He studied the picture from all angles and from beginning to end, combing it for flaws.

There were none.

After a timid knock on the door, Mae poked her head into the office.

"I thought you might like a cup of coffee, Sir."

"That would be lovely, Mae."

She tiptoed across the room carrying a steaming cup.

He smiled. "Are they still calling?"

"I'm taking care of them, Sir, like you said."

"Good girl."

As she leaned forward to set the cup on his desk, he looked down the open throat of her blouse and then to the coffee in the cup. Both were light and sweet, filled to overflowing just as he liked them.

He slowly swirled a spoon in the cup.

"Actually, Mae, I've been thinking. It's been a long week. Maybe we both need a break."

"Sir?"

"I have a bit of business in Rochester this afternoon, some people to see. I could give you your pay early, if you'd like to come along. You can shop while I take care of business. After that, we'll have lunch together at one of those nice little restaurants in Midtown Plaza."

"That would be super, Mr. Matthews."

He smiled broadly. She was so pretty. So much prettier than the last one. Sipping his coffee, he reveled in the power and energy moving inside him, guiding him as it always had. It was a good thing.

He needed all the help he could get.

It would take a lot more than a little arm-twisting to bring Jake Benjamin to his knees.

Chapter Five

Still dabbing at her eyes, Louise walked across the park. Pierce had a way of making even the most glorious morning seem gloomy. It was as if he'd sucked the sunshine right out of the sky. Lord, how she hated him.

She'd married at twenty-three when she was young and pretty, naïve enough to dream her whirlwind courtship would be followed by a lifetime of romance. She laughed, making fresh tears spring to her eyes. Six years later, she awoke. Almost thirty, finding her beauty fading and her marriage a terrible joke. It didn't seem fair.

She unlocked the front door of Panache, her dress shop, to find the radio blaring. Millie, her daytime help, was in the window dancing with a mannequin.

"Millie!" Louise marched to the radio and pulled the plug. Silence filled the room. "Honestly! Why you insist on playing that rot is beyond me."

Millie replaced the mannequin and quickly smoothed her dress. "I'm sorry, Mrs. Matthews. I didn't realize it was getting toward ten o'clock."

"It's quarter past. You'll make up those fifteen minutes at the end of your shift tonight. Regardless of the time, I want that dial to stay on the classical music station, and keep it at a volume that won't make my teeth chatter, if you don't mind."

"Sorry."

Millie's careless shrug showed she wasn't sorry in the least.

Louise assessed the salesgirl through narrowed eyes. At eighteen, Millie was well on her way to becoming a broad. With her false eyelashes and padded brassiere, she was pretty in the same way a tinseled Christmas tree was—for its promise. She had her whole life ahead, a clean slate. All her mistakes were as yet unmade.

How Louise wished she could say the same.

"What do you think of my window?" Millie asked. "Is it all right?"

Louise turned her attention to the bright display of raincoats and scarves and the clever way Millie wound the pearl handles of a spring handbag through the mannequin's fingers. The display was perfect, fresh and young, exactly the image Louise wanted Panache to project.

"It'll do," she said grudgingly.

"I moved the rack of purses toward the front," Millie said, undaunted. "I thought to put these skirts over here by the counter where people can see them better."

She was right, of course. The skirts, the latest from New York, were a huge disappointment in terms of sales. They'd be much more visible near the counter. Millie smiled jauntily, as if to say Louise should have known that.

"No. I want the skirts to stay where they are. We're pushing summer now, not spring."

"All right, Mrs. Matthews. I only thought … "

"Don't think, Millie. Ask."

"Yes, Ma'am."

"I have some paperwork to do in my office. Please don't disturb me unless it's extremely important."

"Yes, Ma'am."

Louise, walking briskly to the back of the store, opened the door to an office the color and sweetness of cotton candy. It was her own creation and she was very proud of it.

After she sank into the crushed-velvet chair behind her desk, her eyes wandered to the silver-framed photograph of her and Pierce on their wedding day.

"The perfect couple," she muttered.

Her copper hair was gleaming and Pierce's eyes were radiant. But his smile was as big a lie as her lacy white gown. With a mean, secret smile, she turned the picture face down on her desk. That secret was her one small victory and the greatest source of her yearning. She sighed, wishing she could know again the sort of love she'd one shared with Jake.

Soon, she reminded herself. *Soon.*

She opened her handbag and fished out the mallet she took from Pierce's toolbox earlier that morning. Running her fingertips over its cool, sleek head, she thought how nice it would be to use the mallet to smash out his perfect, white teeth. Who was he to belittle her as if it wasn't her money that launched his dream in the first place? Did he think he could cast her aside and humiliate her now that he had money of his own?

Louise thought not.

When she felt composed, she tiptoed to the hall and listened carefully, as Millie prattled with a customer while the radio played in the background. Louise hoped it was loud enough.

She opened the back door and glanced up and down the alley. A pair of pigeons cooed softly from a telephone wire and a stray dog sniffed at a garbage can. There were no other witnesses.

She produced a nail file from her bag. Working quickly, she scratched the paint around the lock. After another cautious glance up and down the alley, she took out the mallet and swung it against the doorknob with all her strength.

The crash of splintering wood sent the dog skittering from the alley, its tail between its legs. Louise ducked inside and peered back out, half-expecting the alley to fill with customers and shopkeepers.

No one appeared.

Back in her office, she shoved the mallet and nail file into a desk drawer. When her hands stopped shaking, she picked up the telephone receiver and dialed the police. While she waited, she righted the photo on her desk and stared into her husband's lying face.

He had so many plans; he swept her along in the undertow of his accomplishments and then left her behind treading water.

"Not for long, Darling," she said softly.

Louise Matthews had plans, too.

•

From his vantage point at the front desk of the Heatherfield Police Station, Tom Hopewell shot cursory glances at the door of Matthews Developing. Pierce was up to something. There was no doubt about it.

Tom saw him come out of the old lady's store again this morning, something Pierce did once or twice a month, though Tom couldn't imagine why. He ran a hand across his already-stubbled chin and tapped two fingers against his lips.

When he stopped Pierce in the park, the man was preoccupied. He was a cool one, but Tom noticed how his eyes kept returning to the variety store. Why?

He'd always suspected Pierce had a hand in the death of old James Conswell. The Heatherfield Hotel burned from the top down, all four stories, and the old man slept on ground level. That seemed suspicious to Tom, though it wasn't anything he could prove.

The telephone rang, scattering his thoughts. "Heatherfield PD, Hopewell here."

"Tommy?"

His heart sank. That was Nancy's second call that morning. By Tom's calculations, he could expect at least a dozen more before his shift ended at five o'clock. Pregnancy made Nancy vulnerable and constantly needing reassurance. He turned his attention to the latest crisis. She was planning their meals for the month and wanted to know if he preferred ham or beef next Thursday. He sighed. It would be a long forty weeks.

He managed to pacify her without hurting her feelings, then hung up. The phone rang immediately.

"Heatherfield Police, Hopewell."

"Tom? It's Louise Matthews."

The introduction was unnecessary. He'd have known her breathy voice anywhere and unconsciously sat up straighter.

"What can I do for you, Louise?"

"I'm afraid someone tried to break into the store last night."

"A break-in?" He shuffled through the papers on his desk, a nervous habit he developed during Nancy's last pregnancy. "Is anything missing?"

"I don't think so."

"Sit tight. I'll be right over."

She was waiting out front when he arrived. She took his arm, and he got gooseflesh when she pressed her lips against his ear.

"I was hoping we could do this without a lot of fuss," she said.

He followed her to the back of the store where the doorknob tilted crazily in its slot. Tom squatted to examine the scratches around the lock. "Looks like they tried to use a file to pry it open."

"That's what I thought, too." She stood beside him, her hands balled on her slender hips. "I don't keep any money in the store overnight. I have a sign right on the door that says so."

"Hmm." The doorknob was dented as if it was hit with a hammer. Tom pulled a pad from his pocket and made a note. "When did you first notice the damage?"

"This morning. I came to empty my wastebasket, and there it was."

The wind shifted, bringing the sweet scent of her perfume. He remembered that scent from high school. She'd been such a pretty little thing and Lord, how he'd wanted her.

"You didn't notice anything missing?"

"Not a thing."

He pressed a meaty hand against the carpet.

"I haven't seen much of Jake Benjamin lately," Louise said abruptly.

He squinted at her in surprise. "Jake wouldn't have needed a hammer, Doll, and I doubt you have anything on your racks to fit him, anyway."

"Goodness, Tom. I wasn't implying I thought he did this."

She swept a tiny hand across the wreckage. "I just meant I haven't seen him in town in a couple months. I think about him being all alone on that hill."

Tom studied her face, searching for her meaning. It was a little late in the game for her to be thinking about Jake. He stood. "No one tried to break in here last night." He jotted another note in his pad.

Her face turned pale. "Why do you say that?"

"It rained lions and tigers all night. With the door hanging open like this, the carpeting would have been soaked in minutes. It must've happened sometime this morning."

She smiled. "Of course. Why didn't I think of that?"

"You'll need to stop by the station today and fill out a formal complaint. Meanwhile, you'd better have your husband put a new knob and bolt on this door."

"Sure." Her tone was breezy, but anger smoldered in her smoky eyes. "If he's not too busy with that silly housing project of his."

"Building another tract?"

"Adding to the one at Victory Park, from what I hear. Of course, I stay out of his business dealings just like he stays out of mine."

Tom filed that information in the back of his mind, scribbled a few more notes and turned to leave. "I'll ask around and see if anyone saw or heard something. Get this door taken care of, okay? Remember to stop by the station later."

She smiled sweetly. "Will do."

As he trudged back to the station, Tom's thoughts returned to Jake Benjamin. Like every other red-blooded boy in Heatherfield, Tom was jealous as hell when Jake won the affections of Louise Sharp.

He was also mighty curious. Jake was different, even then—a gentle giant who seemed as comfortable writing poetry as running a field goal. Tom shook his head. He would rather have seen Lou end up with Jake than a swine like Pierce Matthews.

He frowned, remembering the summer of '42 when his own number came up. He, Jake and Stu Gordon lined up outside the draft office along with half the town waiting for their physical examinations.

Pierce was the only one of them who came out wearing a smile.

A punctured eardrum earned him a 4-F classification, leaving him free to build his empire and take his pick of the Heatherfield girls while every other male between the ages of eighteen and twenty-five was shipped overseas. Tom reentered the station, wondering how a man went about puncturing his own eardrum.

Back at his desk, he quickly reread his notes and sighed.

Heatherfield was getting as bad as the city. As the town swelled, so did its crime rate. It was almost like two warring forces that pit the old against the young, the weak against the strong.

It wasn't like that in the old days when his father was on the force. He let Tom wear his cap and ride through town in the patrol car with him. The worst crimes Tom's father dealt with were Sunday drivers clogging up traffic on Main Street and people locking their keys in their automobiles.

Heatherfield was becoming like everyplace else, with thefts, assaults and even an armed robbery a few years earlier. Most of the crimes were committed out of spite, but Louise's was a new one. Tom shook his head.

He'd never known anyone to vandalize her own property before.

He filled out the incident report, swallowed a cup of coffee and took another call from Nancy. All the time, he stared at the front door of Matthews Developing.

When Pierce Matthews' shiny black Frazier pulled out of the lot an hour later, Tom's unmarked car followed a safe distance behind.

Chapter Six

The house wasn't big enough for both of them. There was no place to hide, even if he wanted to. Problem was, he didn't. He was drawn to her, almost against his will, pulled as if by magnetism, compelled to be near her. She was sleeping in his grandmother's bed only twenty feet down the hall. That thought kept Jake tossing in his own bed.

At two o'clock in the morning, he gave up the fight for sleep, pulled on his clothes and quietly slipped from the house. After pausing to glance into the darkened upstairs window, he walked soundlessly down the path.

There was no car. He was certain of it.

He spent most of the afternoon searching the woods with Tory, then most of the evening searching alone. He found nothing amiss, not even a broken twig. He had no reason to doubt her story about amnesia, but he did. She wasn't telling him everything, though the reason was clear. She was afraid of something—or someone.

He cut a path through the woods, pausing again to listen to the shushing of the river and the distant cry of a loon—peaceful sounds, incongruous with the battle raging inside him. Why hadn't he sent her away?

She was dangerous for him, like the chocolate-covered peanuts he once bought from Penny Candy when he was a kid. He remembered standing in her store, face pressed against the glass of the candy case, wanting them while knowing he would pay, not only with his nickel allowance but with a painful case of hives.

He wanted them anyway. Pain and desire went hand-in-hand. He should know that by now.

He also knew what it was like to feel alone and frightened. Running his fingers over his ravaged face, he realized again how the war did him in emotionally and physically. In his darkest hour, in the shelter of a makeshift hospital, an Army chaplain gave him kindness and the courage to continue on.

Could he give Tory any less?

Instead of making his usual trek past the sawmill and through the graveyard, he went downstream, taking the overgrown path leading to the cabin. The night was clear, the cabin steeped in moonlight and memories.

•

"Do you like it, Louise?"

"Oh, Jake! It's super!"

"Not yet, but it will be."

"When will it be finished? I can't wait. Tell me again where everything will be."

"This room is the kitchen."

"It looks small."

"It'll seem bigger once the walls are up."

"We'll have a fireplace in the living room, right?"

"You bet."

"This room?"

"A nursery for little Jake."

"This one?"

"For baby Louise."

"What'll this room be for?"

"Come here. I'll show you."

"Oh, Jake."

"I love you, Lou. Do you know how much I love you?"

•

A familiar ache tore through his chest. He made a damned fool of himself, back then, but it would never happen again.

He'd intended to raze the cabin after the war, tear it apart log by log, stone by stone, leaving no reminders, but he couldn't bring himself to do it. Instead, he let it sit there, a shell of memories, for four years.

That winter, though, he felt compelled to finish it. He worked steadily, caulking and sanding, running electrical wires, installing plumbing. When it was finished, he hauled a few pieces of spare furniture down from the main house, thinking to rent the cabin that fall to the hunters who came from the city, but ...

He had other plans for it now.

He stepped through the front door, bracing himself for the usual onslaught of memories. As he wandered through the empty rooms, his chest ached again when he thought of the children he built them for. While working on the rooms again he almost convinced himself he still had a chance, telling himself his scars weren't that bad. Someday, a woman would be able to look beyond them and see a man she could love.

Tory told him the truth. He'd never lie down with a woman again unless he paid her. He'd seen it in her eyes that morning when the cold light of reality shined on his face. He was hideous.

He turned to the task at hand, taking inventory. He had to bring more blankets and a few dishes and towels. Smiling, he imagined Tory lingering over coffee at the small table in the kitchen, the morning sun in her hair. He imagined Tory spending chilly evenings beside the fireplace, lying down at night in the little bedroom and gazing up at the stars. That last image made the ache in his chest shift to his groin. He'd been without a woman for too long. The sooner he got her out of his house, the better.

An hour later, he slipped back into his own house, creeping up the stairs and down the hall. While passing the room that had belonged to his grandmother, he heard Tory cry out. Though muffled, it was unmistakably a cry of fear, as if she'd awakened from a bad dream.

He pressed his ear to the door, and the sound came again, going right through his heart.

Oh, Child, he thought. I could make it better if you'd let me.

That thought foremost in his mind, he raised his hand to knock.

•

She slept deeply. As if anesthetized by the mountain air, she slipped between the crisp, cool sheets and crashed into oblivion.

Then she was wide awake, her eyes darting around the strange, moonlit room, searching for something—anything—to allay her terrible fears.

She dreamed again. She'd been lying in the forest as a cold, relentless rain pelted her body and face. An assemblage of old men gathered around, staring and silent. Through the trees, she saw her car, blood-spattered and glowing red.

It seemed so real and terrifying, she cried out, screaming until her throat was raw. Then, like a mother comforting a sleeping child, the whispering winds soothed her back to sleep and she awoke.

She lay trembling, her throat parched, heart banging in her chest, unable to shed the nagging feeling someone needed her help, but who? She closed her eyes and concentrated. Someone was waiting for her, depending on her.

It was useless. She turned on the bedside lamp, her gaze wandering around the small, tidy room. A German Bible lay facedown on the night stand beside a pair of wire-rimmed glasses. Beneath the table, a pair of bedroom slippers sat side-by-side. The calendar above her bed was open to January, 1949.

She squeezed shut her eyes. Delirium was a disease of the night, or so she'd read. Would daylight ever come? Her panic returned, threatening to overwhelm her.

Relax, she told herself. *Breathe.*

It wasn't the first time she knew such fear. She'd known it as a child away at summer camp, terrified of night sounds outside her tent. Every hooting owl was a band of rogues, every rustling leaf became a prowling wolf. She cowered in her sleeping bag, fist crushed to her lips, imagining her house, dolls and mother's gentle face. The memories calmed her then. Maybe they would work again.

She tried to remember her apartment. To her alarm, she couldn't see it, not even one room. All she saw was a vast white vacuum of nothingness. She shot up in bed, placing her hands on her temples, forcing herself to concentrate.

As fast as images formed in her brain, they were plucked away like daisies from a summer garden.

She snatched her purse from the night stand and rifled through it, flipping open her wallet to pull out her driver's license. Her name was Victoria Sasser, her address, 107 Overland Drive.

An image came slowly. That time, it remained. She saw an airy white room with a bookcase and cluttered desk. She almost choked on a sigh of relief.

She fingered her ID badge from Women, Incorporated, and then her keys and her gun. Another picture came sharply into focus of a pretty Latina named Frankie with a shy smile and haunted eyes.

"Oh, Frankie, I'm sorry," she whispered.

She started slowly working backward, reconstructing the day of the accident. There was Frankie's urgent call, the book titled *Heatherfield*, visiting Clyde Hardback's store to buy a book that might help her understand the nightmare that plagued her all her life. Instead, she was pulled into it.

A lost, lonely, homesick feeling pooled in her chest.

She had to face it. As incredible as it seemed, she was living in a fictitious world. None of it was real—the mountain, Jake, not even the bed on which she lay. Her thoughts tumbled through a labyrinth of confusion and hit a thick, brick wall at every turn.

If only she could find her car, she'd find a way out of the mess she was in, but how? They searched all day without finding as much as a tire track. It was as if her Mitsubishi had vanished into thin air.

Tory might never get out.

Her homesickness gave way to a feeling of suffocation.

"Take five, Counselor," she told herself. "A panic attack won't help."

Throwing open the window, she gulped cold, night air. When she'd regained her equanimity, she settled back into bed. As sleep reclaimed her, her thoughts returned to her visit with Clyde.

Steamy for the times, he said. Poor Destiny wasn't all that respected in the literary world.

Her eyes flew open. What had he said? She barely dared to breathe lest the memory escape. She focused on Clyde's gnarled hands as they reached for the book she held, willing herself to recreate his words.

She had a nasty habit of tooting her own horn. She liked to write herself into her stories.

Tory gasped. "Of course!"

A tidal wave of relief washed over her. If she'd somehow been written into that strange book, it stood to reason the author had the power to write her out. Destiny Paige died in 1972, but Tory was in 1949. Was it possible Destiny was alive and well, hiding someplace in the story?

As she fell into an exhausted sleep, one thought remained firmly fixed in her mind. Destiny Paige held the key that would free her from this prison. All Tory had to do was find her.

Chapter Seven

The next morning, Tory awoke with a feeling of optimism she wouldn't have thought possible the previous day. Sliding out of bed, she walked to the window and leaned out. The sun rose over the hillside, casting indigo shadows across the forest. In the distance, she heard the faint echo of Jake's ax and smiled. Didn't he ever sleep?

She moved from the window and opened the closet door. Five dresses hung neatly on their hooks, all similar in style to the one she wore yesterday. She selected a yellow gingham shift and padded down the hall to the bathroom, pausing outside the door to Jake's bedroom, which was small and sparsely furnished.

A patchwork quilt spilled haphazardly from a double bed where a pillow still bore the imprint of his head. A book lay facedown on the table as if he'd been reading and set it aside for the night. Curious, she picked it up, read the open page and smiled. She wouldn't have thought he appreciated poetry.

A pair of dog tags glinted from a porcelain dish. Beside them were two medals. Tory picked them up and examined them, seeing one was a Bronze Star, the other a Purple Heart. As she clasped them in her hand, emotions stronger than she'd ever known flooded her senses—fear, sorrow and rage.

Shaken, she replaced the medals in the dish and hurried from the room.

She washed quickly and pulled her hair into a plait, eager to begin her search for Destiny Paige. Where in Heatherfield would an author hang out?

She mulled over the possibilities as she filled the kitchen sink with water to wash out the dress she wore the previous day, along with her underclothes, and carried them outside to the clothesline.

Morning air greeted her, crisp, clean and rife with bird song. A rabbit hopped from the shelter of the trees, sitting inches from Tory as it licked its paws. Tory squatted, her hand extended.

"Come here, Boy."

To her amazement, it did. She stroked its velvety ears while the rabbit accepted clover from her hand.

"Aren't you a sweet little thing?" she murmured.

Standing, she surveyed the beauty of the hillside. At home, she often spent long Sunday afternoons hiking at the nature center, but even the most breathtaking trails Spencer Crest had to offer couldn't compare to what she saw on Jake's mountain.

"What a wonderful world you created, Destiny Paige," she whispered.

•

By the time Jake returned from the woods, Tory had the table set for two. A plate of pancakes steamed in its center, flanked on either side by a bowl of scrambled eggs and a platter of crisp bacon.

He stopped in the doorway, eyeing the scene.

"I hope you're hungry," Tory said brightly. "I made enough to feed an army."

"You didn't have to," he said gruffly, walking past her to wash his hands in the sink.

"It's the least I could do. You've been very decent to me."

His huge form dominated the kitchen. Tory's eyes moved over his big, work-roughened hands, his hair damp with sweat until it curled just below his collar.

Lord God, she thought, *that's one beautiful man.*

He turned to face her and she averted her gaze. "Go ahead and sit down before everything gets cold."

He ate hungrily, saying little and seeming ill at ease, almost angry. She wondered if she'd overstepped her boundaries. Nibbling on a piece of bacon, she felt too excited to eat.

"So," she said casually, "what's Heatherfield like?"

He shrugged. "It's like anyplace else."

"Is it a big town?"

He shoveled a forkful of eggs into his mouth, chewed and swallowed. "It's a whole lot bigger than it used to be. It's changed a lot since the war."

She reached for another slice of bacon. "What war?"

When she saw his incredulous look, she mentally kicked herself for being off guard.

Jake drank some coffee and slowly set down his cup. "The second one."

"Are their any libraries or museums in town?"

His expression darkened subtly. "No museums. They were talking about building a library the last I knew. I don't go into town very often."

"How about bookstores?"

He laughed softly. "There's Penny Candy's place. It's as much a bookstore as anything else."

"Penny Candy? Is that really her name?"

He fiddled with his coffee cup. "Yep."

"That's quite a name."

"She's quite a gal."

"How far is it to town?"

He shrugged again. "About four miles down the hill."

"I might walk down later and take a look around."

He stared at her for a long moment, then wiped his mouth with a napkin before tossing it aside. "Be a hell of a walk back."

"I'm perfectly capable of walking four miles. I—" She stopped before admitting she ran six miles a day. "—would hope."

"I don't think you'll find much open on Sunday." Jake pushed back his chair and stood. "I have to drive to town tomorrow to pick up some things at the grocer's. You can ride along if you want." He retreated to the stairway, then turned back. "Thanks for breakfast."

She watched the doorway long after Jake disappeared through it and smiled. Underneath that grizzly bear veneer, Jake had the heart of a lamb. Then another thought came nipping on the first one's heels.

He's tough and tender, just like the hero in any romance novel, she realized.

•

Jake stood under the shower, welcoming the hot spray of water running over his hair and into his mouth. A man could get used to a warm meal on the table and a pretty girl to share it with.

He scrubbed his skin until it burned.

She was full of questions that morning. Maybe she was bored with the mountain. She wanted museums, libraries and entertainment, the things city girls craved. He ran soapy hands savagely through his curls. It was best to let her go. That would save him the trouble of making the little speech he prepared.

He stepped from the shower, made a fist and rubbed a circle in the steam on the mirror to scrutinize the face that stared back. He came close to making a fool of himself last night.

What was he thinking?

The man in the mirror scowled as he lathered his face. He'd been thinking what any red-blooded man would think. He drew his razor across his face in clean, even strokes, carefully avoiding the scars. She said he'd been decent. God help him, she wasn't making it any easier for him.

He sat across from her at breakfast, not daring to look at her, his senses finely attuned to the fact she wore nothing under her dress. He drew his hands back through his hair. God, he had to get her out of the house. Today.

He returned to the kitchen and found her standing on a chair, rearranging the cupboards. His eyes caressed the smooth, round line of her bottom.

Today, he reminded himself.

She turned, saw him watching and smiled.

"I had quite a time finding things this morning. If we're going downtown tomorrow, I thought I should make a grocery list. You're almost out of sugar, see?" She held out a sack and shook it. "Almost empty."

"Tory—"

She pulled out a can of shoe polish and almost dropped it.

"Shoe polish in with the spices? Who'd have thought?"

"Tory—"

"If I got the cupboards organized, we'd have a better idea of what we need. Why are you looking at me like that?"

"You can't stay here."

Her hand froze, clutching the can of shoe polish, and a look resembling fear flickered across her face before she turned back to the cupboard.

"I'm sorry. It was presumptuous of me. I'll put everything back the way you had it." She quickly replaced the items in the cupboard.

"It's not that."

She turned back, her eyes pleading.

"Let me stay, Jake. Just until I get my bearings? I promise I won't be any trouble."

Trouble? Is she kidding? he wondered.

"I don't intend to freeload, if that's what you thought," she said in a rush. "I could do things for you."

Oh, Child. His eyes involuntarily traced the pleasant fullness of her breasts. I'll bet.

Her face flamed, then her chin raised. "I can make beds, wash dishes, scrub floors—and I'm a pretty fair cook. You saw that yourself."

He couldn't bear it, because he wanted that and more—so much, but she didn't have an inkling.

He crossed the room, took the can of shoe polish from her hands, and deftly lifted her from the chair. Their eyes locked. He heard a soft gasp just before his lips crashed down on hers. He drove his tongue into her mouth, demanding its sweetness. When she didn't resist, he shoved himself closer, trapping her between the cupboards and the hard line of his body.

She pressed her hands against his chest and shoved hard. The kiss was worth every bit of anger he saw smoldering in her eyes.

"How dare you?" she hissed.

She was more beautiful than ever, just then, and he caught his breath. "I've been a very long time without a woman, Tory. It's best for both of us if you don't spend another night under this roof."

His words extinguished some of the angry fire in her eyes.

"I have a cabin just a little ways away. You're welcome to it until you get your bearings."

The relief on her face belied the hostility in her tone. "It's a safe distance away, I hope?"

"Yes."

"I don't appreciate being man-handled. I won't stand for it."

Those were angry words, but he remembered the taste of her lips and how, for a brief moment, she responded to his kiss.

"I won't touch you again," he said, "until you ask me to."

Chapter Eight

His kisses were brutal and degrading. It demeaned her that he used her to play out his sick little fantasies. She once found that exciting, but not anymore.

Louise sat beside her husband in their usual pew at Heatherfield First Presbyterian, three rows back from the pulpit, smiling for her audience. Inside, she seethed with hatred, remembering that morning's game.

Her eyes brushed over the congregation and rested on Tom Hopewell and his brood of four brats, with Nancy, his wife, showing again, the old sow. Better Nancy than her. As if feeling the weight of Louise's stare, Tom glanced at her and waved. She nodded politely.

Tom was one of the few people in Heatherfield Jake considered a friend. She only hoped he'd get it in his thick head to tell Jake about her trouble at the store, and that she'd asked after him. If not, she'd have to invent another excuse to get Tom alone. It cost nearly ten dollars to repair the door, but if Jake took the bait it was worth every nickel.

The organ played *No Greater Love*, as the choir moved single file to the front of the church. Pierce dropped his arm around her shoulders and she shuddered. As the choir sang, she drifted back in time to other embraces and kisses that left her breathless, aching with need.

She smiled at the words, no greater love. Jake had to come to town sometime, whether Tom ran interference or not. When he did, Louise planned to be ready.

•

The music was lovely that morning. In the back of the church, Penny opened her hymnal and added her scratchy voice to the choir's rich harmony. Most of Heatherfield's old-timers were lifetime members of the United Methodist Church on Old Main Street. Penny preferred the Presbyterian with its soft, velvet pews and handsome, young pastor. A strapping man of merry green eyes and booming voice, he reminded her of Dwight.

When they finished the morning's selections, the choir drifted back to their seats. After exchanging bits of gossip with her neighbors on either side, Penny settled back eagerly awaiting the morning's sermon. Pastor Rinds delivered such lovely sermons.

As she lovingly followed his progress to the altar, her eyes fell on a dark figure near the front of the church—Pierce Matthews.

She frowned.

It was a sacrilege such a man would show his face in the Lord's house. The thought kindled a fire in her breast. She pondered the meaning of that sudden heat, intrigued by the knowledge she was feeling hatred. She couldn't say she ever truly hated anyone before. There was no doubt about the emotion, though. It was hatred, plain and simple.

She immediately mouthed an *Our Father*, being at an age when she had to be careful about her eternal soul.

As she stared at the back of Pierce's head, a feeling of despair replaced her anger. It was Sunday, and that meant the next day was Monday. When Monday came …

Despair became a thick swelling in her throat, became a river that coursed down her cheeks. Just when she was certain the river would drown her, the sun crept through the stained-glass window above her head, drenching her in soft, golden light. A limb of a weeping cherry tree tapped softly on the pane. Its leaves fluttered like fairy wings against the glass, almost like a gentle reminder.

She folded the last of her tears into a tattered handkerchief and mouthed another *Our Father*, because she'd doubted. She added a prayer to Saint Francis, and then one to Saint Theresa for good measure.

●

Tom listened to Pastor Rind's sermon, but he couldn't stop his eyes from darting around the church. They kept returning to Pierce Matthews, the scoundrel. He sat beside Louise, playing the role of devoted husband.

Tom knew better.

He had intended to follow Matthews only a few miles to see where he was going in such an all-fired hurry, but he ended up tailing him all the way to a lower-class section of Rochester. What did Pierce want in an abandoned warehouse that took almost an hour to get to?

It seemed mighty suspicious to Tom.

Then there was the business of taking the Davenport girl to a seedy hotel. That really set Tom's kettle to boiling, though he wouldn't make any trouble over it. The girl was of age, though a poor, sweet, naïve kitten. God only knew what sort of bill of goods Matthews had sold her.

He shifted his gaze to where Mae sat, pale and small, between her parents. No, Tom wouldn't make trouble over that. Phil and Chlois Davenport were good, decent people. He wouldn't disgrace them by dragging their daughter's name through the mud. He shook his head at the scandal that would create.

Still and all, that cleared up one other matter. He studied Louise cautiously. If a gal got lonely enough, there was no telling what fool ideas might come into her pretty head. He dropped his arm around his wife, and she smiled and snuggled close. Lord, how he loved her.

His anger flared again.

He sympathized with Louise, but she could've had better if she'd only waited. Jake would have moved hell and high water to come home to that little gal. If she thought for a minute Tom would play messenger boy for her to Jake, she had another thing coming.

Chapter Nine

Who does he think he is? Tory wondered, shooting a sideways glance at Jake's profile as they rumbled down the old logging trail leading through the woods. His big hands, which less than an hour ago touched her, gripped the steering wheel and nearly swallowed it.

At least he was honest about his motives, which was more than she could say about most men. Still, who the hell did he think he was?

He glanced at her, and she quickly turned her face toward the window, inching closer to the door and holding onto her anger.

Unexpectedly, the truck hit a rut. She lurched forward and grabbed the dash to steady herself.

"Easy," Jake said. "Are you all right?"

"I'm fine," she said stiffly.

Those were nearly the first words she spoke to him since the episode in the kitchen. She threw a backward glance at the truck bed, piled high with enough towels, bedding and dishes for a year's visit, though she'd coolly informed him she didn't intend to stay more than a few days, perhaps a week.

Jake pulled into a grove of trees and turned off the engine. "We have to go on foot from here."

Without a word, Tory jumped from the truck and grabbed a box from the bed. The moment she lifted it, she knew it was the wrong choice. Hefting it off the tailgate, she almost stumbled under its weight.

"Let me get that." Jake reached for the box.

"I can do it," she said. Damned if she'd give him the satisfaction of another show of strength.

She shifted the box against her hip and trudged down the narrow, overgrown path, ducking to avoid branches that clawed at her clothes and hair. After a short distance, the path widened into a clearing. She walked through a thicket and froze, nearly dropping the box.

It was a small, tidy cabin surrounded by a ring of evergreens. Two wicker chairs rocked emptily on the porch in the afternoon breeze. Lacy, white curtains swayed in the windows.

It was the house from the cover of the book. She choked back a sob.

"It's not fancy, but you should be comfortable."

She whirled at the sound of his voice. "What is this place?"

He hesitated. "It's a hunting cabin."

She set down the box and took a tentative step forward.

"Is something wrong, Tory?"

"There was a fire here, wasn't there?"

He looked at her quizzically, then shook his head. "What makes you think that?"

Because I saw it burn to the ground, she thought, feeling her knees buckle.

Jake was instantly at her side, his hands at her waist. "Are you all right?"

"I don't know."

"It's all right, Tory. Come here. Look." He led her to the back of the cabin and pointed at the roof and frame. The wood was perfectly sound. "There was no fire. See? There's nothing to be afraid of."

He spoke gently, as if coaxing a small child.

She didn't want or need his concern. She pulled free of his grasp just as a pair of chickadees twittered in the trees, sounding like laughter. The sound mingled with the chortling river flowing a few yards away. A riot of blue and pink forget-me-nots sprawled over the banks. In such a setting, her fears seemed groundless.

"Of course there isn't." Summoning her dignity, she lifted her chin. "I was confused for a minute. That's all." She breezed past him and stepped onto the porch.

The front door opened into a room made of knotty pine. Two easy chairs faced each other before a cut-stone fireplace that spanned the entire wall. The room exuded warmth, peace and masculinity, along with another element she couldn't name.

While Jake went to retrieve the rest of the boxes, Tory wandered into the kitchen where a small table and chairs sat under a window. Red-checked curtains were parted to reveal the river.

She ran her fingertips along a countertop that had been varnished to a glossy sheen. A slow realization dawned. More than the mortar and timber, fixtures or cut stones, the cabin had been built with love.

Suddenly, she remembered the pictures the book had shown her— pictures of a younger, more innocent Jake building a home for the woman he loved. Feeling a pang, she steeled herself against it.

Sensing his presence, she turned to see him in the doorway, his hands in his jeans pockets.

"You built this, didn't you?" she asked.

He shrugged. "Winter project."

The cabin was more than that and they both knew it. Behind his shuttered eyes, she sensed he wanted her to like it and approve.

"I guess we should start putting this stuff away." He indicated the pile of boxes standing against the living room wall.

"I can manage."

The moment to compliment his handiwork passed and she was sorry she hadn't.

He hovered in the doorway for a moment. "I'll stop by, look in on you later and see how you're getting along."

"You don't have to." She opened a box of dishes. "I'm sure I can handle anything that might come up."

She watched from the window as his broad shoulders disappeared down the path, then set about putting the cabin in order. As she put fresh sheets on the bed, deposited a stack of clean towels in the bathroom closet and arranged the cooking items in the kitchen cupboards, memories of his kiss lingered.

She scrubbed vigorously at the inside of a cupboard, scattering particles of sawdust on the floor, trying to rekindle her earlier anger. What bothered her most was that he thought she enjoyed the kiss.

No, she thought. Be honest with yourself. What bothers you most is you did like it. In fact, you liked it a lot.

"Great going, Tory," she said. "You've found the perfect man. The only trouble is, he isn't real." She looked around the cozy room. "None of this is real."

That thought started a headache nagging at the base of her neck. She flopped into an easy chair and reached for her purse. Shaking three ibuprofen tablets from a bottle, she swallowed them dry and opened her wallet. That was becoming her lifeline and only link to reality.

She flipped through a handful of photos, trying to put names to the faces that smiled back at her, but they seemed like strangers.

Her uneasiness returned. She lingered over a black-and-white snapshot of herself with a stout, forty-something woman in a tight jumpsuit. She smiled broadly as she flashed a handful of bills for the camera.

Tory scrutinized the woman's bulldog face and slowly, as if through a fog, a memory emerged. She and the woman had been on the board-walk in Atlantic City. The woman had just won a lot of money at a blackjack table. They ducked into a photo booth to pose.

The picture was ragged at one end, as if torn in half. The woman with the bulldog face had the other part.

Who is she? Tory wondered, staring into her eyes, willing herself to remember.

Better pull yourself together, Kiddo, the woman seemed to say.

Tory grinned. "Hello, Kate."

One thing was certain. The mountain was casting a spell over her that made her forget her real life. She'd better find Destiny Paige soon.

Her thoughts scampered back to the kiss. A pocket of warmth spread through her stomach as she shoved the photo back into her wallet. In the meantime, she'd better steer clear of Jake Benjamin.

•

It was the best thing he could've done, and the smartest thing he'd done in two days. Jake brought his ax crashing down onto the trunk of a fallen tree, then began sawing the limbs to manageable lengths. She didn't plan to stay more than a couple of days. That was fine. Since he needed her on the mountain as badly as he needed a pack of rattle-snakes, why did the thought of her leaving make him feel so incredibly empty?

He leveled a savage blow against the tree, the crash resonating through the forest. She was wearing a wedding band, for Christ's sake! He leveled another. Even if she wasn't, it was only a matter of time before some other man came around to claim her.

Women like Tory belonged to someone.

He wiped sweat from his forehead, opened his canteen and swal-lowed water. His eyes traced the jagged stump of the fallen tree. Light-ning never struck twice in the same place, but love showed no mercy. It would strike a man down repeatedly if he let it.

Hours later, the cut timber loaded snugly into the bed of the truck,

Jake drove home. He stacked half of his afternoon's labor onto a wood-pile beside the shed before going inside to shower.

When he'd dressed in clean slacks and a T-shirt, he returned to the kitchen and prepared a simple meal of bread, cold ham and cheese. Tossing the items into a grocery sack, he drove back down the logging trail.

When he reached the cabin, he saw Tory sitting on the porch with sunlight reflecting off her hair. Golden strands that escaped the braid framed her face like a pale halo. She stared at a photograph, then slid it into the pocket of her dress when she saw him.

"Evenings can be chilly up here," he said, stacking an arm load of wood neatly beside the porch before going back for another load.

When the last piece of wood was added to the pile, he returned with the grocery bag.

"What's this?" she asked.

"Dinner." He handed it to her.

He followed her inside and immediately noticed a change. She had swept sawdust from the corners and spread a gingham cloth over the kitchen table. In the center was a bouquet of forget-me-nots spilling from a Mason jar. On the living room mantel was another jar of ferns.

It was more than the splashes of color and the lingering scents of bleach and flowers. The cabin felt different. It had the subtle, unmistakable suggestion of a woman's presence.

He couldn't take his eyes off her as she sliced ham and cheese and arranged his offerings into sandwiches. That was how it should be. A man returned from a day's work and the woman was there, doing things with bread and meat, but not just any woman. The ache filled his chest again.

It should be *that* woman.

The thought was suffocating. He shoved his way out the front door, angry with himself and her, then waited on the porch. She joined him a moment later bearing a plateful of sandwiches. He reached for one, taking her in from the corner of his eye, seeing the rigid way she sat and the unyielding set of her jaw. She still hadn't forgiven him for the kiss and probably thought he was a wolf.

They ate without speaking. He was a man who valued solitude, but her angry silence was almost more than he could bear. He wondered how to close the distance between them. If he said he was sorry he kissed her, that would be the biggest lie of his life.

"Why don't you make out that shopping list?" he suggested. "We'll pick up anything you need in town tomorrow."

She nodded.

"I have a couple errands to run that'll probably take an hour. Will that give you enough time to look around?"

She nodded again.

He gathered the leftover crusts, shoving them into the sack. "I'll stop by early in the morning, if you don't mind."

She gave another nod.

With nothing left to say or do but leave, he turned reluctantly down the path. He hated leaving like that, but what else could he do? He took four steps, telling himself not to look back. He wouldn't give the little ingrate the satisfaction.

Counting steps, he forced himself to keep walking.

"Jake?"

He turned and saw her coming toward him.

"Thank you for the firewood ... and everything."

Sunlight filtered through the trees and did strange things to her eyes. They were lighter, almost chalcedonic.

"You must think I'm a terrible ingrate."

"No, I don't."

"I guess I'm a bit confused." She lowered her beautiful eyes. "I guess I'm a little afraid."

"I can understand that."

"It's hard to make conversation when you don't know what you know or don't." She smiled. "Does that make any sense?"

"We'll figure it out, Tory."

"I hope so."

He shifted his weight. He didn't want to say too much and push his luck too far.

"I was going for a walk. Want to join me?"

"What's the bread for?"

He smiled. "You'll see."

He led her deep into the forest to where a family of beavers had dammed part of the river, making the water pool into an inlet. It was his favorite place on the mountain, especially in the evening when waterfowl came to feed. The pool was alive with loons, blue heron and a flock of Canada geese.

Her soft intake of breath was gratifying.

"Oh, Jake. This is lovely." She pointed at the loons. "What are they?"

Across the pool, a gander flapped his ruffled feathers, hissing a warning.

"Shhh," Jake whispered. "Sit."

She sat on the ground, folding her legs beneath her, watching. Sensing no threat, the geese returned to their feeding. Jake tore a crust of bread into pieces and threw them into the pool.

The geese marched up the bank, honking a reveille, and greedily gobbled them up. Tory laughed, a soft, tinkling-bells sound that filled Jake's heart with joy.

Not to be outdone, a pair of young beavers tumbled across the bank. They dashed along the length of the dam, bickering, their tails slapping the water. They shot coy glances at Tory as if making certain she noticed.

She laughed again. Jake smiled, feeling glad he brought her. It felt good and right to have her there, experiencing that moment with him. He leaned back against a tree and enjoyed her childlike pleasure as the geese accepted bread from her hand.

When they depleted her supply of bread scraps, the geese marched single file down the bank. As they settled into the water with contented honks, Tory turned a radiant smile on Jake.

"I've never seen anyplace so wonderful. At least, I don't think so."

Her hand rested on the ground only inches from his. He fought the urge to take it. "Nothing's coming back at all?"

"Just the opposite. I seem to remember less today than yesterday."

There was something, or someone, she wanted badly to remember, judging by the way she scrutinized that photo, earlier. He stared across the water, not wanting to know but needing to.

"You were looking at a picture earlier," he said, swallowing hard. "There must be people out there somewhere who care about you." He forced himself to add, "People who love you."

She pulled out the photo and handed it to him. "I found this in the bottom of my purse."

He braced himself as he reached for it. It would be a man, of course, but he couldn't let her see his disappointment.

He turned the photo over, glanced at it, and slowly exhaled when he saw it was a woman—a fat woman in a tight costume, what his buddies in the Corps would have called a real B-19. He wanted to kiss the picture.

"No idea who she is?" He returned the photo to her.

She stuffed it into her pocket and shook her head.

"Maybe we could show it around tomorrow and see if anyone—"

"I don't want to talk about it."

"All right."

Sitting quietly, they watched the day disappear. Tory commented on the river's hypnotic rhythm. Jake told her some of its history.

"The old-timers like to say this land was discovered by fairies," Jake said. "Actually, it was Indians."

He gazed across the river to where the limbs of a beech tree hung low, spreading like a canopy. Jake liked to think that it was in that spot where he sat that the Senecas gave the river its name.

"They called it Conhocton," he said softly. "It means branches in the water."

"I've heard of that." She faced him, rigid with excitement. "There's a town by that name. It's nearby, right?"

"No, there's no such town. Not that I know of, anyway."

Her crestfallen look returned and he cursed himself, wishing he hadn't spoken. "I could be wrong. We can check a map."

"Never mind." She sighed. "We won't find it."

She was sad again. He would've given anything not to have brought that sadness back to her face. His hand crept across the blanket of pine needles to cover hers. She gently pulled free, tucking a stray tendril behind her ear.

"What was it like growing up here?" she asked.

He shrugged. "It was all right."

She stretched out on the ground with her chin propped in her hands. "What's your best memory?"

As they talked, shadows fell, then darkness. Crickets began chirping a symphony. Across the pool, a bullfrog croaked.

Jake found himself telling her things, ideas and thoughts he'd never put into words before. She listened and understood—even the things he couldn't talk about.

"I assumed everyone lived like we did in Heatherfield," he said. "Hell, I'd never even been out of the state until the ...Until a few years ago."

"The war?" she asked softly.

"Yeah."

"It must have been awful for you."

"It was awful for everyone, Darlin."

"But especially for the ones who were there."

There were things a man couldn't discuss. They were hidden deep in his inner recesses because they were too terrible to acknowledge. For Jake, his time in the war was one of those things.

He stood. "It's getting late. Come on. I'll walk you back."

The path was moonlit and eerie with quiet beauty. When they reached Tory's cabin, Jake hesitated, not wanting the night to end. "You'd better close those windows, unless you want unexpected company."

"Company?"

He smiled at her expression of alarm. "Raccoons. They're pretty brave now because no one hunts them anymore."

She gave him a smile like a gift, something he could treasure and take out later to savor when he was alone. He jammed his hands in his pockets, nearly overwhelmed by the desire to kiss her again.

"I'll see you in the morning." He turned. "Sleep well."

"Jake?"

The sound of his name on her lips was music. He turned back.

"I'll make the pancakes. You bring the syrup, okay?"

He smiled. "You bet."

She was a mighty pretty picture there in the moonlight. He tucked that in his heart, too, to savor in the dark later.

Chapter Ten

Before the morning sun chased the shadows from the cabin, Tory was in the kitchen brewing a pot of coffee. She barely slept all night. She lay awake, her mind whirling and stomach aching, rehearsing for her encounter with Destiny Paige. By dawn, she tempered her angry speech into a humble request.

"Please get me out of here. I don't care how."

She set the table for two, then returned to the bedroom to dress. Retrieving a simple white shift from the closet, she tried it on in front of the mirror. As an afterthought, she pulled the belt from her ruined jeans and cinched it at her waist. She turned side-to-side, frowning at her reflection. White ankle socks offset black combat boots. She wore a matronly housedress pulled together with black leather and silver buckles.

Her frown deepened. She was a study in contradictions, sort of like June Cleaver done Nazi style.

As she mixed pancake batter, she thought of the things Jake said the previous night and the easy companionship they shared. When she opened the door to his knock half an hour later, Jake's expression told her he remembered it, too.

He talked easily that morning and ate ravenously. Tory picked at her food, feeling more nervous than ever. A disturbing thought came to her consciousness and refused to leave.

Jake was the most decent man she'd ever met. She'd be leaving Heatherfield soon, maybe that day. To her surprise, she wanted to take Jake with her.

Heading toward town later, she focused on the scenery rolling past her window, the surrealistic beauty of the hillside and rolling fields of heather. As abruptly as they began, the fields ended and became a housing project.

The tract depressed her. She scrutinized the endless rows of houses, identical in color and size, searching for the reason. Although new, the dwellings were cheaply made. Their sameness and close proximity to each other made them seem shabby, but it was more than that. The tract was dreary, as if a dark cloud hung overhead.

In sharp contrast, the project gave way to older homes—charming Colonials on wide, friendly streets where children could play in safety, and where women could walk alone at night without fear.

They rolled to a stop at a red light where a block of abandoned buildings huddled together like wary old men. Jake explained those were the last vestiges of the thirties, when Heatherfield had soup kitchens and hidden storerooms stocked with homemade gin.

Pulling to the curb in front of a park, he let the truck idle.

"I'll let you out here. I shouldn't be more than an hour."

She stared out the window, both fascinated and terrified. Lulled by the tranquility of Jake's mountain, the idea she'd actually been transported to another time seemed an unpleasant but abstract idea.

Suddenly, reality stared her in the face. Packards and Frasiers barged down the avenue, their horns blaring. A milkman darted from his truck, depositing frothy bottles on doorsteps. Women clicked past on stiletto heels, wheeling baby buggies, with small pillbox caps perched jauntily on their heads. Men smiled at each other and tipped their derbies in greeting.

"Tory?" Jake watched her. "Are you all right?"

She gave him a wan smile. "Why wouldn't I be?"

"You look scared to death. Would you rather come with me?"

She moistened her lips with her tongue and gave him a more-convincing smile.

"Don't be silly. Where should I meet you?"

"I'll find you in about an hour, okay?"

She climbed from the truck and sent him off with a small wave. As he drove away, she took a small breath and muttered, "Act natural, Tory. For God's sake, try to blend in."

She pasted on a smile. As she walked, she tried to focus her attention on the bustling shoppers and the bright spring flowers spilling from baskets all along the sidewalks, concentrating on the familiar and not the odd.

She passed a corner market and slowed when she noticed the familiar signs taped to the window advertising waxed paper—Bromo

Seltzer and cod liver oil. But those signs weren't wrinkled or yellowed with age—they were brand new. A wave of bile rushed up the back of her throat, but she choked it down.

The shopkeeper leaned on his broom and eyed her with undisguised curiosity. "You all right, Missy?"

She nodded and hurried on her way.

She hadn't gone more than a block before a movie house caught her eye. She stopped to peer in the window. A red-velvet lobby was decorated with posters of Humphrey Bogart, Spencer Tracy, and Joan Crawford. She smiled.

Then her smile faded when she saw a small, handwritten sign in the glass of the ticket window.

> *Ground floor is for whites only.*
> *Negroes please use balcony.*

Appalled, she whirled from the building and straight into the path of a policeman.

"Whoa, there!" His hands went out to steady her. "You all right, Doll?"

"I'm— Yes. I'm fine."

His hooded eyes showed concern and curiosity. "You must be new around here. You look a bit lost."

That was as good an excuse as any. "Actually, I am. I'm looking for a place called Penny Candy's. Can you tell me where it is?"

"Penny Candy's?"

She caught his look of surprise before he turned to point a stubby finger across the square.

"The only two-story building in the plaza. You can't miss it."

Shielding her eyes with her hand, she peered across the street.

Does he mean that mousetrap across the street? she wondered.

Swallowing her disappointment, she said a feeble, "Thank you," and walked on.

"My pleasure, Doll."

She felt his curious gaze follow her as she went down the block. As she crossed the square, she noticed a throng of teenagers gathered in front of the open door of a department store. She drew nearer, curious to see what had attracted their attention.

Three old women stood on the fringes of the crowd shaking their heads, their lips as rigid as the pencil-straight seams up the backs of their stockings.

"It's getting worse by the day," one said loudly. "What passes for music I—well, I just declare!"

"What's wrong with Kate Smith or Bing Crosby?"

"Now that's music. This, on the other hand—"

"Shocking!"

"It's fit for nothing except to give young girls ideas."

The three women gave Tory pointed glances.

"A snake in the grass," one huffed. "Why, that boy's the devil's messenger, the devil's messenger in the flesh, by God!"

The other two women nodded.

Curious, Tory peered through the crowd of teenagers who stood in mesmerized silence, transfixed by the dim gray glow of a black-and-white TV. A young, zoot-suited Frank Sinatra smiled at her from the screen, crooning about cotton candy wishes.

Tory looked at the three old women in surprise and they frowned back. She shook her head. When had America lost its innocence and cotton-candy dreams? It would take another five years to progress from black and white to color TV, then only another fifty to make the leap from Frank Sinatra to Marilyn Manson.

A young girl with a pixie face and an explosion of red curls sidled up to Tory. "Isn't he the gravy?"

"What?"

"Not what. Who." She pointed at the TV. "Frankie Sinatra. The Voice."

"Oh. Right."

The girl sighed. "He's so dreamy. My friend Betty won tickets to see him in concert in New York City. I was just as jealous as a cat."

"You must be a big fan."

"Natch. Who isn't?"

Tory smiled softly and nodded toward the three old women.

"Oh, never mind them." What looked like a hundred silver bracelets chimed as she waved a dismissive hand toward the old women. "Billy Sunday was in town over the weekend. He gets the old-timers all stirred up."

She tore her gaze from the TV screen and stared at Tory's clothing with open curiosity. "Say, there's a dreamy scarf in the window at Panache. It would be perfect with that dress."

"What's Panache?"

"Only the nattiest dress shop in town. I'm Millie." She stuck out her hand, starting another ripple of chimes from the bracelets. "Top salesgirl. Who are you?"

She smiled. "I'm Tory."

"You're from the city, aren't you?"

"Um, yes."

"I knew you couldn't be from around here."

"What makes you say that?"

Millie shrugged. "We're all the same here. You're different. That's all."

Before Tory could press for an explanation, Millie glanced at her watch.

"Geez Louise! I'm late. Miz Matthews will have kittens. Remember to stop in and look at that scarf, okay? I'll be there all day."

Her grin was infectious. Tory smiled as she watched Millie strut, pelvis first, down the street. When she disappeared into a trim, white shop, Tory turned toward the rickety old bookstore.

•

"Fools rush in where angels … la la dee …" Penny heard the front door open and close. The bottle of cream in her hands shook. It was only a minute past nine. He couldn't be there already, could he?"

She paused for a moment frozen in fear, then uttered an, "Our Father," and hobbled to the front of the store.

Morning sunlight shone through the window, spreading a pool of light around the prettiest girl Penny ever saw. Relief went through her in a breathless rush.

"Hello there, Dearie. Something I can help you find today?"

The young woman smiled. "I've been browsing through your books. You have an impressive collection of romances."

Penny beamed with pleasure. "That's the only kind of book I carry."

"I wonder if you'd have any books by my favorite author, a lady named Destiny Paige?"

Penny's smile widened. "I have every one of them. Which would you like to see?"

"I can't say that I have a favorite."

"I feel the exact same way. Come with me, Dearie."

She led Tory to the storeroom where her favorite books nestled in yellowed tissue in an old potato crate. She lifted the lid and said, "Every one is a Destiny Paige novel." She handed two of the books to the girl. "Will these do?"

"They'll be a start." She slung her handbag from her shoulder and opened the clasp. "What do I owe you?"

"I couldn't sell them to you."

The girl's smile faded. "But you have to."

Penny smiled and shook her head. "No, Sir."

"Please. I'd be willing to pay twice the cover price or whatever you think is fair."

Penny folded her arms across her chest, enjoying the game. "I won't do it."

"Then why'd you show them to me?" the girl asked in exasperation.

"Because you're a fan, just like me." Penny grinned mischievously. "One fan doesn't sell Destiny Paige novels to another. One gives them." She pressed the books into the girl's hands. "When you finish with these, come back. I'll give you another."

"Thank you very much, but I can't keep them. I'll borrow them for a few days, then I'll return them." She tucked the books into her bag.

Penny pushed back her spectacles and regarded the girl thoughtfully, trying to place her. She knew most of the local girls, but she'd never seen that one before.

"You must be new in town."

"Just visiting."

"I'm Penny Candy. I own this store." Thrusting out her hand, she added proudly. "Have done so for almost fifty years."

The girl extended a hand that felt delightfully warm and soft. "My name's Tory."

"Proud to have you, Tory."

"I'll bring your books back in a few days, if that's all right."

"Take your time, Dearie. I have plenty. Can't say as I do much reading anymore, anyway." She tapped her glasses. "My eyes aren't what they used to be."

The girl glanced into the crate. "She's a wonderful storyteller, isn't she?"

"Oh, yes. The best."

"Want to know what I heard?" Tory lowered her voice, and Penny leaned forward eagerly. "I heard she was writing a novel about Heatherfield."

"A novel about Heatherfield?" Penny gaped for a moment, then realization dawned. She was being paid back for her little joke. The new girl was delightful. Penny threw back her head and gave a good, old-fashioned belly laugh. "Mercy, Child! You had me going."

Tory laughed with her for a moment. "Seriously, though. I've been out of touch. When do you expect her next novel to come out?"

"Oh, dear." Penny's laughter died. "You haven't heard?"

"Heard what?"

"She died in January. There won't be any more novels."

"She died?" Tory's eyes widened. "Are you sure?"

"Oh, yes. It was in all the papers. She was in a terrible automobile smash, a limousine, if I recall." She shuddered. "I've never liked automobiles. I only drive if there's no other way."

Tory moaned softly.

"There, there." Penny touched her shoulder, realizing she'd shocked her. Tory's face was white. "I'm sorry to have had to be the one to tell—"

Pitiful howling wafted into the stockroom from the front of the store. "Oh, dear. That's Thomas looking for his breakfast. We'd better skee-do. That boy hates to be kept waiting."

Chapter Eleven

Numb with disappointment, Tory followed as Penny threaded her way back through the clutter. Destiny Paige had been there, but Tory missed her by three months. What should she do?

Out front, an old gray tomcat sat in the window hissing, its ragged ears pulled back. Tory and Penny noticed the man simultaneously, and Penny moaned softly.

"Good morning, Penny." He tipped his hat to Tory. "Ma'am."

"What do you want?" Penny asked.

The man laughed and held out a sheaf of documents. "Come now, Penny. Don't tell me you've forgotten our appointment?"

Penny's face drained of color.

Tory's eyes flicked over the stranger. He was tall and dark, with dazzlingly white teeth and a perfectly trimmed beard. His eyes were an alarming shade of blue. She disliked him instantly.

As a pretty daughter of affluent parents, Tory had been exempt from the schoolyard cruelty inflicted on less-fortunate children. Instead of a benefit, her popularity was a responsibility, a cross she had to bear. More than once, in a fit of rage, she threw herself into the paths of playground bullies and took their wrath on herself to spare a friend.

She realized she was looking at another bully.

"I—" Penny stammered. "No, of course not."

He waved the documents under her nose. "Time's up."

"What do I have to do?" she asked in a small voice.

"This is a Bill of Sale for the store." He pulled one document from the stack. "This one is a voucher. Mere technicalities, Old Gal. I've seen to everything. All you have to do is sign."

Penny held the papers close to her face, squinting. The man pompously handed her a pen. "Right on the dotted line at the bottom."

Penny held the pen in trembling hands.

Tory had seen enough. "May I?" Stepping forward, she snatched the documents from the old woman's hands.

The man gave her a look of surprised annoyance. "All due respect, Sister, this is none of your business."

Tory ignored him and scanned the documents. "Why, this is a Bill of Sale. Shame on you, Penny." She stacked the papers neatly and returned them to the man. "Penny must've been confused, Sir. In any case, she shouldn't have made arrangements for the store without speaking to me first. I'm sorry to have wasted your time."

"Pardon me." His eyes flashed with anger. "I really don't see how this concerns you, Miss."

"It concerns me plenty. As Penny's business partner, I can't possibly allow her to sell."

"Business partner?" He choked on the words.

"Silent, until now. I've recently moved to the area and intend to take a much more active roll." She smiled sweetly. "Sort of a hobby."

He folded his arms across his chest. "Where is it you moved here from, exactly?"

Tory's smile wavered and she hoped her face didn't betray any panic. She wasn't sure where Heatherfield was, let alone what existed around it. "The city."

"Which city?"

Millie's comment about the Frank Sinatra concert came to her in the nick of time. Silently thanking her, Tory smiled broadly and said, "New York, of course."

His look of hatred went to Penny. "Now listen here," he said. "I don't know what kind of scam you girls are cooking up, but—"

Before he could complete his threat, a large man's bulk filled the doorway. Tory recognized him as the policeman she'd bumped into in front of the theater.

"Good morning, Penny, Pierce." He tipped his hat to Tory. "I see you found your way all right."

"Yes," she said brightly. "Thank you."

The floor groaned under his weight as he entered the store and crossed to the candy case. "Nancy's craving these licorice sticks something fierce," he said, pulling a handful of change from his pocket. "I'd better take all you've got."

"Certainly, Tom." Penny hurried to the case and clumsily filled a paper sack with licorice.

Pierce glanced at Tom then shot Tory a poisoned look. She met his gaze unflinchingly and smiled. "'Bye, now."

He shoved the documents back into their folder and slammed out the front door.

When Tom left, Penny collapsed against the counter and exclaimed, "Mercy!"

"What was that all about, Penny?" Tory asked. "Who was that awful man?"

Penny frowned at the dark figure stalking across the park. "His name is Pierce Matthews." Her voice lowered to a grumble. "He shows up every month just like the gas bill, and wants to get hold of my store."

"You don't want to sell."

"Lord, no! It was a wedding gift from my Dwight. It's all I have in the world, all I've ever had."

"Why does he want it so badly?"

"He says it's in the way." Her voice wavered. "Says he aims to tear it down and build a roller rink."

Tory touched her shoulder. "Don't worry. We got rid of him—for the time being."

Penny sank into a nearby rocking chair. "You shouldn't have crossed him. He'll make things bad for you."

"I'm not worried about that. I know how to handle a bully."

Penny sighed. "I don't know how much longer I can hold onto this place, anyway. Those licorice sticks I sold to Tom Hopewell were my first sale in three days." She laughed pitifully. "Twenty-six cents won't even pay the ice man." Her eyes darted to the window. "He's used to getting his own way. He'll make it bad for you, for us both."

"If he comes back here, you let me handle him."

"How will I find you?"

"I'm renting a cabin on the mountain. You can call and leave a message with Jake Benjamin."

Penny's eyes widened. "You're renting from young Jake?"

"Do you know him?"

"From a bean sprout. Jake's a lovely boy."

Tory gathered her bag. "I'll be back in a couple of days. Call if you need me before then, okay?"

Penny shook her head. "He's a bad sort, that Pierce Matthews. You have no idea who you're dealing with."

"No," Tory said firmly. "He has no idea who he's dealing with."

That statement struck a chord. Penny clasped Tory's hand and peered into her eyes. "Mercy," she whispered, "he doesn't, does he? No, Sir. He has no idea at all."

Chapter Twelve

"Let's see what we've got." Tom Hopewell sifted through the stack of papers on his desk and shook his head. "Nope. No reports of any missing persons in the last seventy-two hours. When did you say she turned up?"

His old friend towered above the desk, one of the few people who could make Tom feel small. "Late Friday night or early Saturday morning, whichever you want to call it."

"She said she was heading where?"

"A place called Savona. Ever heard of it?"

"Savona, New York?" Tom pulled out a map of New York State and traced his finger down it. "Doesn't exist." He thought for a moment, tapping his finger against his stubbled chin. "Come to think of it, I took a strange call on Saturday morning around seven o'clock. A young lady reported a stolen car. When I asked for details, she hung up on me. I thought it was just a prank."

Jake hesitated. "She claims she went over the embankment. I searched my property three times. There's no car."

Tom pulled a notepad from his breast pocket, reached for a pencil, and licked the end. "What sort of car was it? Did she say?"

Jake hesitated again, then said, "She said she came in a Mitsubishi."

Tom whistled softly. "Nutcase, you think?"

"I don't know. She doesn't seem to remember anything about her life before the accident."

"I'd better call the asylum and see if they're missing anybody."

As Tom's fingers curled around the receiver, Jake placed a restraining hand on his arm. Startled, Tom glanced up into Jake's fierce eyes.

"I don't want her to come to any trouble, Tom."

"I'll be discreet. If she doesn't prove a danger to society, she won't have any trouble."

Jake considered that. "Fair enough."

Tom's hand slid from the receiver. "Is she a pretty little thing with blue eyes and blonde braids?"

Jake's expression softened. "That's her."

Tom whistled again.

"I'd appreciate it if this stays between us," Jake said. "If word got out she was, well, you know. It wouldn't be good."

"You got it."

"You'll let me know first if you find out anything?"

"Yes."

Tom watched Jake leave the station. Waiting until Jake passed the window, he picked up the receiver and dialed.

•

Tory stepped from the porch of Penny Candy's, her mind reeling. Pierce Matthews was a brutal man. She'd gone head-to-head with his kind more often than she cared to remember. She'd done the right thing to step in, hadn't she?

She cast a nervous glance across the park. She was a stranger in town, and Pierce was a powerful man. His name was all over the plaza.

What was she thinking to play God like that?

The thought stayed with her as she hurried down the block. It wasn't until she reached the department store that the full impact struck.

Playing God.

The nape of her neck prickled. She paused to sort out her thoughts. Her first instinct had been to protect the old woman from a bully's strong-arming, but the germ of another idea was forming in her mind.

Destiny Paige had been there. For some reason, she was playing dead, but she hadn't died in a car wreck in January '49 like Penny said. She died of liver sclerosis on Tory's birthday in June '72. Technically, she had to still be alive.

Destiny obviously had an agenda for Penny Candy's, a plan that would no doubt affect the outcome of the story. If Tory caused enough trouble in Heatherfield's plot, something that upset the balance of the novel, Destiny Paige had to come looking for her.

That makes sense, doesn't it? she wondered with a sigh.

Even a long shot was better than none at all.

She walked on, feeling curious eyes peeping at her from store windows and across the tops of newspapers. She sighed again. If she was going to be stuck there for awhile, she needed to duck into a dress shop and find something less conspicuous to wear. A few pairs of underwear wouldn't hurt, either.

She entered the first store she found and a chorus of tinkling bells announced her arrival. Millie's head poked out from behind a display of culottes. She grinned.

"I didn't think you'd come."

Despite her best efforts, Tory's nose wrinkled. The store reeked of Tabu, a scent as overpowering as the décor, which was entirely pink. It looked like a Pepto Bismol explosion with pink walls, pink carpets and pink on most of the clothes.

"I can't wait for you to see this," Millie bubbled, pulling a pink scarf from a mannequin's hands and affixing it to Tory's head in a floppy bow.

She turned Tory toward the mirror. "There. What do you think?"

Tory winced and wanted to wretch. "Wow. You're right. It's really something, isn't it?"

Millie grinned. "I knew you'd love it."

Tory removed the scarf and looked at the price tag. The scarf was thirty-five cents. "Put it on the counter for me, will you, while I look around?"

Millie's eyes followed Tory's movements as she pulled dresses from the racks, held them up, and replaced them. Across the store, a pair of Donna Reed look-alikes whispered behind their hands.

Tory hurriedly selected a blue cotton dress, two pairs of lightweight slacks and a matching blouse for each. As she unloaded them on the counter, she calculated her bill at around twenty dollars.

Millie rang up the sale, exclaiming over Tory's choices.

"Eighteen dollars and sixty-three cents." She winked, and whispered loudly, "I gave you a preferred customer discount."

Tory opened her wallet, glad she'd cashed her paycheck on Friday. She would insist on helping Jake buy groceries and gas for the truck. As she fingered a crisp, fifty-dollar bill, a warning bell shrieked in her mind, and she remembered a clerk in the Market Street florist shop asking, "Did you just print it today?"

Her heart sank as she shoved the bill back into her purse. She had plenty of money, and it was as useless as Monopoly money. She had three hundred crisp new dollars—all dated 1999.

"Something wrong?" Millie asked.

"I—I seem to have forgotten my wallet."

"No prob. We take checks, too."

"I don't seem to have my checkbook, either."

"Oh, dear." Millie's brows knit together, then she brightened. "We'll set you up with a charge account, then. How'll that be?"

"Don't bother. I'll return another time."

"Don't be redic!" Millie shuffled through a stack of forms. "I can have it ready in a jiffy."

"Have we got a problem here, Millie?"

A pretty woman appeared beside the counter dressed entirely in pink. Her eyes were the color of smoke and her auburn hair was luminous under the bright store lights. Tory searched her face because she seemed vaguely familiar.

"No problem, Ma'am. I was just going to set up this lady with a charge account, on account of she forgot her wallet and checkbook."

"That's fine." Her gaze flicked over Tory's shabby dress and scuffed boots, and her lips drooped in contempt. "Just show three forms of identification. After you've filled out the credit application, we'll contact your references. You do have references?"

Tory's cheeks stung with embarrassment.

"That won't be necessary. There's nothing here I can't live without."

"I suspected as much."

That sparked Tory's anger. She fought to keep her voice even. "What's your point?"

"My point?" The woman laughed harshly. "I've seen it all before, Sister." When her voice rose, the Donna Reeds stared. "If you're looking for the thrift store, it's down the street."

"Excuse me?"

The bells of the front door chimed. The Donna reeds gasped, while Millie's face drained of color.

Tory turned and saw Jake in the doorway.

"Problem, Louise?" he asked.

Louise's face burst into a smile. "Why, Jake! What a lovely surprise. No, no problem. At least nothing I can't handle." She laughed. "This woman seems to have a champagne taste on a soda-pop budget."

Jake's expression clouded. He strode to the counter and pulled out his wallet.

"This woman is my guest. From now on, you sell her what she needs and send the bill to me." He faced Millie. "What do I owe you?"

Millie swallowed her gum. "Eighteen sixty-three, Sir."

"Forget it, Jake," Tory said, taking his arm. "I don't want them."

Ignoring her, he handed Millie a twenty. "Bag them up."

"Yes, Sir." Millie's gaze flicked admiringly over Tory before it returned to Jake.

"Your guest? Why didn't she say something?" Louise's voice took on a wheedling tone. "I asked her if she had references. She should've told me she was a friend of yours."

As Tory watched the exchange, a slow realization dawned.

Louise? Is it possible? she wondered.

Jake shoved the change from Millie in his pocket and slung the bag over his shoulder. Taking Tory's arm, he said, "Let's go."

They were halfway down the sidewalk before Tory asked, "Why did you do that?"

Jake shrugged. "Lots of reasons."

"I wish you hadn't. I owe you too much already."

"You don't owe me a thing, Tory."

Curious eyes followed them down the street, but they weren't focused on her. She noticed furtive glances and solemn nods from those who met Jake's gaze. The realization struck her they were afraid of Jake.

They were almost to the truck before she asked, "Who was that woman who owns the dress shop?"

"Her name is Louise Matthews." His voice caught slightly on the last word.

"Pierce's wife?"

Jake whirled to face her. "How do you know about that?"

"I met him this morning at Penny Candy's. He was giving her a rough time, trying to force her to sell the store. I stepped in."

"You stay away from Pierce Matthews!"

She saw the anger in his stance, and his scars deepened to crimson. "What should I have done? Stood by and let an old woman be bullied out of her property?"

"That's exactly what you should have done."

"Would you?"

He flung open the truck's door, got in and started the engine. "He does what he wants. I don't concern myself with what goes on in town. If you're smart, you won't, either."

He slammed the door. The subject was closed.

•

When Jake was safely gone, Louise whirled on the salesgirl. "We do not extend credit without three forms of identification, Millie. I've told you that time and time again!"

Her tone chased the grin from Millie's face. "Yes, Ma'am."

"One more slip-up and you're back to jerking sodas at the Stardust Diner, understand?"

"But it turned out swell, Miz Matthews."

"No thanks to you!"

Millie gazed wistfully at the door. "Did you see the way he looked at her? It was just like in the movies."

"I saw nothing of the sort."

"He's crazy in love with her," Millie whispered. "Tory's tamed the Bogeyman."

Louise felt faint. Her stomach ached. She'd have to have been blind to miss that. "I—I'm not feeling well, Millie. I'll be in my office lying down."

She stumbled to her office, drew the blinds and stretched out on the chaise lounge. Fishing a bottle of Bromo Seltzer from her handbag, she popped open the cap as she recalled Jake's words.

This woman is my guest.

It was too awful.

She laughed, a pitiful little bleat. His kept woman was more like it. Louise knew a tramp when she saw one. Pressing her palms to her throbbing forehead, she whispered, "Oh, Darling, when I think how you loved me ..."

For a heart-wrenching moment, she did, and the thought of that love lavished on another woman made her cry in deep, racking sobs. Knife blades of jealousy tore through her heart.

She sat up and blew her nose, flipping open her compact and assessing the damage. Puffy eyes stared back from a pale face. She'd never been strong. She was a weak, foolish woman who let herself be dragged along by the whims of powerful men. First it was her daddy, then her husband.

She vowed it was over. This time, Louise Matthews would make a stand. She'd grab happiness by the seat of its pants and gain control of Benjamin's Mountain to build her own housing project. What would Pierce think of that?

She took a shaky breath and smiled. She'd win Jake back. But first, she had to get rid of that awful woman, whoever she was.

•

Who the devil was she?

Pierce glowered from his office window as the couple got into Jake's Model A and drove off. He might've guessed Jake was behind it. Was there no end to what the man would do to torment him?

Wadding the useless Bill of Sale, he hurled it into the trash. The phone rang constantly. Mae quit without notice. Pierce had plans for her that afternoon. It seemed all his plans were falling apart.

He buried his head in his hands, trying to think. A picture came to mind that he'd struggled with for most of the day. The truth was, the men he met in the city scared him. He'd thought the deal was too risky, too much money, but now …

He drummed his fingers on the desktop, waiting for the phone to stop ringing. Turnabout was fair play. If it was a fight Jake wanted, Pierce would give him one.

He took a deep breath, yanked the receiver from its cradle, and dialed the number he'd committed to memory.

After two rings, a gruff voice asked, "Yeah?"

"Matthews here. I spoke with you the other day regarding a job."

"Right."

Pierce moistened his lips. "I've decided to hire you."

There was a brief silence. "One shot, two G's. No guarantee."

"I understand."

"We'll be in touch."

With sweating hands, Pierce dropped the receiver into its cradle and sat back with a smile.

Jake Benjamin's fate was sealed.

Chapter Thirteen

After midnight, Tory set down the second of Penny's books. Her eyes felt cat-scratched. Her brain was numb with boredom. She never read anything so silly and pointless before.

She scanned the book's cover. A woman in a low-cut dress and come-and-get-me expression struggled unconvincingly in a pirate's massive arms. Tory sighed. She enjoyed a good romance from time to time, but this definitely wasn't a good one.

She turned off the bedside lamp and stared at the ceiling, knowing it would be hours before she slept. Her head was crowded with thoughts. It was inconceivable the woman who created those bodice-ripping rotters had also created Jake Benjamin.

His face swam before her eyes. Like the characters in the books, he was virile and handsome, but he was complex. His ruggedness was layered with integrity and decency. He was the perfect man.

Don't go there, Tory, she warned herself.

She quickly set her mind on track. Destiny made center-stage appearances in both novels. In one scene, she wrote she'd been recognized by a character in a Manhattan nightclub and asked to read excerpts from her novels. Tory chuckled. Storytelling didn't get much lamer than that.

Her smile froze at the rustle of footsteps outside. For a pulse-pounding moment, they stopped. When they moved on, Tory slowly exhaled. The so-called heroes in the two Destiny Paige novels she'd read would have barged in and demanded satisfaction. Why had Destiny given Jake a conscience?

She rolled onto her side and gazed at the moon, picking up an earlier train of thought. Destiny was the epitome of self-importance. If Tory were to create an event that called for a star, she might be able to lure the author back into the book. It was another long shot, but it just might work.

Meanwhile, Tory had to see what she could do to stir up the situation. Surely, Destiny's vanity wouldn't allow Tory to tamper with her creation. She had to intervene.

A small voice added, Unless it was all planned in advance, and your own words and actions are part of an intricate plot.

It was unsettling and infuriating. Tory Sasser wasn't out of control of her life and never had been. There was no way in hell she'd start now, either.

"What should I do?" She stared at the sky as if the quiet darkness held answers. Disheartened by its silence, she turned her face away from the moon and drifted into a fitful sleep.

•

She was still awake, reading the books she got from Penny Candy. Jake watched from the shelter of the trees, a fierce longing tearing at his guts. It was torture. What was this magnet or pull of the moon that drew him to her?

Her hair tumbled across her shoulders as she bent over the book. He saw the covers peeking out of her handbag that afternoon. Why would a woman like her need that sort of vicarious thrill?

"Oh, Child. I could give you the real thing if only you wanted me." She didn't want him. She made that perfectly clear.

She extinguished the bedside lamp, pitching the room into darkness. Jake reluctantly moved on. Tom Hopewell would've made his phone calls by then. Jake turned for a last, longing glance into her darkened window. It didn't matter. Whatever Tom discovered, Jake would protect her.

As he trudged toward home, something she said that afternoon returned to him. He could well imagine what Pierce Matthews intended to do with Penny Candy's store. He would tear it down to create more so-called progress. The man was like a steamroller, devouring everything in his path.

Jake scowled. The thought of the man's filthy eyes on Tory incensed him. He wouldn't let Tory go to town again.

He strode to his porch and threw open the door. It crashed like a shotgun blast behind him. He rummaged in the icebox for a bottle of beer and returned to the porch. Unscrewing the cap, he took a long swallow as he silently chided himself.

As if he could stop her. Tory was a strong woman who knew her own mind. That was one of the things he loved about her.

He sat on his porch for a long time, listening to the night sounds of the forest. He knew those sounds as well as he knew his own heartbeat—the hypnotic swelling of the river, the haunting cry of a loon and the restless wind that swirled around him in pockets of uneasiness. Draining his bottle, he looked up at the stars. They, too, seemed uneasy.

He shivered unaccountably. The night had a strange feel to it, deceptively calm, urgent, deep, dark and quiet. It was in the air. It would be a night of visions and dreams.

Chapter Fourteen

It was a perfect day for a wedding. The sky stretched across the valley, sailor blue and cloudless. The sun sat like a benevolent God in its kingdom above the cobblestone chapel. Penny smiled and murmured softly in her sleep.

The chapel doors were thrown wide. Penny heard the sweet swell of music coming from inside. The bride was coming! Penny's dream-self stood on tiptoe at the fence, straining for a closer look. There she was.

The bride stepped daintily across the threshold, the endless white train of her gown flowing behind her. The wind lifted her veil and she smiled. Penny's breath caught. Her eyes were clear blue lakes, her skin the color of peaches. Her hair was as gold as corn. Penny, hiding her face in her hands, wept for the sheer beauty of her.

A white dove circled in the air above her and a voice came from the center of the sun. "Behold, the Fair One."

"Oh, yes," Penny whispered.

"The beloved. Chosen for a very great love."

"Yes. Yes."

"You must help us."

"I must? How?"

"You must help guide her to the one who was created for her, the one who is worthy of her."

"Who?" She squinted at the sun. "Who would be worthy of such a creature?"

"Behold."

Barely breathing, Penny watched as the groom appeared. He was a good, big, beautiful man, who took his bride's hand.

"Young Jake?" she whispered.

"Yes, Sweet One. That is the way it must be, but there are those who are against us."

"Who? Who'd be against …?"

"Behold!"

Wind descended, a deep, swirling blackness. Penny clutched the fence, crying out in horror as the gale tore the bride from Jake's grasp and carried her away. Wounds appeared on his face, pulsing red.

"Do you see the wounds, Sweet One?"

"Please. I can't bear them."

"Nor we. That was not our intent. He wasn't created for sorrow. Sweet One, lover of love, time is short. You must help us."

"What should I do?"

As suddenly as they appeared, the clouds blew away. The picture of Jake and his bride reappeared, hand-in-hand. A voice thundered from the midst of the sun, "It must be!"

"Saints preserve us!" Penny sat up, rubbing her eyes. She never should have had that nip of whiskey before bed, but she'd been sleeping poorly of late.

Pondering the dream for a moment, she remembered the solemn words that still hung in the air, then padded to the kitchen and prepared a cup of warm milk, drinking it standing up. By the time she rinsed the cup and set it on the drain board to dry, the admonition was wandering from her mind, the dream becoming unreal. She walked back to bed and turned off the light, lying in the dark as she concentrated.

She mouthed the words the dream entrusted to her, lest she forget. "It must be," she whispered. "It must be … it must."

•

Wind raged in the trees, a terrible, sorrowful moaning. Icy teardrops pelted her from above. She opened her eyes. A quarry of old men gathered about her, watchful and solemn. She shivered.

Intermittent flashes of red pulsed through the forest. In the trees something caught their light, glinting and disappearing. What was it? What was the light trying to show her?

She tensed. There it was again, something silver. A car? She struggled to understand but failed. She hurt everywhere. Her throat was raw as if from screaming.

"Help!" she cried. "Please help me!"

"Shh," the wind whispered. "Sleeeep."

Her eyelids became heavy as if she were drugged. She moaned,

"No. Please. I want to see."

"Shh."

Someone spoke to her, but it wasn't the wind. It was a man with a devil-red face. "Stay with me."

"Who are you?"

Big hands reached. "You're all right. Stay with me."

She moaned again, the sound mingling with the wailing wind. Big hands touched her. "Stay with me now."

"Shh. Shh."

The sound of her own screams awoke Tory from the nightmare. She was shaking, drenched in sweat, too terrified to turn on the light. In the darkness that enveloped her, she heard the man's voice, but it was faint as if coming from far away. It grew fainter until it was not a voice, just an impression.

"Stay with me. Staywithmestaywithmestay ..."

•

"Jake? Are you there?"

Heavy mist hung in the foul green air. Jake turned toward the voice. "Stu? Where the hell are you? I can't see a damned thing."

Stu's icy hand clamped on his shoulder as he crawled from the water. "It's too quiet, isn't it?" he whispered.

Waves lapped at his thighs, polluted with tension, as one hundred fifty Marines crawled soundlessly onto shore.

"It's too quiet," Stu repeated in a hoarse whisper. "Something's going to happen. I can feel it."

"Shh. It'll be all right." Jake knew he was lying. He, too, felt something bad about to happen.

They dropped to their bellies and crawled toward the rendezvous point. Then he saw the flash of gunfire and heard shots ring out just before a bullet tore into his chest.

"Christ!" the commander said. "It's an ambush. Open fire!"

Half the company was still in the water. The other half fumbled for their weapons.

Jake moaned, trying to pull out of the dream. The movie rolled on, as dull and grainy as a homemade picture show.

Strafing planes flew low overhead, their shadows like vultures circling in the mist. He felt the vibration of bullets striking the ground around him.

Stu called his name. He had to go back for him. There was nothing to lose.

He saw himself crawling, leaving a trail of blood in the sand, to where Stu lay bleeding from the throat. Stu Gordon was his best friend.

"No!" He reached out and clamped his hands over the wound. Warm, sticky blood pulsed between his fingers and covered his hands. Strafing planes flew low overhead, showering them with bullets.

Jake came closer, sheltering Stu's body with his own. "No! No, no no!"

He didn't want to look anymore, but he didn't know how to make the pictures stop. He saw himself dragging Stu's body to a trench.

"Jake." Stu wet his lips with a bloody tongue. "Tell my mom and dad—"

"Don't talk."

"—that I died brave."

He cradled Stu'd head, both hands clamped on the wound. "Don't do this to me, you bastard! Don't do it!"

Blood gushed between his fingers. His body was filled with holes. His own blood pooled on the ground, then he drifted away, floating. There was an end to the fighting. All he saw was light.

Jake swung his legs over the side of the bed, forcing his head between his knees while he waited for the nausea to pass. Of all the war dreams, that was the one he feared most, the dream of undeath.

What he couldn't face during the day, his mind showed him at night, forcing him to look, demanding an explanation for his existence. He didn't have one, because he knew the truth.

He had died in that trench beside Stu Gordon.

A soothing breeze drifted through the open window, cooling the beads of sweat on his flesh. He found his footing and eased himself from the bed.

Moments later, he sat on the porch, thoughtfully sipping a bottle of beer. He'd been dead. For reasons he couldn't fathom, his life had been restored. He should've felt grateful, but he didn't. What was the point in living only to grow old and die alone? Was that life?

His thoughts returned to his old friend and their carefree days of hunting squirrels and climbing trees. At eleven, Stu had already lived half his life, but he died a hero. He believed in something enough to go to the wall to defend it. Jake would've gladly done the same. What was worth having was worth fighting for.

The wind picked up the thought, whispering it into his heart. He thought of Tory, asleep in her bed, safe. He felt the now-familiar yearning pool in his chest.

In that split second, he made up his mind. What was worth having was worth fighting for.

Chapter Fifteen

They weren't on the same frequency that morning. Their conversation was stilted and careful. It seemed they were back at the beginning, acting like strangers.

Tory sat across from Jake at the breakfast table, thinking of a million things she wanted to say. She couldn't say one of them. Jake cradled his coffee cup in his hands, staring vaguely at the river. Dark shadows circled under his eyes. He looked as drained as she felt.

Their hands brushed together as they both reached for the last slice of toast. Tory felt as if she'd touched a live wire. A current of electricity crackled in the air between them. Jake must've felt it, too, because he jerked his hand away.

"Take it," he said.

"I don't want it."

They finished their breakfast in silence while the piece of toast grew cold on its plate. Finally, Jake cleared his throat. Tory glanced up and saw that his eyes were fixed intently on her face.

"Is there something on your mind, Jake?" she asked.

He cleared his throat again. Tory shifted uncomfortably. Why was he acting so peculiar that morning?

"There's a library over in Watson on the other side of the valley. I'll take you there this afternoon if you don't have other plans."

She stared in surprise. That was hardly what she'd been expecting. "A library?"

"You asked the other day if Heatherfield had a library. It turns out they're building one but it isn't finished yet."

She'd forgotten that conversation. "Oh. That."

"There's a museum, too, if you're still interested."

"I found what I was looking for at Penny Candy's."

"Oh." He seemed disappointed.

"Maybe some other time," she said.

He shrugged.

"Actually, I planned to return to town today," she said.

He drained his coffee cup and set it aside. "I have some brush to clean up and a couple trees that were hit in the storm the other night. I'll take you when I'm through, if it's not too late."

"No problem. I'll walk."

"You can't walk four miles straight uphill, Tory," he said testily.

She smiled. "You'd be surprised."

"I don't want to be surprised, and I don't like the idea of a woman walking along that road. Too many blind spots."

She tapped a finger against her lips and counted to ten, reminding herself he didn't know any better. It was 1949 and a woman was expected to defer to a man's judgment automatically.

"I'm a big girl," she finally said. "I can handle it."

He tried to stare her down, but she met his gaze without flinching. He threw his napkin aside. "The brush can wait until later. When will you be ready?"

It was a good try, but she wasn't giving in that easily. "I'd really rather walk, Jake. I could use the exercise."

He stood, dug a crumpled bill from his pocket and threw it on the table.

"What's that for?" she asked.

"For anything you might need."

She flicked it back toward him. "I won't need it."

"You can't wander around without any money, Tory." He was clearly at the end of his patience. "You'll be arrested for vagrancy."

She considered that and wondered if the threat was valid.

"If you don't use it, you can give it back, okay?"

He was learning how to compromise. She reluctantly slipped the bill into her pocket.

She hurried through cleaning the breakfast dishes, hung a load of laundry on the line and set out. She felt Jake's eyes on her as she started down the winding mountain road, watching from somewhere in the trees. She strolled until she rounded the first bend, then quickened her pace to a brisk walk.

Her combat boots prevented the run her body craved. Her muscles were going slack. She hadn't had a good run in... God, had it only been four days?

As she walked, her mind wandered back to the variety store. Penny Candy's store definitely had an image problem. It was no surprise the old lady was going broke. From outside, it resembled an abandoned building.

That was her first priority. A bit of paint and elbow grease would go a long way.

Inside was going to be a piece of work. All that outdated merchandise took up valuable floor space. She frowned, knowing without asking that Penny wouldn't want to part with so much as an Ace comb.

As she considered her dilemma, an image fluttered through her mind of a store similar to Penny's in layout, but that was where the similarity ended. The store she imagined was swank. It had deep, comfortable chairs, music and rows and rows of books.

It was a place she knew well. Her footsteps slowed. Concentrate, Tory! she told herself.

The image fluttered away, as elusive as a butterfly.

The plaza was quiet when Tory arrived. She strolled across the park, enjoying the sun on her back and the scent of hyacinths on the morning breeze. Scanning the storefronts, she took a mental inventory. Most of the shops appeared to cater to women. To survive, Penny would have to do the same. What did women in 1949 want?

That was easy. They wanted the same things women had always wanted—respect, nice homes and good lives for their children. As she passed a corner newsstand, a headline screamed at her from the morning paper.

De Beauvoir to Speak to Local Women's Group. Irate Husbands Protest: "We Don't Abide Troublemakers Here!"

She smiled. A new age was dawning. Women were hungry for knowledge and a way to express their individuality. She intended to give it to them.

She sprinted onto Penny's porch, determined to make the old woman see reason. As usual, the front door was wide open. Penny napped in her rocking chair.

Tory gently touched her hand. Penny's eyes flew open and she gasped as if seeing a ghost.

"I'm sorry. Did I startle you? Look. I brought back your books."

Penny stared uncomprehendingly.

"Your romance novels." Tory held them out.

Penny came out of her trance and smiled. "So you did, Dearie, so you did." She stifled a yawn. "I'm all fogged up this morning. I don't believe I slept a wink last night. Did you enjoy the books?"

"They were every bit as good as I expected."

"Wonderful." Penny pulled herself from her chair. "I'll go right out back and fetch you another. That's what I'll do, by God. Which one would you like to read next?"

"Bring me your favorite."

As Penny shuffled off to the storage room, Tory wandered through the aisles, assessing the stock. She didn't know where to begin. Every shelf was a haphazard collection of junk. She saw yellowed greeting cards, faded papier-mache party decorations and Toni home permanents all coated with three inches of dust.

She pulled a dog-eared paperback from a shelf, blew off the dust, and opened the cover. Her earlier vision returned, showing a warm room, a cheerily gurgling coffee pot and rows of books.

She coked her head to one side, studying the store's layout. It was a perfect match for the one in her mind.

She shoved the paperback into its slot, her excitement growing in proportion to her new idea. She'd transform Penny Candy's into a bookstore. Romance had its place, oh definitely, but there would also be books on cooking, child rearing, gardening and poetry. Suddenly, another picture flashed through her mind of a bright-red poster taped to an oversized window. She thought for a moment and a slow smile spread across her face.

"Hello! Anybody home?"

The screen door slammed, scattering Tory's thoughts. Millie bounded into the store wearing a simple green smock cinched at the waist with a wide belt. Her frizzy curls were pulled into a plait and her feet were clad in a pair of scuffed brown boots.

Tory choked on her surprise. "Hello, Millie."

Millie grinned. "It's true! My friend Betty heard it in the diner, but I said to myself I had to see a classy dame like Tory working in the rat shack 'fore I'd believe it."

"Rat shack?"

"Oh." She lowered her gaze. "Sorry. I don't have anything against the place personally, see? My ma don't like me coming in here, 'cause it's a firetrap. Here." She held up two lemon sticks from the candy case and dropped a dime onto the counter. "I want to be your first customer."

Tory smiled and slid the candy into a bag. "Actually, Millie, you can help me."

Millie leaned forward eagerly. "I could?"

"You could be part of my market analysis."

Her brows furrowed. "I don't get you."

Tory took a sales pad and pencil from under the counter. "Start by telling me what your favorite magazines are."

"That's easy. Teen Miss and True Story, when I can get them. Grimley's don't carry but two copies of each, and everyone's positively crazy about them." Her lower lip curled into an impish pout. "Except the old-timers, of course."

"We want this store to be everyone's store, Mille. What if I told you Penny Candy's would stock a dozen copies of both magazines starting next month?"

"That would be super!"

Tory jotted down the names of the magazines onto her pad. "What about books? What's hot these days?"

"Hot?"

"I mean, you know, cool?"

Millie gave her a puzzled glance.

"I mean, what's hip? What's happening? What do kids like to read?"

"Why didn't you say so?" The girl eagerly recited a list of current favorites, which Tory scribbled onto the pad.

The sound of tolling church bells wafted in through the open door. Millie grabbed her bag of candy. "Gee, I'd stay and help you some more, but I can't be late for work on account of Miz Matthews is looking for a reason to give me the scoot."

"Tell your friends about us, okay? Let them know we're open to new ideas. Will you do that for me?"

"Sure thing, Tory. You can count on me." She tossed her last words over her shoulder as she bounded from the store.

Tory watched from the window as Millie strutted importantly across the square. She dallied in the park to speak to a gang of teenagers, hands waving excitedly toward Penny's store.

Tory smiled. She keyed the dime into the cash register and turned the crank. The register blinked, shuddered and obliged with a cheerful ding-ding. Tory, smiling again, dropped the coin into the drawer.

"Mercy!" Penny puffed to the counter bearing an armload of books. "I couldn't decide which was my favorite, so I brought them all. Did I hear the bell just now?"

"I made my first sale," Tory said, grinning. "Millie from the dress shop stopped by for some candies."

"How lovely. I don't seem to get many of the young people any-more."

Tory saw her opportunity and seized it. "I might know how to change that if you're interested."

"By all means, Child. If you have an idea, tell it to me." Penny sank into a chair, her eyes glued to Tory's face, as she laid out her plans.

"Just give them what they want," Penny echoed when Tory finished. "It sounds simple enough, but the changes you're talking about will cost a lot of money."

"You've been in business for fifty years, Penny. I'm sure we can set up accounts without any problem."

Penny frowned. "You mean credit, don't you? I've never done busi-ness on credit."

"You may have to start," Tory said gently. "It might be the only way to save the store."

"No, Sir." She folded her arms across her chest. "I won't do it."

"All right. We can apply for a small business loan."

"No, Sir! I won't do business with banks. Don't trust 'em." She glanced around and lowered her voice. "I'd rather keep my profits in a pouch under my mattress where they're safe."

Tory groaned inwardly. She knew it wouldn't be easy. "We won't use a bank, then. What if we found a backer, someone we could trust, to front us the money we need. What about that?"

Penny threw back her head and laughed. "Oh, Child! You do get me going. Who with a lick of sense would back me?"

"Let me worry about that, okay? Trust me?"

The old woman fished a tattered handkerchief from her sleeve and dabbed at her eyes. "The curious thing is, I do."

"All right." Tory reached for her sales pad and flipped to a clean page. "The first thing we need to do is order new merchandise. Where do you do your buying?"

"Well, now, let's see." Penny closed her eyes and cocked her head to one side. "I haven't gotten anything new in quite some time. There's a wholesale warehouse in the city, but I don't like to go. I can't seem to keep my wits about me in all that traffic."

"I'll drive," Tory said quickly, then thought better of it and shuddered. "I've heard horror stories about New York City cab drivers running people off the road. Is it really as bad as they say?"

The question made the old woman collapse into peals of giggles. "Mercy, Child! I wouldn't know."

"But you said—"

"You didn't really think I was talking about the city of New York, did you?"

"What city were you talking about?"

Penny fished out her handkerchief and held it to her nose, honking loudly. "Why, Rochester, of course."

Tory went numb. "Did you say Rochester?"

Replacing her handkerchief in her sleeve, Penny gave her a curious glance. "Of course, dear. What did you think?"

"Rochester, New York?"

"The only one I know of."

A tremor of excitement quivered in Tory's stomach. She gripped the old woman's hand. "Penny, this is wonderful! How soon can we go?"

"Most any time, I suppose. How about tomorrow?"

"Tomorrow." Tory blinked back tears and kissed Penny's hand. "Thank you, Penny. Thank you so much."

"There, there." Penny awkwardly stroked Tory's hair. "I only wish I'd thought of it sooner. I've been overdue. Just this morning, I said, 'Penny, old gal, what you need is some fun. An outing's what you need, by God.'" Her eyes sparkled. Her words, gaining momentum, came rapidly. "We'll put a sign on the door and go, as free as a couple of bluebirds. We'll shop the whole day. I know of a cunning little restaurant where they serve the dearest little sandwiches."

Tory wasn't listening. Out on the porch, she paused to catch her breath, wrapping her arms around herself in a secret hug. Rochester, New York, was the city Destiny Paige called home. Tory's plan was working.

Feeling lighter than air, she stepped into the tool shed behind the store. A ray of dusty sunlight filtered through the gaps in the wall, showing an assortment of rusting garden tools lining a shelf along the back. Most of them looked as if they hadn't seen daylight since World

War One.

Moments later, she emerged with a pair of moth-eaten gardening gloves and a wheelbarrow full of equipment. She set to work clearing the lot of debris, whistling cheerfully as she pulled out a stubborn tangle of ragweed.

She smiled as she collected trash from the overgrown flower beds, the word tomorrow ringing through her mind.

Tomorrow she had a date with Destiny.

Chapter Sixteen

It was the busiest day the store had known since the Heatherfield Hotel burned down. Penny spent the morning scooping candies, wrapping doodads and packaging whatnots. Newcomers streamed in as steady as water from a leaking faucet, buying hair nets, push pins and the like.

Penny knew what they really came for. They hoped for a glimpse of her new partner.

She paused to consider the word and say it aloud, then nodded. Yes, indeed, she liked the sound of it. Her partner was a fairy princess who dropped out of heaven and captured the mountain man's heart.

The thought gave her gooseflesh.

There are those who are against us.

"What's that?" She cocked her head, listening intently. A frown creased her brow. She could well imagine the gossip being passed over the counter at Grimley's like so much spare change. Her frown deepened to a scowl. Loose lips sank ships. Everyone knew that.

She thought guiltily of the satisfaction she took in telling the news 'round the bingo hall the previous night and of the surprised looks from the old-timers.

"I'll not tell another soul."

Startled from his nap, the tomcat blinked at her and testily licked his paws. "No, Sir, Thomas. I won't."

The fire whistle blew, chasing away the thought. "Gracious! Noon already?"

She hobbled to the kitchenette out back and compiled a tray of soda crackers and cheese. Pulling a pitcher of iced tea from the lukewarm Frigidaire, she added that to the tray. In a balancing act she thought quite remarkable, she carried them through her disheveled store and onto the front porch.

She stared in disbelief. All across the lot, pale tufts of grass poked up where a decade's worth of rubbish had been. She glanced left and right. Where they once blossomed unseen behind the weeds, clusters of hyacinth nodded their graceful heads. An old straw broom leaned against a porch post like a sailor standing sentinel over his freshly swabbed deck. A dozen bulging trash bags were queued at the curb. Penny smiled at the golden-haired figure who wrought that miracle.

"Come take a break, Child. Gracious. It saps my strength just to look at all this work you've done."

Tory set aside her trowel and ambled over to join her. She plopped into a porch rocker and gratefully accepted a glass of iced tea from Penny's hand.

"I've barely begun," she said, downing the tea in one gulp. "A fresh coat of paint would work wonders for this porch, don't you think?"

"Indeed, it would." Penny arranged her humble lunch tray and sank into her chair. A persistent little voice buzzed in her ear.

She inclined her head to one side to listen. Tory reached to refill her glass, and a silver band on her finger glinted in the sunshine. Suddenly, Penny knew what was bothering her. She glanced askance at her new partner.

"I have to chuckle at the thought of the two of us trying to get around in New York City."

Tory smiled and bit into a cracker.

"Funny," Penny said slowly, "but I could've sworn I heard you tell Pierce Matthews you're from New York City. That can't be right, can it?"

Tory's shoulders slumped almost imperceptibly. After several seconds, she said, "I don't know."

"You don't know?"

"Can you keep a secret, Penny?"

"Oh, yes." She leaned closer eagerly. "I'm a grand secret keeper."

"I'm going to tell you something, but you mustn't tell a soul."

Penny listened in fascination as Tory related the story of her car accident and resulting amnesia.

"But that's dreadful! You have no idea who you are?"

Tory shook her head.

"You don't know but what people are worrying themselves sick over you? A husband? Children?"

"I don't think so. I have a handful of pictures in my purse. No men or children."

"I wonder about that ring." Penny pointed to the silver band on Tory's index finger. "There's no doubt it's a wedding band."

"It does appear to be one, doesn't it?"

"May I see it?"

Tory slipped the ring off her finger. Penny held it close to her face, adjusted her spectacles, and peered at the inscription. "Six fifty-one. What do you suppose that means?"

Tory grabbed the ring and hurriedly replaced it on her finger. "Who knows? Probably just a bunch of scratches."

Penny thought for a moment, then brightened. "Why, there's only one thing it can mean. Lordy, I haven't seen one of those since the First World War." She slapped Tory's knee in triumph. "You aren't married. You're promised."

"Promised?"

"Six, fifty-one. Don't you see? You're promised to be married in June of 1951. That's two years and two months away."

"Maybe you're right."

"I wonder that your intended hasn't come looking for you."

Tory shrugged and reached for another cracker.

"Why, I'll bet he's dead!" Penny said happily. "I'll bet your young man gave his life in the war, God rest his soul, and that's why you wear it on your index finger, not your ring finger."

"That's an awful thing to say."

"I suppose it was. Forgive me, Love." She waited for a solemn moment, and then added, "Since you don't seem to remember him, anyway, maybe you should consider finding someone else. It's not good for a young woman to be alone. Not right."

When Tory didn't respond, Penny screwed up her courage and plunged ahead. "I don't believe you could do better than young Jake."

Tory choked on her cracker. "What makes you say such a thing? I'm only renting from Jake. There's nothing between us."

"Of course not, Dearie." Penny smiled knowingly, reaching for a wedge of cheese. Tory could say whatever she liked, but the truth was written all over her face. Penny swallowed the last of her tea and set the glass on the tray. A soft breeze whispered its thanks.

With a satisfied yawn, Penny closed her eyes and dozed in the sun's warm approval.

Moments later, she awoke to find the lot empty of debris and the grass freshly cut. The sun sat low in the sky. Tory was nowhere to be seen. Penny hobbled into the store and set about closing for the day.

She'd just zipped the day's earnings into her bag when a long shadow fell across the floor. She glanced up with an expectant smile, expecting to see Tory. Her smile froze, and her heart skipped a beat.

"You," she gasped.

Pierce Matthews strode into the store. His eyes swept the room. "Where's your new partner?"

Penny clutched the bag to her breast. "She's not here."

"Pity. I was hoping to talk to her. I guess I'll have to talk to you instead."

Penny inched closer to the wall, still clutching her bag.

Pierce stepped closer. "I've tried to play fair, Old Gal. Lord knows I have. Why did you double-cross me?"

She shook her head, unable to speak.

"You've left me no choice but to fight dirty."

She gripped the sack so tightly, her knuckles ached. "Wh—what do you mean?"

His eyes gazed about the room and then returned to her face. He smiled. "When was the last time this building was properly inspected?"

Heatherfield's code-enforcement officer was Dwight's boyhood friend and passed Penny's store for fifty years on that principal. Penny relaxed slightly. "Terry Riley stops every year."

"That old fool can't see the nose in front of his face. I mean a real inspection." His hand swept the room with a flourish. "Sagging floors, bare electrical wires, inadequate lighting." He clicked his tongue. "Not good, Penny."

She looked around as if seeing the store for the first time, and her heart sank. Every word he said was true.

"I'd hate to think what would happen if a real inspector dropped by unexpectedly, say, someone from the insurance company? You'd be ruined, Old Gal, unless ..."

"Yes?"

His hand shot out to grip her wrist. "Agree in writing to sell it to me today."

He was hurting her badly, cutting off her blood supply. She couldn't breathe or think. "I can't. Let me be."

"What a dirty shame." His eyes bored into hers. "This place isn't up to spec, Lady. It's not safe. I'd hate to see it go up in flames some night, say while you were sleeping up there in—"

"That'll do, Pierce."

He released his hold abruptly and addressed the figure in the doorway without turning. "This isn't your business, Jake."

Jake stepped across the threshold, his gaze going to Penny. "You all right, Mrs. Candy?"

"Fine, Jake," she squeaked. A glance at his face told her he wasn't listening. His stony gaze was back on Pierce Matthews.

Penny edged closer to the wall, terrified of the hatred that swirled in the air between the two men.

"You take too much on yourself, Old Boy," Pierce said. "Always have. People can get hurt mixing in where they've no business."

"Is that supposed to be a threat?"

Pierce turned to face him. "It's a fact."

"I guess I'll take my chances." Jake's tone was breezy, his hands resting casually in his pockets. But the rigid set of his jaw and the stretched look of his biceps spoke of barely tethered fury.

Pierce smiled. "I'd think again if I were you. That pretty little gal of yours, well, it would be a shame if she were to get hurt just because you took your damned fool chan—"

Penny barely saw Jake cross the room or perceived the smooth motion that sent Pierce toppling to the floor. Jake's foot ended up on Pierce's neck. When he spoke, his voice was like the growl of an angry dog.

"If anything happens to her," Jake said, "you'll answer to me. Understand?"

Pierce hissed an obscenity. Jake increased pressure on his neck. Penny, pressing her fist to her mouth, watched in horror as Pierce made small, gasping sounds.

"Do you understand?" Jake enunciated the words carefully.

When Pierce didn't answer, Jake's foot went down harder, and Pierce's face began to turn blue. His lips puckered, desperately sucking air.

"Jake, don't!"

Penny was surprised to hear the words spoken. She hadn't thought herself capable of speech. It wasn't until Tory streaked past her and grabbed Jake's arm she realized she hadn't spoken.

"He's suffocating!"

Jake didn't seem to hear. His eyes were glued to Pierce's face, burning with hatred.

"Let him go!" Tory shook Jake's arm fiercely.

He reluctantly released his hold. Pierce, wheezing badly, scrambled to his feet. Dusting off his pants, he strode to the door and turned back. With a murderous look in his eyes he said, "You're a dead man, Benjamin."

•

Jake, still seething and white-knuckled, drove home. Tory sat beside him, silent and disapproving. He glared at the road that stretched before his windshield, unable to face her any more than he could face himself. He made a promise when he returned from the war that he'd never lift his hand against another human being again. That night, he almost killed a man.

They were halfway up the mountain before he trusted himself to speak. "I want you to stay away from Penny Candy's."

"I can't do that."

"You don't know who you're dealing with, Tory. He isn't human. He doesn't care who he hurts."

"That's exactly why I can't abandon that helpless old woman. I can take care of myself, Jake."

He cursed under his breath. "No, you can't."

"Yes, I can," she said sharply.

He turned to her in anger. Seeing her cheeks aglow with fresh air, her eyes sparkling with indignation, every ounce of fight in him fled. He loved her and wanted to tell her so badly—right at that moment.

He turned into the driveway and switched off the engine. The truck shuddered to a halt. Jake wet his lips. "Listen, Tory, I—"

"What would you like for dinner?" She climbed out of the truck.

"I already made dinner for us."

"You did?"

He shrugged. "A couple of sandwiches. I thought we'd eat by the river. We don't have to."

Her expression softened. "I'd like that."

When they reached the inlet, Tory spread a blanket on the bank while Jake unloaded the picnic basket he prepared earlier that afternoon. He tried to ignore her amused expression, as he pulled out jars of pickles, containers of salad, and a chocolate cake.

"I thought you said it was just a couple of sandwiches."

He shrugged.

"There's enough food in that basket to feed the whole town."

His hands were shaking as he set a thermos of coffee on the blanket. He hoped she hadn't noticed. "I wasn't sure what you wanted." He raised his eyes to meet hers. "What you liked."

"I like most everything here."

"Me, too."

Their eyes locked, and he searched hers for a hidden meaning. She quickly averted her gaze.

He could barely eat for the sick churning in his stomach. Words of love swirled in his mind like autumn leaves. He held them in, waiting for the right moment.

When she finished eating, Tory lay back on the blanket. Jake's eyes traced her movements as she ran a hand across her midriff.

Tory groaned softly. "I ate too much. Why'd you let me eat so much?"

He noticed a smidgen of chocolate on her cheek and gently wiped it away with his thumb. "You worked hard today."

"Not nearly hard enough." She rolled onto her side, cupping her chin in her hand, studying him for a moment. "The place needs more help than I can give. Which reminds me, have you got plans for that can of paint in the pantry of my cabin?"

He hesitated, weighing his options, not wanting to encourage her. "I guess not."

"Thanks." She grinned, melting his heart. "Would you mind if I dug up some of these daffodils? Penny's is the only store in the plaza without flowers.

He sighed. *Please*, Tory, he thought. *For God's sake forget about Penny Candy's.* When he opened his mouth, all he said was, "Take all you want."

"The store has so much potential. The problem is, Penny doesn't have the cash to back it up."

He snorted softly. He didn't doubt that at all. It was a miracle Penny even kept her doors open with the shiny new stores clamoring for a newcomer's attention.

"I'm trying to persuade her to take out a loan," Tory continued. "She's afraid to deal with the banks."

"That's the way the old-timers are." Jake drained his coffee cup and tossed the grounds onto the bank. "You have to remember how hard they were hit when the banks failed. They lost their homes and businesses. Most came out of the Depression with nothing but the shirts on their backs, and those were the lucky ones."

"That was ages ago. The banks are sound now. The economy's never been better."

Her optimism echoed that of the nation. He wondered how people were able to forget so easily. Images of the Depression years still haunted him with their poverty and hopelessness. He remembered drifters showing up at their door, begging his father for work or a glass of milk for their children.

"The only other way would be to find an independent backer," she said, "someone to front her the money she needs, then collect payments once the store was on its feet. I might be able to talk her into that."

Jake leaned back against the tree and closed his eyes. He had an uneasy feeling he knew where the discussion was headed.

"Being a stranger here, I wouldn't know who to approach with the proposal. Do you know of anyone?"

"Nope."

"What about you?"

A few tense moments passed. "I don't mix in with the town, Tory. Nothing that goes on down there interests me in the least."

"You wouldn't have to mix in. All you'd have to do is put up the cash, just a few hundred dollars, then we'd—"

"No."

"But you have nothing to lose and Penny has everything to gain. I know she could make a go of it if you'd only—"

"I said no."

"But why?"

He steeled himself against her wounded expression, though it wasn't easy. He would give her anything and do anything she asked—except for that. "I have my reasons, okay?"

"Tell me."

"You wouldn't understand."

"I want to try."

He sighed. How could he explain what he himself didn't understand? He wouldn't and couldn't be a part of that world. Too many things had changed, including himself. He didn't fit in anymore. He was afraid to try.

As if hearing his thoughts, she gently touched his arm. "Things change, Jake. Ignoring that won't make it any less true."

"What's the truth, Tory?" He dug a fistful of soil from the ground and held it in his clenched hand. "For me, it's this land. It's the trees, the sky and the river. That's the truth I fought for. It's the only truth I care about." He tossed the soil into the river. "They can keep their shopping centers, movie houses and wars. None of it can touch me. Not anymore."

For a moment, the only sound was the splashing of geese on the water. "This is all you want from life? Isolation?"

"That's right."

"You want to sit up here, secluded in your own little world and not give a damn? Not help someone even if you can?"

He stared at the river, weighing her assessment. It wasn't exactly the portrait he wanted to paint of himself. "Yes," he said finally.

"Then why are you helping me?"

His eyes met hers in a head-on collision. *Because I love you. You're all I think about or care about anymore.* The words burned on his lips. It was the right time to tell her, but he couldn't do it.

"What choice did I have? Sending you out there?" He waved toward the hillside. "Not knowing your name or what state you were in, for Christ's sake?"

"You feel sorry for me."

"Yes."

"Is that the only reason, Jake?"

He looked away and shrugged. "What did you think?"

"I didn't know. Now I do." She stood and brushed off her dress. "Good night, Jake."

He watched her disappear down the path. He ached to call her back and tell her the truth, but it was too late.

•

Tory blinked back tears as she hurried toward the cabin. Half of her prayed he'd follow. The other half was ready with a tongue-lashing if he tried. He was sheltering her out of pity, nothing more. She should've been glad. Why was she brokenhearted?

Because she was lovesick, burning with a fever she never felt before. Jake obviously got over his initial attraction, while hers grew stronger every day.

She climbed the porch stairs, sank into her favorite rocking chair and embraced the coming darkness. An owl hooted in the trees, a sad, lonely sound. A host of stars twinkled in the sky millions of miles away. Jake's words echoed in her mind.

They can keep their wars. None of it can touch me.

Sitting there with him, she could almost believe it, could almost buy into the optimism that hung in the air over the plaza, could almost deny the coming reality of Korea and Vietnam and a nation that somehow lost its innocence.

She was lonely in the knowledge, crushed under its weight. Unchecked tears streamed down her face. She wished she could believe in the simplicity Jake embraced and deny the existence of the world as it would become, a world where children gunned down other children in their classrooms and where women were brutalized just for being there.

She'd be going back to that world soon. For the first time, she wondered why.

Chapter Seventeen

Destiny Paige lay on her davenport dreaming of bees.

It was summertime, a time of lazy, happy days on her grandparents' farm. She lay in the meadow, chin propped on her hands, experiencing the joy of being barefoot, the sweet earth scent of clover and the buzzing of bees in a nearby honey tree. She was writing a silly, happy poem about bees.

Bizzing and buzzing … What was that?

She sat up, listening attentively. The sound changed. It wasn't bees. It was the dull roar the ocean made when heard in a conch shell. The change in tone confused her.

She groggily opened her eyes. Dirty fingers of light spread through the cracks in the blinds, pointing out piles of dirty clothing and a mound of discarded whiskey bottles. Destiny flung an arm across her eyes, concentrating on the sound in her head, trying to return to her dream.

"Where are we?" she slurred. "Oh, yes." Waves slapped against the shore and she heard sea gulls.

She smiled. It was nice. It was absolutely delicious.

"Destiny!" a sea gull shrieked as it circled.

Her eyes flew open.

"No," she whispered. "It can't be."

She broke out in a cold sweat.

"Destiny!"

"Oh, help me. Someone please help me."

"Destiny! Destiny!"

The horrible sound came from everywhere, the ceiling, the walls and battered carpets. She trembled. The spirits, stirring in the deep cavern inside her where they lived, were restless, trying to get out.

"Go away!" She choked on a sob, fumbled beside the davenport for the radio, and turned up the volume high. The sudden noise and movement made a blinding pain explode behind her eyes. She cried out in agony, fumbling for the cord until she yanked it from the wall.

"Destiny!"

"She's dead!" she shouted. "Destiny is dead! I killed her!"

Pressing her hands to her ears, she tried to block out the voices. The effort hurt. She groped on the floor beside her until she touched the neck of a bottle. She pulled it to her lips, caressing it like a lover as sweet, burning liquid poured down her throat.

She took a shaky breath, wiping her mouth with the back of her hand. It would be all right soon. The bottle would make the horrid voices go away.

She tipped it on end to coax the last drop from it, then scowled.

"You're worthless."

She threw it across the room where it crashed in a pile with the others.

She tried to sit. Her stomach lurched in rebellion. Rolling onto her side, clutching her aching middle, she tried to think. There had to be an unopened bottle in the kitchen, perhaps a sweet little bottle of brandy or a lively nip of gin.

Strengthened by the thought, she placed her feet squarely on the floor and willed the room to stop spinning. As she wobbled toward the kitchen, her stomach buckled at the musty, closed smell in the room.

"That's a girl," she murmured. "Only a few more steps, a few tiny steps."

She propelled herself down the hall, past stacks of food-encrusted dishes and another mountain of whiskey bottles. The voices called to her, persistent and shrieking.

She stubbed her toe on a broken chair, cursed, and dropped to her knees beside the liquor cabinet. Opening the door, she pulled the lone bottle of brandy from its shelf, broke the seal and tipped it to her lips.

The voices fell silent.

Halfway through the bottle, her mutinous stomach threatened to erupt. She barely made it to the bathroom in time.

After she was sick, she flushed the toilet, cursed the loss of perfectly good brandy and crumbled to the floor in a heap. She sat on the cool marble tile, her head cradled between her knees. From somewhere deep inside her, a voice called her name.

"Why won't you stop?" she moaned. "Why won't you leave me

be?" Repeating the singsong words, she tapped a rhythm on her thigh. "Why won't you stop and leave me be? Why won't you stop and leave me be?"

She glimpsed a woman in the mirror and laughed wickedly. "Who might you be?"

Weeks ago, she covered the mirror with a sheet. She'd been afraid of the demons in her eyes. If she looked too long or too hard, they might come out again to torment and hurt her. In her haste to reach the toilet, she'd knocked a corner of the sheet loose.

She considered for a long moment the skinny leg that protruded from her gown and the stubby, unpainted fingernails.

"Who might you be, Miss Missy?"

She reached out with a bare foot, curled her toes around the edge of the sheet and yanked it free. The sight of the broken woman huddled beside the toilet made her gasp.

Her hair hung in limp, greasy strands around her dirty face. Her once voluptuous figure was rail thin, like a scarecrow. She screwed up her courage, took another gulp of brandy and looked at the woman's face. The eyes staring back were haunted.

They were still in her.

She sobbed long and hard. They took everything she had—her beauty, her dream and her family.

Still, they stayed.

With a strength born of fury, she grabbed an empty bottle and threw it at the looking glass.

A spider web of cracks spread across the surface. In every splinter, she saw reflections of her former life. One showed a haunting, bittersweet image of her youngest daughter, chubby hands reaching as she crawled into Destiny's lap with a Crayola drawing. Destiny impatiently brushed the gift aside, wanting to work and be left alone.

She wept brokenheartedly. For the rest of her life, alone was the only thing she'd ever be.

"What do you want?" she sobbed. "What more do you want from me?"

"The work! The work must be completed!" a voice shrieked.

She wept beside the toilet long after light faded to darkness, and sorrow rendered her sober. She carried her bottle to the living room, took a swallow for courage and knelt beside the davenport. Pulling a box out from underneath, she shook it and her heart sank because it was too heavy. After a deep breath and another swallow of brandy, she opened it.

The pages were there, but there were at least a hundred more than last time. With trembling hands, she carried the box to the fireplace and opened the grate.

The voices shrieked, pleaded and shouted dark threats as she tore the manuscript to shreds. Bullets of pain rippled through her head as she doggedly continued her work.

When the last page was in pieces, she heaped the confetti onto the floor of the fireplace, opened the flue and struck a match.

The pages hissed and flared as they caught fire. The voices screamed. An acrid odor filled Destiny's nostrils.

She howled with laughter as she watched them burn.

When Heatherfield was nothing more than a pile of smoking ash, she slept.

Chapter Eighteen

Bumping toward the city in Penny's Chevy Stylemaster on Wednesday morning, Tory was as nervous as a sixteen-year-old with a brand new learner's permit. The car was like a tank, big, broad and deep-chested. There was no power steering or power brakes.

"How can you drive this boat, Penny?" She ground the gears and winced. "I can barely see over the steering wheel."

Penny smiled. "You're doing fine, Dearie."

As they left the graveled roads behind, Tory relaxed her grip on the wheel, turned on the radio and let her mind wander. A sixth sense told her she was close to locating Destiny Paige and was almost home free. Her conscience said she had a responsibility to Penny before she left.

In a town like Heatherfield, image was everything. She had to point Penny in the right direction, show her how to make the store more appealing to the new American woman. She was pretty sure she knew how to do it. The answer came to her the previous day. The store needed a poetry forum, a showcase for talent and culture. She wondered how to sell Penny on the idea.

She considered her options as Penny hummed along with Tommy Dorsey's orchestra. When the song on the radio ended, Tory plunged in.

Penny seemed dubious. "Do you think folks would turn out?"

"I know they will, because we'll make it irresistible."

Penny frowned. "What about that rat, Pierce Matthews? What if he calls in the dogs like he said he would? He can have the insurance people shut me down."

"He won't."

"How can you be so sure?"

"Because we'll shut ourselves down first."

Penny's brow wrinkled in confusion.

Tory smiled. "You need to make repairs anyway. I'm guessing two weeks should do it. That'll give us time to promote the event and re-stock the shelves. The poetry reading will be the grand reopening of an all-new Penny Candy's."

"But we need workmen," Penny fussed. "Electricians and what-have-you. Those men don't work for free."

Tory reached across the seat and patted Penny's hand. "If things go the way I think, you'll have plenty of money to pay them."

"I hope you're right."

Tory glanced at her sweet, troubled face and bit her lip. *So do I, Sweetheart*, she thought.

"There's your turn just ahead!" Penny flapped her hands nervously toward the exit ramp.

Tory made a sharp left turn, entered the city limits and succumbed to her second wave of culture shock in a week.

She kept her eyes fixed on the road, taking cautious sidelong glances up and down the Main Street Bridge, digesting the city one bite at a time. It opened its arms to her, enveloping her like a long-lost friend. It was totally changed, totally wrong and familiar enough to give her gooseflesh.

She cruised pristine streets, gazing in wonder at proud homes that would in half a century be reduced to crack houses, charming mom-and-pop markets destined to be shamed, broken and boarded up. Passing a group of children skipping rope, she felt a pang of sadness for the Mr. Roger's neighborhood so soon to fall from grace.

Caught up in her musing, she barely noticed the subtle change taking place inside her. She was remembering. As she inched the Chevy back into the swell of traffic, she was barely able to concentrate on driving for the tidal wave of memories washing over her. Crystal-clear images clamored for space in her brain, as sharply as if the events occurred that morning.

She recalled her college days and the conversations she once had with Kate. *How can that be?* she wondered. Earlier that morning, she was barely able to remember Kate's name.

"Right over there, Pumpkin," Penny said joyously, intruding on her thoughts. "That warehouse just across the boulevard."

Moments later, they walked into a squat, windowless building.

"Isn't it exciting?" Penny said, as awed as a child in a toy store. "It's awfully big, isn't it?"

Tory stared at the endless rows of shelves stocked to the ceiling with books, paper products and beauty supplies, and her heart sank. How would she ever keep Penny on task?

She hustled the old woman to the romance section and assigned her the job of selecting a suitable line, then wandered up and down the aisles, taking notes. She perused the sections devoted to cooking, gardening and fashion.

Two grueling hours later, armed with her stock list and bogus credit references, she walked to the order desk. The clerk, a tired, balding little man, wrote up her orders with barely a glance at her paperwork.

"Nothing but books," Penny said wistfully as they left the warehouse. "You're sure we did the right thing?"

"Of course we did." Tory felt a twinge of guilt when she looked at the old woman's trusting face. If Tory made the wrong decision, Penny was ruined.

As they strolled through the business district, Tory felt her trepidation melt away. It was a glorious day. The sun was warm on her back. The city was scented with lilacs. She scanned the crowded sidewalk in search of a faceless woman, but she'd know her when she saw her.

In one of the second-hand shops on Monroe Avenue, Penny selected a phonograph and some classical records. Tory insisted on a worn but colorful Oriental rug, a pair of brocade drapes and six easy chairs with matching fabrics. Having made the arrangements to have the items shipped to the store, she and Penny got back into the Chevy and drove across town.

Penny twittered like a spring robin. Tory barely listened. She peered into passing cars and shop windows, studying the sea of faces, gripped by a mounting sense of urgency.

She'd know her when she saw her.

•

Dotty's Luncheonette sat quietly on the corner of Union Avenue and Forbs Street. A gray, tin structure with a curved roof, the building resembled an old-fashioned lunch box. Spanking white window boxes hung cheerily from the diner's windowed front with bright-red geraniums breaking up the somber aluminum siding.

Inside, Tory's senses were assaulted by the odors of greasy French fries and roasted chicken. She slid into a red leather booth in the window, her stomach churning. Glancing at the clock, she saw it was past two. The luncheonette was the last stop on their trip. Surely she'd know her when she saw her, wouldn't she?

Her eyes darted around the room, taking in the gleaming black-and-white linoleum and shiny chrome lunch counter. There was a red pay phone in the back hall. A waitress approached their booth and merrily ticked off the lunch specials. Tory listened distractedly. The sounds of clinking silverware and murmuring voices magnified to a dull roar in her head.

The pay phone beckoned.

When Tory's sandwich came, she forced it down without tasting it. Waitresses scurried past, the rubber soles of their work shoes banging on the black-and-white floor. The phone booth seemed to loom in its corner.

"Aren't you going to eat your apple pie?" Penny asked hopefully, reaching for Tory's plate.

Tory's eyes drifted back to the phone. She pulled in a sharp breath. "Of course!"

"Oh." Penny's hand fell away. "I noticed you haven't touched it. That's all. It'd be a dirty shame to let good pie go to waste."

Tory's attention snapped back to the older woman. "What?"

"Your pie. I said it would be a shame to let it go to waste."

Tory slid the plate across the table and neatly snatched up the bill. "I'll go take care of this. Be right back."

She paid the tab with Jake's five-dollar bill, asking for the change in coins, and then walked on trembling legs to the rear of the diner. She leafed through the heavy directory hanging on a chain beside the pay phone.

There was no listing for Destiny Paige.

She leaned her forehead against the cool glass partition of the booth and sighed. She should've known it wouldn't be that simple. "Okay, Counselor. What now?"

This isn't the first time you've searched for this broad.

"What?"

Think about it, Kiddo.

Tory heard Kate's voice as clearly as if she stood beside her. She thought back to the night she searched her computer for Destiny Paige and tried to remember what the screen had shown.

The memory came easily. She slipped through two pages of P's, tracing her finger down the column of names. She grinned at Pratt, Dierdra.

"Bingo."

She dropped a nickel into the slot and dialed. The phone rang three times while she crossed her fingers. Four rings sounded, then five. "Come on, Destiny," she whispered. "Be there."

A husky voice answered on the sixth ring. The voice suggested sleep or years of heavy cigarette smoking.

"Yeah? Hello?"

She had chosen her words with utmost care, but at the sound of Destiny's voice, Tory found herself speechless.

"Who's there?"

"I'd like to speak with Dierdra Pratt. Is she there?"

"Who's asking?"

"My name is ..."

A waitress idled near the counter, waiting impatiently to use the pay phone, a pretty woman with waist-length auburn hair.

"Julia Roberts," Tory said. "I'm a student at the university."

"What's that got to do with me?"

Tory hesitated. The one thing she counted on was the woman's vanity. She crossed her fingers, uttered a silent prayer and threw out her trump card. "I'm doing a paper on great contemporary authors. I'd love to interview Destiny Paige. Someone said you might be able to put me in contact with her."

"I can't help you."

The line went dead.

Tory hung up and redialed. With every unanswered ring, her anger grew. When the woman snappishly answered, Tory's carefully prepared speech went out the window.

"Why'd you hang up on me?" she demanded.

"I told you I can't help you. I don't know any Destiny Paige."

"I think you do. I think you know her very well. In fact, I think you are Destiny Paige."

Silence answered her.

"Aren't you?"

The woman sighed. "I was. Not anymore."

"You're not a writer anymore? Is that what you're saying?"

"Yes. That's it."

"I think you are." Tory trembled with rage. She came too far and was too close to give up. "I think you're working on a project right now and I'd love to talk to you about it."

"No, I'm not!"

"You're writing a book called *Heatherfield.* "

She shrieked as if in pain.

"Destiny?"

The line went dead a second time. Tory grabbed a napkin from a nearby table and jotted down the Lyle Avenue address listed in the directory. She rushed back to the table where Penny sipped a cup of tea.

"Sit tight, Penny." She grabbed the keys to the Stylemaster, kissed the startled woman's cheek and hurried out of the diner. There was no time to lose. She sprinted down the block to the car. With her heart hammering in her chest, she gunned the engine and thundered across town to Lyle Avenue.

•

Jake laid the ax aside and turned questioning eyes toward the sky. Storm clouds danced across the sun. The wind moaned in the trees, trying to tell him something. He closed his eyes, listening. Something brooding and ominous was in the air.

A raindrop slapped his cheek. Hurriedly collecting his equipment, he turned the truck toward home.

By the time he arrived, the sky was as black as midnight. Rain poured down in torrents, while thunder rocked the hillside. He cast an uneasy glance north, praying Tory was all right. The thought stayed with him, nagging at him as he changed into dry clothes and made a pot of coffee. Moments later, he carried a steaming mug into the living room and stared out the window.

Across the hillside, sturdy trees bowed low in the wind. Bits of debris flew past the window like wayward doves. A power line snapped, pitching the room into darkness.

He tipped the scalding coffee to his lips and drank, barely noticing the heat. He was troubled, held fast by irrational fears. All centered around Tory. There were so many things he wanted to tell her and experiences he longed to share with her. Suddenly, he had the terrified feeling he'd never have another chance.

He moved away from the window, lighting a kerosene lamp until the room flickered. Taking a novel from the bookshelf, he opened it and tried to concentrate. The words swam before his eyes. Danger was coming. He smelled it in the air and heard it on the howling wind.

Closing the book, he moved back to the window and told himself he was being stupid. Tory was fine. She was in the city, shopping with Penny. It probably wasn't even raining that far north.

"Come home, Baby," he whispered. "I need you here."

He ached for her, to take her in his arms and shelter her from such a formidable enemy. He wanted to protect her from the danger, whatever it was.

Chapter Nineteen

Tory slammed to a stop in front of the house on Lyle Avenue. A quick glance at her napkin confirmed that was the address she wanted. As she stared at the house in disbelief, a finger of fear traced a path down her spine.

The ancient Victorian sat forlornly on a square of overgrown lawn. She stepped cautiously from the Chevy. Shading her eyes with her hand, she peered at the darkened upstairs windows and shivered. Something was wrong. The house looked empty—or haunted.

From the corner of her eye, she caught a flicker of movement behind a dormered window. Tory hurried up the cobbled walk, noting the neglected flower beds and overflowing mailbox. Taking a deep breath, she stepped briskly onto the porch and raised the brass knocker. It fell into place with a hollow crash.

Tory pressed her ear to the leaded-glass windowpane, listening for movement inside the house. She stepped back and peered up at the dormered window. A face appeared and quickly moved away.

"Hello?" she called. "Hello?"

Her greeting echoed in the silent street. The house stared at her, dark, somber and forbidding.

"I won't go away, Destiny!" she shouted. "Come out and talk to me. Come out and face what you've done!"

The house seemed to hold its breath.

Incensed, Tory grabbed a rock from the garden and threw it at a window. It struck the shutters and crashed back into the bushes. Picking up another rock, she drew back and aimed again. Before she could throw it, the front door opened and she found herself face-to-face with the most used-up woman she ever saw. Sunken eyes regarded her from a bloodless face.

"Please," she said wearily. "Don't."

Tory, dropping the rock, stared in shocked silence. Destiny was as grossly untended as the house in which she lived—not at all the egotistical artist Tory expected. An expensive ball gown hung on her emaciated frame. At her scalp, three inches of regrowth peppered her platinum hair.

"If I talk with you, will you go away?"

"That's just it, Destiny. I can't go without your help."

The woman cast uneasy glances up and down the street. "We mustn't talk out here. Come inside. Tell me what this is about." She stepped aside and waved Tory in.

The house was filthy. A sour stench rose from the carpet to permeate the air. Tory, squinting into the dark living room, took a wary step inside.

"Come, come." Destiny hustled her in and closed the front door. She brushed past her and stood before the shuttered picture window. Without facing her guest, she tipped a whiskey bottle to her lips and drank.

"Talk."

"Let me start by being honest with you. My name isn't really Julia. It's—

"I know who you are." Destiny whirled toward Tory, her eyes wild with fear or madness. "Don't you think they started in, whispering and moaning?" Her voice broke off in a sob. "You're Victoria, aren't you? The Beloved."

"I've heard the voices, too, but I'm not who they think I am. I'm just an ordinary person. At least I was until—"

"Just an ordinary person." Destiny laughed wildly and turned back to the window, gulping from the bottle again. "God help me. God help us all."

"Destiny, please. You've got to tell me what this is all about."

"I swore I'd never tell anyone. Who'd believe it?"

Tory stepped forward. "I would."

"I can't talk about it. Please go. Please leave me alone."

The dismissal resparked Tory's anger. She leapt at the other woman and held her bony arm. "Go away? Don't you think I'd like to?" she shouted. "My God, one minute, I'm living my life and I have it all together, and the next minute I'm fifty years in the past and I don't even know my own name! You know the reason for it! I know you do, and I won't leave until I hear it."

"They thought I was crazy." Her eyes searched Tory's face as she clutched the bottle against her breast. "I can hardly believe it myself. They actually pulled you in from the future?"

"Who are they?" Tory demanded.

Destiny sighed. "You'd better sit down."

She sank into a worn chaise recliner, rested her head against the back of the chair and closed her eyes. Tory sat in a mustard-colored Queen Anne chair opposite, waiting in tense silence while Destiny gathered her thoughts. When she finally spoke her voice was hollow, tinged with exhaustion.

"It started five years ago," Destiny began. "The war was in full swing, all over the newspapers and on the radio." She drank more whiskey, wiping her mouth with the back of her hand. "I read a story in the Democrat about a young Marine who was killed in an ambush while dragging a wounded comrade to safety. That story broke my heart."

She hesitated. "What made the story doubly tragic was that the soldiers who killed him were the same ones his unit were sent to reinforce. They were United States soldiers. Evidently, there was a terrible mix-up."

She opened her eyes, reached for the bottle and drank deeply. "That boy haunted me. He was twenty-three, engaged to be married. He hadn't even had a chance at life. It seemed sad and senseless.

"I despise unhappy endings, so I decided to write his story as if he'd lived. I gave him a town, a girl and a new name. His real name was Ben Jacobsen."

"Jake Benjamin," Tory whispered.

Destiny nodded.

"I was more than a hundred pages into it before I realized it wasn't working. I couldn't cheapen that boy's story by reducing it to a tawdry romance." Noticing Tory's surprised expression, she smiled sadly. "Oh, yes. I admit it. My characters are silly and superficial. It was my chance to create someone beautiful, someone important." She leaned forward, searching Tory's eyes. "Can you understand?"

"I want to. Help me understand, Destiny."

She stood and walked to the window, prying open the blinds with her bony finger. Slivers of light sliced through the dusty air. "I went to New York City to consult a medium. I thought if I could summon Ben Jacobsen's spirit, I could capture his essence. Then I could write his story with authenticity." She turned to Tory, her mouth settling into a thin, white line. "Instead, I unleashed a nightmare."

"How so?"

"Ben Jacobsen was a good, gentle boy. His wrongful death provoked the spirits."

"What spirits?"

"The ones living inside any young man—love and hatred, vengeance and yearning. I set them free, the whole gamut of them." She buried her face in her hands. "They wouldn't leave me alone. Everywhere I went, I heard their terrible voices—at the grocer's, the dry cleaner's, the savings and loan. One day, I realized the awful truth." She peered at Tory through splayed fingers. "They weren't in those places. They were in me."

"You mean …?" Tory shuddered, trying to take it in. "They were inside you?"

"I'd wake up in the morning, exhausted, and find myself sitting at my typewriter beside a stack of pages I couldn't remember writing. They were creating their own world, one in which they could avenge themselves and resolve that boy's death." Her voice broke. "They wouldn't stop. I lost my husband and children. I burned the pages, but they rewrote them. No matter how many times I destroyed them, they always came back."

She drained the bottle and tossed it aside. "I was afraid for my sanity and my life. I broke the connection the only way I could by writing myself in. Then I wrote myself out."

She crossed the room, her skeletal fingers gripping Tory's hand, her eyes pleading for forgiveness.

"I can't help you, Victoria. As far as Heatherfield is concerned, I don't exist. I gave up any power I had over the story on the day I killed Destiny Paige."

A tension headache crept up the base of Tory's neck.

"But if you don't exist, how can I sit here and talk to you?"

"You're in a very dangerous place, Victoria. You've crossed over into the real world."

"I'm in the real world now?"

Destiny nodded. "You're a disconnected spirit, a wandering entity."

Tory bolted upright, freeing her hand from the woman's grasp. "If I'm in the real world, then Corning exists. I can get there from here."

"You can go to it as it exists now, but this is 1949. You haven't been born yet."

Deflated, Tory sank into her chair. "It's so confusing. Heatherfield is in New York State, yet there's no Corning or Buffalo. Why?"

"It never occurred to me to write them in. I gave Heatherfield route numbers and surrounding towns purely out of my imagination. I wrote in Rochester because it's my hometown and it gave the men of Heatherfield a place to work."

"Then everything that exists is here because you wrote it?"

"Exactly."

"But you didn't write me in?"

"I didn't know you existed. Technically speaking, you didn't. They wanted you, don't you see? Above all, the spirit of Ben Jacobsen yearns for love."

"Why me?"

"They must've had reasons. You must be special or unique. Once they selected you, they created a venue in which to present themselves, which was my novel, and simply waited for you to find it. To draw you into their world, they needed a physical component."

"My tears," Tory said softly. "I cried while I read. Some of my tears fell into the book."

"Once they had them, they had your essence. As simply as that, you became part of Heatherfield."

Tory massaged her throbbing temples. It was beginning to make sense. She thought of her mother's complicated pregnancy and Tory's birth at twenty-nine weeks. She'd been touted as a miracle child, rushed to the finest neonatal care center in the state—Strong Memorial Hospital in Rochester where she lived precariously under an oxygen tent while Destiny Paige lay dying of liver sclerosis. Released by Destiny's death, the spirits brooded over Tory, sending her dreams and waiting for her to grow up.

It was too much.

"I can't go home?" she asked tremulously. "Ever?"

"Hold onto your identity, Victoria, with all of your strength. As long as you do, Heatherfield can't own you."

"I'm beginning to forget who I am. They're stealing my memory."

"This is war. Don't think for a moment it isn't. There's a fearsome battle being waged, one as old as time. It's justice versus wrongdoing, love versus hatred and good versus evil."

"That's where Pierce Matthews comes in, isn't it?"

"Watch out for him. He's dangerous for you."

"He's nothing but a common bully," Tory scoffed. "How can a fictional character possibly hurt me?"

"You can feel pain. All fictional characters experience human emotions."

"Jake Benjamin is real, then, at least to some extent?"

Destiny smiled tenderly. "Beautiful, isn't he?"

"He's everything a man should be. I have to hand it to you, Destiny," Tory said wryly. "You did a bang-up job."

"I only began him. The loving spirits made him what he's become, someone good and kind."

"Wounded."

Her expression clouded. "Yes, I suppose he is."

"I'm falling in love with him."

"You mustn't do that!" she said fiercely. "If you give him your heart, you'll never be free to leave Heatherfield."

"Then I have to go soon. There must be a way. Please help me find it, Destiny. You're the only one who can."

"Go back to Heatherfield and wait. Concentrate on your true identity. Go now, while you still can." Her shoulders drooped. "I'll do what I can from here."

"How will I know …? How can I reach you?"

"You can't."

"But—"

"Go now, Victoria. Be who you are. Above all, don't ever come back here."

"Why?" Tory's voice wavered.

"Right now, Penny Candy is your link to Heatherfield. Lose that link and you'll be trapped here, forever sealed in this reality.

•

Tory drove back to Dotty's Luncheonette thoroughly shaken. Her only hope of survival rested on the shoulders of a drunken poet. If Destiny returned to drinking and forgot her promise, Tory was doomed.

She thundered across town feeling like Cinderella at ten minutes before midnight, but it wasn't fear of losing contact with Penny that drove her. She scanned the streets, one thought on her mind—one crucial errand she must run before the opportunity was lost forever.

When she saw what she was looking for, she nosed the Chevy into a parking spot, praying she had the courage to do what needed to be done.

Her hands shook almost uncontrollably as she dropped a nickel into the pay phone.

"Bell Telephone. What listing, please?"

"Yes, Operator. I need to reach a party at Trixie's House of Curl on Denison Parkway in Corning. Can you connect me?"

"One moment while I look for that listing."

She waited, her thoughts adrift in the sea of time.

"Did you really used to work here, Mommy? In this scary old building?"

She was eight years old, standing on tiptoe, trying to see inside the news papered windows of the beauty salon in which her mother once worked. A rusted sign hung crookedly over the front door and read, Trixie's House of Curl.

"It wasn't so scary then, Love." Her mother smiled, patting her head. "Actually, it was quite wonderful."

Tory tried to imagine the salon as her mother described it, when the salon hummed with hair dryers while women in curlers let cigarettes dangle from their lips. She tried to imagine her mother at twenty-three, doing comb-outs and permanent waves, saving money for a wedding gown.

The call rang through, chasing away the memory.

"Trixie's House of Curl. Darcy speaking."

Tory wasn't prepared for the flood of emotions her mother's voice evoked, and she choked.

"He—Hello?" Get a grip, Counselor. Do not blow this. "Yes, is this Darcy Parker?"

"That's right."

"Um, you probably don't remember me. In fact, I'm sure of it. My name's Julia." It was going badly. What made her think she could do it?

"What can I do for you, Julia?"

The kindness in her tone instantly set Tory at ease, giving her the courage to continue. That was her mother and friend, the only person in the world who ever made her feel safe. "The thing is, you set my hair for my freshman dance. It was a long time ago."

"Julia?" She could almost see her mother's brow wrinkle in thought. "I'm sorry. I don't remember."

"I've always hated my hair," she blurted. "It's naturally curly. I've never been able to do much with it. The way you brushed it—no one has ever made it shine like you did." Despite herself, Tory choked on a sob.

"Are you all right, Honey?"

"The thing is, you listened when I talked and made me feel important. It meant a lot to me."

The confession was met by silence. Tory wondered what her mother thought.

"I guess what I'm trying to say is, I think you're a beautiful person. I'll always remember you," Tory finished.

"What a lovely thing to say."

"Yeah, well, I have to go now."

"Stop by again when you get the chance. We'll give you a hot oil treatment. That'll really make your hair shine."

Tory smiled through her tears. "I'll do that."

"'Bye, now."

Tory's next words slipped from her lips just as Darcy Parker rang off. For the rest of her life, Tory would wonder if her mother heard her say, "I love you, Mama."

It was well past four o'clock when she walked back through the doors of Dotty's Luncheonette. Penny dozed against the window in her booth. Tory gently shook her awake.

"Gracious!" Penny bolted upright, rubbing her eyes. "I was beginning to wonder if you'd pinched my Chevrolet." Her smile died when she saw the look on Tory's face. Her brow wrinkled in concern. "Mercy, Child. What happened? You look like you're all in. Are you all right?"

"Not yet." Tory shook her head and smiled through her tears. "But I've got a feeling I will be."

Chapter Twenty

Something was wrong.

On Saturday morning, Jake sat across the breakfast table from Tory, trying to pretend he didn't care he was being ignored. The truth was, it bothered him a lot. He forked the last of his scrambled eggs into his mouth and complimented her on the potato pancakes.

She barely nodded. The trip to the city changed her. In the three days that had passed, she'd barely said ten words to Jake. Was that because he refused to give Penny the loan, or was it something else?

He moved to the stove to refill his coffee cup and carry it back to the table. She didn't even look up. He studied her across the table, contemplating. Every morning, she rumbled into town in Penny's god awful automobile as if she were on her way to a fire.

Jake didn't like the idea of a woman owning her own car. He wished Penny hadn't given it to her. Tory didn't need him anymore. There were no walks, talks or quiet moments alone. She spent all her time working on signs with words like, *Express Yourself.*

He intended to.

"So, how are things coming along at the store?" He tried to sound pleasant, but even to his ears the question sounded like an affront.

"Fine." She added the finishing touches to the sign she was working on and held it up to study.

"I've been feeling like a day off. There's a pretty park nearby if you're interested. We could hike the trails and bring a picnic lunch."

"Penny needs me in town. Our grand opening is two weeks away, and we haven't even decided on workmen."

"Maybe we could go this evening, then. The sunsets are beautiful from the gorge. They nearly take away your breath."

"I'm sure I'll be busy for most of the day." She cleared the breakfast dishes from the table with a clatter. "You go ahead, though."

He sighed. She wasn't making it easy on him. "I haven't seen much of you lately. Can you sit for a minute, at least?"

He got to her. Something flashed across her face. It was pleading and mysterious, but it immediately vanished.

"I really can't, Jake. In fact, I'm late now." She stacked the dishes in the sink and fled, as elusive as the wind.

•

Tory loaded her posters in the car, trying not to dwell on Jake's hopeful expression and how it crashed to one of disappointment when she said no, but it was for the best. She was doing the right thing—in the end, it was the kind thing.

She checked the back seat to make sure she hadn't forgotten anything, checking paint, brushes, rags and repeating the chant that was always in her thoughts.

"I'm Victoria Sasser. I live at 107 Overland Drive. I work at—" That was the tough one. She strained her memory. "—Women, Incorporated," she finished in triumph.

Her brow furrowed. What was Women, Incorporated? She sighed. It was so hard to remember. Even when she came up with the right words, they were just words without meaning.

"One more time. Say it like you mean it. I'm Victoria Sas—"

"Tory?"

Startled, she whirled.

Jake stood at the edge of the path with an amused expression on his face.

"What do you want?" she asked sharply.

He held out her car keys. "I thought these might come in handy."

She grabbed them from his hand, ignoring the sparks she felt as skin met skin, and the musky scent of the cologne he wore. Did he wear it for her?

"Hey, listen." He moistened his lips with his tongue. "If you change your mind and want to go after all, well, I'll be here."

The hopeful expression returned to his face. Tory couldn't bear it. "I'll keep it in mind," she said brusquely.

She watched his broad shoulders disappear down the path and she angrily wiped away tears. Lord, she missed him.

She climbed behind the wheel of the Chevy, staring wistfully at the forest as she took a moment to compose herself. From somewhere far away, she heard the angry thumping of Jake's ax. Maybe she should take him up on his offer. They could go as friends. There couldn't be any harm in that.

She considered setting out on foot to find him, and then thought better of it. She'd leave a note on the kitchen table instead.

As she neared the house, a black sedan pulled slowly into the driveway. Two men sat in the front seat wearing black fallout hats and dark glasses. Strange, she thought. They almost look like gangsters. What business would they have with Jake?

The two men stepped from the car and started toward the house. Tory rolled to a stop at the end of the driveway and unrolled her window.

"Something I can do for you fellows?"

They glanced at each other, then at her. An inexplicable chill raced down her spine. If they were looking for Bonnie and Clyde, they were in the wrong story. She addressed them again sharply to hide her fear. "What's your business?"

The taller one spoke, his voice as gritty as sandpaper. "We seem to have taken a wrong turn. We were hoping to use your telephone."

"We don't have one." She immediately wondered why she lied.

Maybe it was because they lied first. The county road that cut through the mountain ran directly between two towns. There were no turns, wrong or otherwise. She regarded the men with a growing sense of uneasiness. She couldn't fathom their reason for the visit, but she was pretty sure it wasn't good.

They tipped their hats, climbed into their sedan and drove away without a backward glance. Tory followed a safe distance behind. At the intersection, they turned left, taking the road leading to Rochester. She watched until the sedan was nothing more than a puff of exhaust on the highway before turning right and driving toward Heatherfield.

She was still pondering the incident as she stepped onto the porch at Penny Candy's. When she opened the front door, all thoughts of gangsters fled. The store had a cheerful, holiday feel that morning. Snappy music played on the newly installed phonograph, but it was more than that and the freshly whitewashed walls. The store echoed with laughter and girlish chatter.

She followed the sound through the store, smiling when she located the source. Millie and her friend, Betty, lay belly-down on the floor, combat boots dangling from their feet as they colored the flyers Tory drew up. A finished stack lay between them.

"You girls are here early," Tory said brightly.

Millie glanced up with a grin. "We've been here for ages, practically." She held up a flyer for Tory's inspection. "How do they look?"

"They're perfect, Millie. Thanks a million."

Millie's bracelets chimed as she waved away Tory's thanks. "Don't mensh."

"How many have we got?"

"This makes a hundred, even. That's not counting the fifty we finished yesterday."

One hundred fifty flyers in three days. Tory sighed. There were at least a thousand to go and the invention of color copiers was twenty years in the future. She wanted a flyer for every door, windshield and telephone pole in the city. The fate of Penny Candy's depended on it.

"You want we should take these around now, Ma'am?" Betty asked.

"The sooner the better," Tory replied, adding her own flyers to the stack. "Put them everywhere."

"Yes, Ma'am."

"The post office, the diner and don't forget the window at Grimley's Market."

"No, Ma'am."

"Betty?"

"Yes, Ma'am?"

She smiled. "My name's Tory, okay?"

Millie gave her friend an I-told-you-so wink and scooped up her stack of flyers.

When the two girls left on their mission, Tory wandered out back looking for Penny. She found her sitting at a battered table, talking on the telephone. A list of crossed-out names lay on the table in front of her.

"I see. No, of course not." Her shoulders slumped as she drew a line through the last name on the list. "Thank you, just the same."

Tory took a tentative step into the room. "Any luck?"

"No one will do the work unless they're paid in advance." The old woman blinked back tears. "It doesn't matter. Their rates are too high, anyway."

"We'll get someone, Penny." Tory's voice was full of a confidence she didn't feel. "I'm sure we will."

"I don't know who, Lovey." Penny shook her head. "I surely don't know who."

Tory returned to the front of the store and pried open a can of paint. Concentrating on her mantra, she spread a fresh, white coat over the lacquered shelves. "My name is Victoria Sasser. I was born in 1972. My best friend's name is—is …"

She reached into her pocket, pulling out a creased photograph and stared at the smiling woman.

She didn't know her.

Tears of frustration came to her eyes. What was the use? She turned away from the spanking-white walls and flamboyant drapes, ignoring the cheerful music that rolled from the phonograph. It was too little, too late. The store was doomed.

She'd been a fool to think she could change that.

•

She wasn't going to change her mind.

He stayed near home all day, working quickly while he cleaned gutters, stacked wood and mended broken slats in the fence. Every moment, he kept his ears pricked for the snort of exhaust that would announce Penny Candy's Chevy coming up the road, but it never came.

At three o'clock, Jake grabbed his toolbox and headed for Tory's cabin with one last task in mind. He'd seen suspicious footprints in the woods last night. They were too large for hers and too small for his own. When he built the cabin, he hadn't thought it necessary to install locks on the windows.

The footprints changed his mind.

He stepped on the porch, still listening for the sound of the car, but for a different reason. She wouldn't like his being there or the thought of his nosing around her possessions.

He hesitated as he pulled the spare key from his pocket. It was for her own good. If she said anything, he'd point out that it was her privacy he wanted to protect. With that thought firmly in mind, he slid the key into the lock and let himself in.

Even in her absence, the house was full of her. He closed his eyes and breathed in her sweet, earthy scent. Opening them again, he drank in every detail, noting the serving dish on the coffee table filled with pine cones and sprigs of evergreen, the bouquets of lilacs crammed into drinking glasses and an abandoned robin's nest in a place of prominence on the mantel.

He smiled. The small touches were nice. He plucked an apple from a bowl, held it briefly and replaced it. Who but Tory could make a bowl of fruit look like a decoration?

While he worked, he played out his favorite fantasy, the one where he and Tory lived there as man and wife. The cabin was filled with children, laughter and love. There was no fear, no dark threat looming on the horizon, telling him someday Tory would leave.

He moved from room to room, lost in his daydream, whistling as he secured and double-checked the locks. He saved her bedroom for last.

As he screwed the final lock into place, a blue jay smacked against the pane and plummeted to the ground. He opened the window, leaned out and scanned the earth below. The blue jay flew off shrieking, but as Jake closed the window, something caught his eye and tore the smile from his face.

He looked again more carefully. The set of man's footprints down in the dirt were too small to be his.

He sank woodenly onto the bed. What man would be prowling so far from town peeping into windows? He tried to convince himself it was one of the migrant workers who farmed the potato fields on the other side of the hill. Maybe he staggered home from town, drunk and wandered off course. Maybe it was a teenager on a dare. There wasn't much harm in that.

Then another, more painful, thought occurred to him. Maybe Tory'd had a guest.

Her clothes lay in a pile at his feet. He picked up the blouse she wore the previous day, one he bought for her in town. Holding it close, he inhaled her scent.

The pain was ferocious. He cast the garment aside and it landed beside a wadded sheet of paper. He picked it up, carefully smoothing out the creases, seeing Tory's bold handwriting.

> *You are cordially invited to EXPRESS YOURSELF!*
> *At a poetry Form*

She misspelled the word forum. He scowled at the advertisement. Where did she get such highbrow ideas anyway? Why hadn't she told him about the forum? She must think him an uneducated clod, a bumpkin.

The icy feeling that told him she'd never be his returned to his gut.

Glancing at his reflection in the mirror, he tried to see what she saw—a mountain man, unshaven and coarse. Thought she was too good for him, did she? Couldn't deign to spend an afternoon with him?

Wadding the sign, he hurled it into the wastepaper basket. Who needed her? She could stay in town all night and live there for all he cared.

He stomped from the cabin and slammed the door behind him so hard the frame splintered. Cursing, he retrieved a hammer and a handful of nails from his toolbox and smacked a nail into place. He'd let her go, then. He was better off without her.

He drove another nail. She only complicated his life. Did she lie in bed at night and dream up ways to piss him off?

He held a third nail in place as a dark shadow crossed the sun, catching his eye. The hammer fell squarely on his thumb and pain shot through his hand.

"Damn it all to hell!" he shouted.

He hurled the hammer into the woods and sucked his thumb. A falcon circled in the sky, the picture of loneliness. It uttered a mournful cry as it disappeared over the crest of the hill. Jake buried his head in his hands. "Damn her."

From somewhere in the distance, the falcon's lonely cry pierced the air again. Jake fleetingly wondered if it knew it was alone and if it cared. He doubted it. Birds didn't waste time pining after love. He, unfortunately, was a different animal.

Returning his gaze to the sky, he stared into its vastness as he contemplated his empty, pointless existence. All that time, he'd been wrong.

He squared his shoulders and hurriedly gathered up his tools. It wasn't right for a man to live alone, and he intended to do something about it—right damn now.

•

Penny dug a quarter tip from her change purse and sent the delivery man on his way. She turned to Tory, a tremulous smile on her lips. She'd been secretly hoping the supplier would recheck her credit references and delay her shipment or not send it at all.

No such luck. There it was, all sixteen cases of it.

"My, that certainly was fast," Penny said.

"Yes, it certainly was." Tory neatly slit the sealing tape, pulled a stock sheet from a drawer, and checked it against the items in the boxes. "Looks like we're in business."

Penny ran her hands over the glossy romance novels, carefully avoiding the invoice tucked into the box. When she spoke, she forced a cheerful note into her voice.

"Looks like we're in business, all right. Five hundred nice, new books and clean, white shelves on which to put them." She glanced hopefully at Tory. "The all-new Penny Candy's, right?"

Tory smiled. It seemed to Penny that some of Tory's earlier enthusiasm had evaporated. Was she losing confidence, too? Penny cautiously opened the invoice and her heart sank almost to her built-up shoes. Thirty-six dollars for that box alone! What had she been thinking? She'd lose the store for sure.

She felt her blood pressure soar to a dangerous height and began her deep-breathing exercises, telling herself to simmer down. She tried to look on the bright side. It was always darkest before the storm, or something like that.

She squinted at her store, trying to see it as an insurance adjuster might, and smiled.

It had never looked lovelier. With the tidy white shelves and pretty new drapes, the inspector probably wouldn't even notice a few shortcomings. She glanced upward and noted the troublesome wires that stretched across the ceiling, and her shoulders slumped. Then again, maybe he would.

A sharp tapping at the window made her jump. She hurried across the store, peered out and groaned when she saw Beatrice Paisley's scowling face on the other side. Two of Bea's cronies frowned at her from the sidewalk.

"Now what do you suppose they want?" she grumbled.

"Only one way to find out." Tory wiped her hands on her dungarees and walked over to where Penny stood.

"We could pretend we aren't here," Penny said hopefully.

"Don't be silly. They've already seen us."

To Penny's dismay, Tory flung open the door and invited the women inside. "What can we do for you ladies?"

Ignoring her, Bea barged straight over to Penny and shoved a flyer under her nose. "What's the meaning of this propaganda?"

"Propaganda?" Penny wasn't sure what she meant by the word, but it made her angry. Wasn't it like the old busybody to try to spoil her lovely shindig? "Now listen here, Bea," Penny said, drawing herself up,

"I won't have—"

"We're so glad you received our invitation," Tory said quickly. "Aren't we, Penny?" Penny's head swiveled in Tory's direction and Tory winked at her. "We were just saying we hoped that people like you would attend our little get-together."

Bea shifted her beady eyes to Tory. "What do you mean, people like us?"

"Oh, you know." Tory lowered her voice. "Some of Heatherfield's more mature citizens, those who could add wisdom and insight to the forum. We'd be honored to hear your work."

Bea blanched. "My work?"

"I'm sure a cultured woman like yourself holds deep truths and beautiful thoughts and has committed them to paper. That's what the forum is about, self-expression."

"Well, I don't actually write my truths and insights down." Bea straightened her shoulders and added haughtily, "But I appreciate culture as much as the next person."

"Perhaps you'd honor us by reading someone else's work, then, say Dickinson or Browning?"

To Penny's amazement, Bea's waspish face crinkled into a smile. "I adore Emily Dickinson."

"I'd be willing to read the essay I wrote for the sunshine Club Newsletter," Viola Hanwell piped up. "I don't like to toot my own horn, but if I recall, everyone thought it was quite good."

"It says here you're serving refreshments," Gertrude Simms added. "What did you have in mind, if I may be so bold?"

"Rum balls," Penny said smugly. "I'll bake 'em myself."

"Good heavens!" Viola gasped.

"Nonsense!" Bea said. "Surely an event of this caliber calls for something a bit more delicate. I'll make my famous lemon cake. It won four years in a row at the annual bake-off, if you recall."

"Three," Viola said. "Don't forget my Brown Bettys beat you out in '47. I'll whip up a batch or two just to help out."

"We can count on you to be here, then?" Tory asked.

"With bells on," Bea said.

Penny hid a smile as the three women hurried away, clucking like chickens in a henhouse. "Glory be," she said. "I don't know how you did it. Those old gals buzzed in here just as ornery as mud wasps and you turned them into honey bees."

Tory laughed. "It's called reverse psychology."

"I'm not sure I understand."

"It's sort of like, if you can't beat 'em, let 'em bake the lemon cake."

A sliver of sunlight splashed through the window and danced across Tory's face. Her hair picked it up and threw back tiny prisms of glittering indigo, red-gold and green. Penny cast her eyes to the floor in shame. How could she have doubted, even for a minute? She had her very own fairy princess. Everything would work out splendidly.

•

It was nearly five o'clock when Jake's Model A pulled to the curb in front of Penny Candy's. He saw Tory through the window, looking beautiful even in mended dungarees and one of his old T-shirts. She was laughing.

He tightened his grip on the steering wheel. What if her sunny smile turned to storm clouds at the sight of him? What if she sent him away?

For a moment, he considered driving off before she noticed him, but only for a moment. He turned off the engine and climbed from the truck, striding into the store with his hands balled into fists in his pockets.

Penny saw him first. "Why, Jake, how lovely of you to come."

Tory's smile faded. She set aside her paintbrush to wipe her hands on her dungarees. "What are you doing here?"

"I've got our supper in the truck. If we leave now, we can still make it to the gorge in time for the sunset." In a tone that left no room for argument, he added, "Go ahead and change while I talk things over with Mrs. Candy."

Ignoring the questioning glance that passed between the two women, he assessed the store's damage. He fingered the electrical wires that stretched, exposed and frayed, across the ceiling, the brown splotches and the sagging floors. Shaking his head, he estimated the project would take weeks.

Penny followed at his heels. "Jake?"

"The whole building has to be rewired. That's your first priority. You need a new roof, too. The foundation could use some help, but that'll have to wait."

Penny stared at him uncomprehendingly. "What are you saying?"

"If you haven't hired a workman yet, I'm available. I can start first thing in the morning."

Tory's smile was worth every dime the project would cost him. She threw her arms around him. "Thank you, Jake."

An arrow of desire shot through his veins, neatly hitting its mark. He gave her a small shove. "Go get cleaned up, so we can go," he said gruffly. "I'm damned near starving."

⋄

Pierce drummed his fingers on his desk, his eyes darting from his wristwatch to the telephone. It was ten minutes past five. He should've heard by then.

He lit a cigarette and swiveled his chair toward the window. The town was buzzing but not with the news he'd expected. A group of young girls scurried around the square, littering telephone poles and storefronts with their silly flyers. He scowled. He'd found two of the blasted things on his door that morning.

He pulled one from the pile of papers on his desk and frowned as he read, "Express yourself." It wasn't bad enough that the little witch was mucking up his plans. She was also filling the young wenches with ideas. Women should know their place.

He jumped when the phone rang at quarter past five.

"Matthews here."

"I thought you said he lived alone."

His hand tensed on the receiver. "Did you do the job?"

"There's a woman."

"I know there's a woman!" he exploded. "Take her out to the country."

"That'll cost."

"I don't care what it costs!" He fought to regain control. "When can you do it?"

"Week or two."

"That's what you said last week."

"We didn't know about the woman last week."

Pierce sighed, his eyes going to the flyer. "Can you make it any sooner? I'm working against a deadline."

"We'll be in touch."

The line went dead. Pierce slammed down the receiver and lit another cigarette. He should've known better than to hire a hatchet man. He should've done the job himself, consequences be damned.

He grabbed the flyer from his desk and scanned it for the date. Penny Candy's was scheduled to reopen in two weeks. With that little

shrew in charge, it might have a chance at something resembling success. Wadding the flyer, he threw it out the window.

Stubbing out his cigarette, he fingered the tender spots on his neck.
There wasn't a snowman's chance in hell he'd let that poetry reading
take place.

•

Louise counted out the day's earnings and tucked them into the
bank bag with a frown. There wasn't enough to bother with a deposit.
It was nearly May. By then, the culottes she ordered from California
should be walking out of the store to the tune of six dollars a pair,
but instead, young girls paraded around town in thrift-store rags and
men's boots. Would the madness never end?

She heard a soft thump against the window and glanced up in time
to see Millie's impish face sprint past. Her hands tightened into fists.
Millie had taped another of those ridiculous signs to the door for the
third time that day.

Louise marched out of the room, flung open the door and tore
down the sign, casting furious glances up and down the street. Millie
was gone.

She stared at the variety store with hatred. It didn't seem possible
that Millie quit Panache to work for the likes of Penny Candy. It was
humiliating.

"You'll come crawling back, Millie," she hissed to the empty street.
"And when you do—"

Her thoughts were diverted by the sight of Jake's Model A pulling from the curb. He drove past her without a glance, that wretched woman sitting beside him. Louise tore the flyer into shreds and
stomped on them. Two words stared back from the sidewalk—*Express
Yourself*. A wicked smile twisted her lips.

"Count on it, Honey," she whispered. "Count on it."

•

Tom Hopewell sifted through the papers on his desk until he found
the one he wanted. The little sweethearts were on every windshield in
town. His eyes went across the street. He had to hand it to that little
gal. Penny Candy's place looked better than he would've thought possible. What was her motive?

Fishing the notebook from his pocket, he scanned what he wrote
earlier that afternoon. Two men in a black sedan pulled over for a soft
tire. He shuddered. They were the sneaky, shiftless kind that made a

cop's hackles want to stand up and take a bow. He tucked away the notebook with a shake of his head. He couldn't arrest a man just for looking suspicious, could he?

His gaze returned to the variety store and his eyes widened in surprise at seeing Jake in town again, which made three times that month. His eyes narrowed to thoughtful slits. His cop's instincts told him there was a connection between the men in the sedan and the pretty blonde. Was it a scam of some kind? What did it have to do with Jake?

He sat back, rubbing his eyes. Heatherfield was going to pieces. Gangsters prowled the streets, poetry readings were being planned and women were getting uppity. Just that morning Nancy jumped all over him about buying her an electric mixer. She told him from then on, she would express herself.

He scratched his head. Something was going on and he intended to find out what it was.

PART THREE
HEATHERFIELD
1949

Chapter One

April burst into May with a blaze of restless energy. Things were unsettled and turbulent. It was as if a cloud of discord hovered over Heatherfield city.

Above Tory's head, a pair of blackbirds argued on a telephone wire. In the window boxes lining the square, tulips turned their backs on each other and softly wept petals. Even the traffic light was at odds with itself, simultaneously flashing red and green.

She shivered despite the humidity, casting an uneasy glance along the stillness of Crescent Street. It was almost six o'clock. The stores were shuttered for the evening. Children were called back from the park by the aroma of hot dogs sizzling on backyard grills. It was the hour when Heatherfield sat down to dinner, but still, the silence had a sinister feel to it.

Maybe it was her imagination. She stood back and surveyed the bright red, white and blue banner Jake hung across the storefront. Deciding it was perfect, she wandered back inside.

Dragonflies swirled and danced in her stomach at the sight of the burnished podium and gleaming rows of chairs. They borrowed one hundred fifty from the fire department and as many again from the First Presbyterian Church. Would it be enough? The dragonflies fluttered again while the empty chairs grinned mockingly. If nobody came, there were three hundred too many.

"What time is it, Penny?" she asked.

The old woman looked up from the display of books she was rearranging and smiled. "Six-fifteen, Love. Precisely five minutes later than it was five minutes ago." She hobbled across the store and laid a gnarled hand on Tory's shoulder. "We're getting close now. Why don't you go upstairs and draw yourself a warm bath? You're as nervous as a cat."

"I can't imagine what's the matter with me. The store looks wonderful, so clean and bright ..." Her voice trailed off.

"Jake did a lovely job with the lighting."

Tory said nothing.

"I can't thank you enough for pleading my case."

"I had nothing to do with it, Penny. I told you that."

"You persuaded him to give me the loan. Don't try to say otherwise."

Tory sighed and waited for Penny to come to the point. It didn't take long.

"He's a fine man. If I were forty years younger, I'd set my cap for him. Any woman would be lucky to have Jake."

The words were painful, making Tory turn away. "Maybe I'll have that bath now."

Upstairs in Penny's apartment, she sank into the footed bathtub and savored the silky feel of the bath oil she bought at the five-and-dime. Her eyes slid to the dress she bought for the occasion, hanging on the doorknob in a fussy profusion of cream-colored taffeta and lace.

She made a face. The dress was awful. No, it was worse than awful. She'd look like a child playing dress-up in her grandmother's cocktail gown, for heaven's sake.

She scrubbed her skin until it was pink, then stepped from the bathtub and toweled herself dry. Slipping into the dress, she hummed loudly and tried to block out Penny's words. A woman would be lucky to have Jake, but she could never be that woman.

After struggling into a pair of stockings, she saw that the seams ran crookedly up her calves. She adjusted them twice before taking them off and throwing them in the garbage pail. She applied a thin coat of lipstick, frowned and wiped it off with a square of toilet paper.

She pulled her hair into a plait, shook it free again and arranged it loosely around her shoulders. Opening her purse, she dabbed the last of her jasmine perfume on her wrists and studied her reflection in the mirror, frowning.

She didn't know herself.

Across the river, the factory whistle mourned the coming hour. Tory took a deep breath. It was time to go.

She heard a soft murmur of voices filling the store as she descended the stairs. The dragonflies danced in her stomach again and she took another deep breath.

Relax, she told herself.

Church bells tolled raucously as she crossed the yard. In the street, a calico kitten chased a dog. She pulled out her notes, scanned them, and stepped onto the shop's porch. A cricket screamed a lullaby as the church bells died. Tory pulled in one last lung full of air and opened the door.

It was show time.

•

It looked like there were a thousand people in the room.

Jake Benjamin, tough Marine and decorated war hero, was quickly losing his nerve. From the safety of the sidewalk, he peered into the window and saw a mob of people overflowing the rows of folding chairs and spilling into the aisle. Mostly female, he noted, with the exception of a starched, miserable-looking Tom Hopewell.

The clatter of woman talk drifted to him on the humid air, making his stomach ache. After that night, they'd have plenty to talk about. He stepped back. There was no way in hell he could do it. After two more backward steps, he knew he'd been a fool to think otherwise.

With his fifth step back, he froze. Tory glided across the lawn, a white dress swirling at her ankles, her hair tumbling freely across her shoulders.

She walked past without seeing him, her eyes glued to the sheet of paper in her hand. He tried to speak her name but couldn't. She knocked the breath from his lungs. He trailed behind as she stepped onto the porch and disappeared inside.

He crowded into the doorway, standing with his hands jammed in his pockets, feeling dizzy from the heat, potpourri of perfumes and the drove of voices. The room swam in and out of focus. People scurried for their seats as Tory slowly walked down the aisle.

She smiled. "Good evening, everyone, and welcome to our first annual poetry forum."

Her voice was hauntingly beautiful, as hypnotizing as a movement from Beethoven, practiced to perfection. Their eyes met, and unspoken communication passed between them when she smiled at him. People turned to stare.

"Tonight is your night, Heatherfield, a time to open your soul and share what moves you. Tonight is your night to express yourself."

There was a smattering of applause from the rear of the store, and she smiled at the row of teenagers.

"I'd like to remind you we have a lot of great books on sale tonight. We hope you'll take a moment to browse after the readings."

"Isn't she lovely?" a voice said softly in Jake's ear.

The touch of a hand on his arm startled him.

Penny leaned closer. "She'll make some lucky man a wonderful wife."

He nodded, his eyes on Tory's face. "Please, God," he muttered, "let it be me."

She unfolded her paper and began to read. He recognized it as Whitman. Though he'd heard the words before, they'd never been spoken so beautifully. He thought fleetingly of long winter evenings with his grandmother reading him poetry by the light of a kerosene lantern. She had loved Tennyson, Shelly and Lawrence. He felt the hard weight of the book concealed in his pocket.

Could he do it?

Tory finished reading and neatly folded her paper. "The forum is officially open. Whenever you're ready to share, we're ready to listen."

She walked to a seat in the front row and sat down. Several seconds passed. Silence, like a fog, enveloped the room. Someone coughed, and somewhere a woman twittered.

Jake's heart hammered in his chest. He was nervous as hell for Tory. She'd pinned all her hopes on that night. He was also nervous for himself, because so had he.

That thought propelled him up the aisle. He died a thousand deaths as the sound of his name rippled across the silence. He squared his shoulders and lifted his chin. So what? He died before and survived, hadn't he?

Ignoring the sea of curious faces, he pulled the book from his pocket. Opening it to a well-worn page, he cleared his throat. He moistened his lips with his tongue, cleared his throat again and spoke aloud the words that were engraved on his heart.

"If I pledged my love to you would you give yours in return?"

The silence in the room was total. Beads of sweat formed on his upper lip. Searing hot flames engulfed him as he burned the last of his bridges behind him. There was no turning back.

He cleared his throat a third time, raking his fingers through his hair, and forged ahead.

"Or like a tender blade 'neath a bitter sun
would you leave my soul to burn?
If I said your smile is bright as summer's day
illuminating a heart's dark night
... would you then agree to stay?
Or would you leave me imprisoned—"

His voice cracked. He chanced a look at her and saw her watching him intently, a thousand questions in her eyes. He quickly averted his gaze.

"—in sorrow, alone and ever sealed
in restless chains of longing
a broken heart unhealed?
And if I tempted fate,
if I came on bended knee
to offer adoration
would you give the same to me?
Or would you, like a cruel wind
push me away,
chained in unrequited yearning
for all my days?
And if it was your destiny,
eternally,
to look on me with eyes of palest blue, would you
forsaking all others
be my eternal lover—"

Their eyes locked. He couldn't read her expression. He swallowed hard and finished with a whisper.

"—if I pledged my love to you?"

The ensuing silence was broken by a smattering of applause. It quickly built to a roar. His eyes went to the floor, unable to look at her or bear the rebuke he might see in her eyes.

He shoved the book into his pocket and left the podium, striding down the aisle past Penny Candy's beaming face, past raised eyebrows and widely grinning lips. He walked past questions he had just plainly answered and hurled himself through the door to escape into the night.

There was no going back.

•

It was worse than she ever thought, much worse. It was her worst nightmare come true. He was in love with her.

Louise sat in her folding chair, stunned into immobility. She wanted to run but couldn't. It was as though she were cemented to the wretched metal seat.

Two thoughts collided in her head. It couldn't possibly be true, but it was. She knew she had to act immediately or lose it all, but what could she possibly do that would alter it?

He was in love with her, or thought he was. Her eyes stung with furious tears at the thought of such humiliation. At first, like everyone, she thought the poem was for her, a public declaration of his love. The melody in his voice carried her back to long afternoons spent by the river. She languished on a blanket while Jake read to her from that silly book of verse. Stupidly, she thought he remembered, too, at least at first.

Reality crashed into her daydream when she and everyone else saw the naked yearning in his eyes directed at her, the she-devil.

Louise turned her head, dabbing at her eyes with a handkerchief. Four readers awaited their turn at the podium, while a dozen more streamed down the aisle, as if this were some sort of literary altar call. She'd intended to give a little message of her own and sat up all night preparing it, but it would be wasted. After Jake's shocking display, the point would be blunted.

Besides, she had to admit, the she-devil was a damned tough act to follow. She shifted her jealous gaze to the back of Tory's blonde head. That broad really packed a wallop.

Where'd she learn to speak like that?

The next two readings only served to underscore the thought. The people stammered and were self-conscious, bad enough in themselves, but a disaster when compared to Little Miss Perfect—Heatherfield's own Rita Hayworth. It was almost as though …

A hint of a smile began at her lips as a thought occurred to her. She fidgeted through two more readings, feeling ready to burst. When the next break came, she fought her way through a sea of knees and elbows and hurried from the store.

She tread lightly down the sidewalk, softly calling Jake's name, stopping to listen carefully. There was no answer. He had to be hiding somewhere nearby, waiting for the god awful event to be over.

She hurried toward the park, her spiked heels clicking purposefully on the pavement. The she-devil wanted a fight, did she? Well, Louise Matthews didn't back down so easily. She would check every shadowed doorway and look under every park bench until she found him and made him listen to the truth.

She smiled wickedly—her truth, that was.

•

It was after ten o'clock when Beatrice Paisley, the last of forty-two readers exited the podium. A handful of men mopped their sweating foreheads and loosened their ties. Women retreated to the ladies' room to powder their noses. A contented hum settled over the store, as folks left the world of culture and reentered the more comfortable realm of exchanging baseball statistics and recipes.

While Millie and Betty doled out glasses of punch, Tory passed plates of lemon cake. She longed for a moment alone to contemplate Jake's reading, but it wouldn't come any time soon. People were lining up for seconds.

Poor Penny was barely keeping up at the register. The shelves were emptying quickly. Everywhere she looked, Tory saw books tucked into shopping bags and clutched in eager hands.

She passed the last piece of cake on her platter and hurried to the back room to fetch another. Millie followed, bearing an empty platter of cookies.

"These rum balls are really hip," Millie exclaimed. "This is the third time I've refilled my damn plate."

Tory bit down on the inside of her cheek. "I see what you mean."

Millie waved a hand across the room and grinned. "Would you look at that?"

Tory's eyes followed Millie's jangling bracelets to the front of the store where two women fought over the last copy of a volume of D. H. Lawrence poetry.

"We'll have to order more poetry books," Millie said. "Who'd have ever thought they'd be so hot?"

"I'm just relieved this thing went over," Tory admitted. "We had an awful lot riding on it."

"Went over?" Millie whooped. "Why, it took off like a helium balloon after big daddy made the scene."

"That'll do, Millie."

"How'd you get a fellow to look at you like that, anyway?"

Ignoring the question, Tory returned to the refreshment table, a cordial smile fixed on her face. Her thoughts were miles away. It hadn't been her imagination after all. Millie saw it, too. The feelings she'd been denying were mutual.

It was no high-school crush. It was the big league—love. She didn't know whether she could stave it off anymore, or if she wanted to. The implications terrified her.

It was nearly midnight before Penny shooed the last guest out the door. Millie and Betty set about cleaning up the plates and cups that littered the store while Tory emptied the register.

"Gracious!" Penny raked the pile of money close to her with a disbelieving grin. "This is more loot than I've seen in five solid years."

Tory smiled. "We did it, Penny."

"I don't know how to thank you, Child."

"You can start by letting me drop this in the night-deposit box." Tory nodded at the pile of cash. "Having that much dough stashed under your mattress won't make for a good night's sleep for either of us."

"Phooey." Penny's grin became a pout, but to Tory's relief she didn't protest.

Tory locked the store for the night and followed the old woman upstairs where they toasted their success with mugs of warm milk. Once Penny was safely tucked in for the night, Tory locked the apartment door behind her and headed for the bank.

She whistled softly as she strolled through the empty streets, jumping at every imagined movement. Though the evening went off without a hint of trouble, the dragonflies in her stomach were still active. She couldn't shake the feeling of danger.

She dropped the bank bag into the night-deposit box, breathing a little easier when the door clinked shut behind it. As she rummaged in her purse for the keys to Penny's Chevy, a dark figure stepped from a doorway. Tory froze, stifling a cry of fear.

The figure came closer.

"How'd it go?"

She slumped against the building, dizzy with relief. "You scared me senseless. What are you doing, hovering out here in the dark?"

Jake stepped from the shadows. "Just keeping an eye on things, Darlin."

The endearment went straight to her heart. They walked together without speaking until they reached the corner, where his Model A was parked.

Jake turned to face her. "So …?"

"So."

"Pretty decent turnout, huh?"

"Phenomenal. People are already asking about the next one."

"That's good."

"Uh-huh."

He leaned against the truck. She felt him watching her. She shifted uneasily, grateful for the darkness.

"You look different tonight." He reached for a strand of her hair.

She purposely dropped her keys, ducked and groped for them beside the truck.

He picked them up and slid them into his pocket. "Why don't you ride home with me tonight?" When he opened the door for her, she realized it wasn't really a question.

The four-mile drive up the mountain seemed to take hours. Tory began a dozen conversations in her head and rejected all of them, because all led back to the poem Jake read that night.

Staring out the window, her hands in her lap, she knew she should break the awful silence but she didn't know how.

•

Why didn't she say something?

Jake's truck lumbered up the hill, barely staying on the road. He was acutely aware of her perfume, the soft rustle of her dress and her silence. Maybe she hadn't gotten it.

He cast a sidelong glance at her. Of course she had. Why else would she sit there with her hands in her lap like that, not speaking?

Instead of continuing down the narrow road to her cabin, he pulled into his own driveway and turned out the lights, reminding himself he wasn't the awkward kid she reduced him to. He survived the jungles of Guadalcanal, malaria and a face full of shrapnel. If she rejected him, he'd survive that, too, somehow.

He moistened his lips and swallowed hard.

"Feel like company?"

The words chased the smile from the moon's face. It turned away, shyly cloaking itself in clouds. Silence and shadows tumbled around them, as all of nature awaited her answer.

"Well, maybe for a few minutes."

She followed him onto the porch and waited while he fumbled with his key. He slid it into the lock, thinking of the bottle of wine on the coffee table and the soft music he left playing on the radio. Catch them off guard, and the battle was half-won. Any soldier worth his rations knew that.

He shoved open the door, watching her carefully for a reaction.

She took an uncertain step and froze in the doorway, as tense as a beaver approaching a trap. "What's this?"

"I wasn't sure which way it would go tonight."

She stared at him.

"I mean the grand opening." Hell, he was botching it. "I thought wine would be good in either case. We could celebrate victory or drown our sorrows."

"Oh."

She sat on the sofa and tucked her dress primly around her knees. He retrieved two goblets and a box of matches from the cabinet, conscious of her eyes following him. He lit a candle, poured a glass of wine and handed it to her without shaking. He sat down beside her on the couch, but not too close.

He waited for her to speak, but she didn't. When he tried to read her eyes, he couldn't. He held his goblet in both hands. He couldn't stop wanting to touch her hair and the curve of her cheek. Instead, he drained his glass.

"Get a new dress?" he asked.

"Yes. Bonner's was having a fabulous sale. Only nine dollars ..." Her voice trailed off as she fiddled with the hem.

"It's pretty."

"Thank you."

She tossed back her drink and he poured another, noting her rigid posture, as if she were ready to bolt. He was blowing it, but what should he do, advance or retreat?

"Your hair looks nice." He held a strand in his fingers. "I like it this way a lot."

She smiled stiffly, pulling away and hooking her hair behind her ear. "Thanks."

He cleared his throat. "Sell a lot of books tonight?"

"Tons."

"That's great."

She stared at her hands, twisting the silver band on her finger. He was looking for another lame stab at conversation when she spoke.

"Thank you for getting things started," she said.

His heart leaped.

"No one was going to read. You got the ball rolling. I know it must've been hard for you."

He sat forward and refilled his glass, then sat back a little closer than before. "It wasn't so bad."

"Oh, not at all. You have a wonderful speaking voice. I know you don't like to be in the public eye, that's all."

He slid his arm along the back of the couch. "I didn't mind that much."

"Well. Thanks just the same."

"You're welcome." He moved dangerously close, dropping his arm around her shoulder.

She stiffened.

He moved his hand along her neck, caressing her cheek with his fingertips.

"Please don't."

"Why, Tory?" he whispered. "Why can't I touch you?"

"I can't tell you." She turned her head away, but not before he saw tears glistening in her eyes.

"Hey." He took her face in his hands, forcing her to meet his gaze. A teardrop splashed his wrist. Christ, what had he done?

"I'm sorry."

"For what?"

"Evidently, I did the wrong thing."

She shook her head. "You did everything right, Jake. Everything."

He stared at her.

"It was for me, wasn't it? The poem?"

His gaze went to the floor. "Yes."

She began to sob.

He raked his fingers through his hair. How could he have been so thoughtless and stupid? She made her position clear a long time earlier. Why had he pushed the issue?

"I was out of line," he said softly. "I didn't mean to—I'll back off. We'll go on like we've been, as friends."

The words only increased her tears, which broke his heart. The last thing he wanted was to hurt her. He struggled with himself, wanting to touch her, not knowing if it was right. What could he do? What could he say that wouldn't make it worse?

"I won't do it again. I promise." He gave up the fight and pulled her into his arms. "Please don't cry."

"I'm scared."

She was scared? He stroked her hair, contemplating that new development. He never understood love, but he knew fear.

He pulled her closer. "Me, too."

"It would change everything."

"I know."

"No, you don't."

She was trembling, and he held her tightly. "Things change. You said so yourself."

"Oh, Jake. You don't understand."

No, he didn't. He didn't understand anything at the moment except for being drunk on her jasmine skin, the softness of her hair, the feel of her arms around him, her cheek against his chest, the whisper of her breath against his neck and the gentle pressure of her lips on his scars.

She traced the line of his jaw all the way to his earlobe. The action set his senses on red alert and he tensed. It wasn't a kiss, was it? Surely it wasn't that.

Her hands crept along his back while her lips traced the jagged scars across his cheek, stopping where they stopped at the corner of his mouth. It was agony. He fought back hard, holding himself in check because he didn't know if it was a kiss.

He shut his eyes tightly and prayed like he hadn't prayed in years. *Let it be a kiss. Please, God, let it be a kiss. Oh, God.*

•

"Oh, Child."

Better use your head, Kiddo, because he's got two, and he's definitely thinking with the smaller one.

Tory was vaguely aware of the voice in her head, shrieking to be heard above Jake's whispers. She didn't know whose it was and didn't care. She ached everywhere.

She knew how badly he wanted her. With that knowledge came a heady feeling of power, yet the intensity of his desire rendered her powerless to fight him. She faced a paradox. She couldn't kiss him, and she couldn't not.

"Child." His eyes searched her face, asking a question. Then his lips covered hers without waiting for the answer.

It was different from their first kiss. His tongue entered her mouth shyly, like a polite visitor, and she didn't push him away.

She melted against him. Lips blended with lips, denim with taffeta, until nothing existed but that moment and that kiss. He gently leaned her back, covering her body with his. Curtains swayed softly in the window as the wind breathed pine scent and cricket song into the room.

A feeling of well being swept over her. Every breath and heartbeat were in tune with his. They were in perfect harmony with each other and the rhythm of the mountain. Nothing had ever been more true or right. He moaned softly, his hand sliding under her dress. A loon raised its haunting cry.

Something deep inside her shrieked a warning. That broke the spell and brought her crashing back into herself.

"No." She pushed him away, trying to sit up. "We can't do this." She might as well have slapped him for the angry, hurt look in his eyes.

"Tory." He wound his fingers through her hair. "Please."

She steeled herself against him. "It'll change things, important things."

He tried to draw her back into his embrace. "I love you. Nothing will change that."

The words hit their mark and her eyes filled with tears. "You don't know. You don't understand. If we were to make love, it would alter things irrevocably."

A look of realization dawned in his eyes. He took her face in his hands. "I'd never hurt you."

"No! That's not what I meant." She pushed him away and jumped to her feet. How could she possibly explain?

He stood before her, holding her captive with his gorgeous eyes. "What did you mean? Explain it to me, Tory. I'm going crazy."

"I can't promise you anything, Jake, and I know you want me to. I can't say I'll stay forever or even tomorrow." Her voice cracked. "I wish I could, but I can't."

"You don't have to promise me anything. I don't care about yesterday or tomorrow, only who you are right now, tonight. I need you." He pulled her into the warm, safe haven of his arms. "Be mine," he whispered, "if only for tonight. If you decide you want to leave tomorrow, I won't do anything to stop you. I swear it."

He kissed her less gently than before. It was almost as if he knew and understood.

The voice in her head shrieked, *Run! Run!* She knew she should listen, but she didn't.

Jake took her hand and led her upstairs. With hands that wouldn't stop trembling, she turned back the sheets on his bed. He came to her in the darkness and undressed her in the pale shaft of moonlight that filtered through the window. She stood before him, naked and afraid.

He whispered her name, and it seemed as if the whole mountain spoke. He drew her close. She was hypnotized by the sound of his voice and the warmth of his body next to hers. He laid her down, pulled her close, and touched every part of her.

She laid her cheek against his chest and listened for the beating of his heart, hearing it with her soul, not her ears. Every beat spoke her name until there was nothing left to fear, nothing left to hide.

•

Long after the heat of their lovemaking cooled, he clung to her, afraid to speak, fearing he'd cry and disgrace himself. He'd forgotten how good it felt to be wrapped in a woman's arms and enveloped in the soft flesh between her legs, to be wanted.

Long after her breathing deepened in sleep, he held her, head cradled against his chest, stroking her hair and the creamy softness of her cheek. He couldn't sleep for the fierce tenderness that filled his heart. She'd clearly never been any man's wife. He was overwhelmed by the responsibility she bestowed on him, the supreme honor of being her first lover.

As the first rays of dawn bruised the morning sky, he replayed the night in his mind and felt again the warm thrill of the words she spoke, along with the lonely sadness of the ones she hadn't said. In the shadows of uncertainty, his insecurity reared its ugly head, whispering that a day would come when another man would take her from him.

He held her fiercely, peering into her sleeping face. He made a promise the previous night he couldn't keep. He'd never let her go.

Chapter Two

Morning came gently, like a watercolor painting of blue skies and pale sunlight. The dark clouds drifted away in the night, carrying all traces of discordance with them. A mild breeze whispered across the mountain. Tickling the treetops, it chased ripples of laughter across the surface of the river. All was well again.

Tory hovered on the brink of consciousness, wrapped in a hundred-year-old quilt and the sensation of being cherished. She murmured in her sleep, turned and slid her hands along the sheets beside her, still warm from the heat of Jake's body, and smiled. She hadn't been dreaming. The realization floated into her consciousness, and her eyes flew open. What had she done?

She lay still for a moment, taking stock of her situation, trying to determine whether any damage was done. She reached deep inside herself and found the leftover embers of passion, still glowing, love, and fear. Dear God, what had she done?

She groped beside the bed. Rejecting the rumpled party dress, she pulled on his T-shirt instead. As she padded downstairs to the kitchen, lured by the scent of perking coffee, she saw the table set for two. A pan of bacon warmed on the stove with a skillet of scrambled eggs. The room was just as it had always been. Everything was the same, yet overnight, everything changed. She sensed a presence and turned. Jake stood in the doorway, a bouquet of goldenrod clasped loosely at his side.

"I wasn't sure what the protocol was for this sort of thing." He handed her the bouquet. "Best I could do."

She was barely able to speak for the love radiating from his eyes. "I'd say you got it just right."

She removed a drinking glass from the drain board and filled it with tap water. As she placed the bouquet in her makeshift vase, an image flitted through her mind of a drinking glass, a brown hand, and a bouquet of daffodils.

She closed her eyes, concentrating on the memory. Jake's arms went around her waist. Then a sharp voice that wasn't Jake's spoke to her.

"Stay with me."

She turned abruptly. "Who said that?"

Jake pulled her closer. "Who said what?"

She wrenched free and went to the window, lifting the curtain. Except for a handful of squirrels, the yard was empty. She turned back to Jake. "How strange."

He shrugged. "The wind's playing tricks on you. Sometimes I hear it speaking, too."

She shook her head. "No. It wasn't the wind. I clearly heard a man's voice, as clearly as if he was in the room with us."

The corners of his mouth lifted in an amused smile. "What did he say?"

"He said, 'Stay with me.'"

Jake's expression changed. "You heard that?"

"Yes."

"Then you've learned to hear my thoughts." He pulled her back into the circle of his arms and kissed her. A thousand points of light exploded in her head. She was overcome by the strange sensation she was beginning to disappear.

"Jake, about last night—"

He murmured softly and gently bit her neck. Warm shivers of desire raced down her spine, but she steeled herself against them.

"We should keep it in perspective and see it for what it was, a moment of mutual need."

That time, he was the one who pulled away. "It was more than that, Tory."

"I could be a married woman with twelve children for all we know."

A small, self-satisfied smile tugged at his lips. "You're not a married woman."

Her cheeks grew hot with embarrassment. "You don't know that."

He cupped her face in his hands. "I know I made love to a beautiful girl last night, and there's probably not a chance in hell she doesn't belong to someone." His hand caressed her cheek. "If it turns out she doesn't, I'll do everything I can to make her mine."

His words started a tug-of-war raging inside her. She wondered how a body could hold so much joy and pain simultaneously. She moved to the table, pulling out her chair.

"Let's eat our breakfast before it gets cold," she said without looking at him. "I'm damned near starving."

•

He was starving, too, consumed by a hunger that would never be satisfied no matter how much of her he got. He couldn't stop looking at her and could barely believe she was real. He was so lovestruck he couldn't eat or bear the thought of the straggling underbrush that awaited him at the lower end of the forest. All he wanted was to sit at the table and look at her for the rest of his life.

She glanced at him from over her coffee cup. "Remember that we rode home together last night."

He liked the way she said home and smiled. "How could I forget?"

Her cheeks colored. "What I meant was, I'll need a ride into town this morning."

His hand crept across the table, covering hers. "I'd hoped you might stay home today."

She looked at him as if he'd lost his mind. "I can't stay home, Jake. It's the first day of our grand reopening. Penny will need all hands on deck and then some."

"Anything I can do to help?"

"No," she said quickly. "I'm sure you have your own work to do."

He shrugged. "It can wait."

"Don't be silly. You don't have to rearrange your life just because we had sex."

The words hurt. His hand slid away from hers.

"Did I say something wrong?" she asked.

He shrugged again. "I didn't like the sound of it. We had sex. That makes it seem cheap."

"Should I have said we made love?"

He met her eyes. "Didn't we?"

A long moment passed.

She sighed, sliding her hand across the table to cover his. "Listen, Jake, I—"

His phone rarely rang. The fact it chose that moment to intrude made him want to rip it from the wall.

Tory removed her hand. "You'd better answer that."

He cursed under his breath, shoved back his chair and walked across the room. "Hello?"

"Jake?"

The breathy voice caught him off guard. He wondered why Louise Matthews would call at such an hour on Saturday morning—or at any time for that matter.

"Jake, is that you?"

"It's me."

"Are you alone?"

He felt Tory's eyes on him. "What's on your mind, Lou?"

"We need to talk. It's extremely urgent. Any chance you'll be coming into town today?"

His eyes slid to Tory. "As it turns out, I will."

"Can you stop by the shop and see me?"

"I suppose."

"In an hour?"

He sighed. "I suppose."

"Park at the alley and use the back door. I'll meet you there."

His irritation flared. He was in no mood for her nonsense. "What's this about?"

"I'll tell you when you come. Jake?"

"Yes."

"Don't tell anyone you're coming, okay?"

Tory gave him a questioning look as he hung up. "Anything wrong?"

He shrugged. "Business."

She stood and cleared the breakfast dishes from the table. "I should go and change. Don't bother with these. I'll do them tonight."

Driving into town he tried to find the road that would take them back to where they'd been before Louise phoned, but Tory cut him off at every turn.

Though it was barely nine o'clock when he pulled to the curb in front of Penny Candy's, a line of customers was already waiting.

"Oh, boy," Tory said. "Looks like we're in for it."

"Sure you don't want me to stay and help?"

She opened the door. "We'll be fine."

"What time shall I come for you?"

She slid from the truck. "Don't bother. I can drive Penny's car."

He grasped her hand. "It's no bother."

"Jake, please. Let me go."

He stared at her for a moment, trying to read her meaning. It was clearly written on her face—back off.

He released her hand, letting her slide from the truck.

"Tory?"

She turned back, her eyebrows raised impatiently.

"Have a great day."

To his surprise, she got back in. "What you asked earlier, we did, okay?"

His heart soared. He leaned over to kiss her, but she pressed a fingertip to his lips.

"I'll try to get away early," she said. "We'll talk when I get home."

Home.

He watched until the screen door of Penny Candy's swallowed her up, then shifted gears and drove toward the dress shop. More annoyed than curious, he took the back alleys to Louise's summons. Whatever it was, he wanted to get it over with. After that, he'd stop at the grocer's and pick up something special for dinner, maybe another bottle of wine. After that, he'd go to a jeweler's and find something even more special to replace the silver band on Tory's finger.

•

Louise hovered near the back door of her shop, checking her wristwatch. What was keeping him?

She went through her story one last time to make sure she had it straight. She was up all night, trying to remember what Millie told her, which she thought was nonsense at the time. Every detail was vital. She went over it point-by-point, checking for flaws, but found none. Would he believe it?

When Jake's truck rumbled down the alley, she hurried to her office and sat at her desk, shuffling through purchase orders. Moments later, she heard a knock at the door.

She modulated her tone to that of a successful businesswoman who was busy but not too curt.

"Yes?"

The door opened and Jake walked in. The room instantly filled with the scent of pine and an overt masculinity that nearly made her swoon.

She glanced up from her desk and feigned surprise. "Jake. Goodness, has it been an hour already?"

He faced her and folded his arms across his chest. "What's on your mind, Louise?"

"Come and sit. Would you like a cup of coffee?"

He remained standing.

She sighed. "This is difficult."

"Let me make it easy on you. If it's about the fifty acres at the bottom of the hill, you can tell him the answer is still no."

"It's not about that." She averted her gaze. "Well, not directly."

He shifted impatiently.

"It's about the poem you read last night at Penny Candy's."

"What about it?"

"It was lovely." She squeezed a tear from her eye, a trick she learned as a child. "Honestly, it was. I sat there thinking how wonderful it would've been had you meant it for someone who was deserving of you."

"What are you trying to say?"

"She's not what you think she is, Jake."

"Yes, she is."

"I'm telling you she's not." She stared at her hands, adding softly, "I know things about her."

A muscle twitched in his jaw. "What things?"

"Things you should know. I'm taking a big chance, telling you. Pierce would kill me if he found out that I—"

He grasped her wrist firmly enough to let her know he meant business. "What things?"

She saw something akin to fury in his eyes and shivered, remembering how people said the war changed him, taking away his conscience. For the first time since she'd known him, she feared him.

"Think about it, Jake. What do you really know about her?"

A shadow of doubt flickered across his face. "I know all I need to."

She shook her head. "All right. I can see your mind's made up."

He tightened his grip on her wrist and his scars deepened in color. "You're on dangerous ground, Sister. You called me down here to tell me something, so tell it. You'd better make yourself plain."

Her cry of fear was only partly affected. "She's an actress from Broadway, hired by my husband to get control of your land. Her name is Victoria Lane."

He tightened his grip even more. "You're lying."

"I wish I were."

Jake said nothing. She could almost see his mind furiously trying to work it out.

"Think about it, Jake. She shows up here out of the clear blue sky and just happens to crash on your mountain. She strikes up a friendship with Penny Candy and gets control of the store, something that Pierce happens to want."

Jake shook his head, trying to block the sound of her voice, but the sickly pallor on his face showed he believed her.

"She's smooth as silk, Jake. That's what she's paid for. I'm sorry." She held out her arms.

He didn't fall into them as expected. Instead, he strode toward the door. "We'll see about that."

Louise scrambled to block the doorway. "Where are you going?"

"To talk to your husband," he spat.

"You can't!" Her fear became genuine. "He'd kill me if he knew or even suspected I meddled in his affairs. I told you only because part of me still cares for you and loves you." She broke off with a sob. "Please, Jake, for the sake of what we once had, don't confront him."

His eyes swept over her, stony and untouched, but the lines in his face softened. She had won.

"I'll be here all day, Darling, if you want to talk," she said softly.

He pushed past without a word and slammed the door as he left. Moments later, she heard his truck roar. She smiled. The poor darling was still so easy to break, but this time, she'd be around to help put him back together.

His first impulse was to barge into Penny Candy's and make Tory explain herself, to say it wasn't true. It couldn't be when he loved her so much. He'd been the first to love her, hadn't he?

He shoved the truck into gear and coasted from the alley, angrily blinking back tears. It was better to be alone and think it through.

He rumbled through the glorious spring countryside without seeing any of it. Images came to mind of his foot on Pierce's neck and Tory rushing to his defense.

Was she protecting her meal ticket?

He remembered Tory reciting poetry with her strong, polished voice, feigning innocence at his touch like the accomplished actress she was. How long had she planned to lead him on?

Unchecked tears ran down his face.

It was true, every word of it.

He pulled the Model A into the woods, laid his head against the steering wheel and cried without shame. Pain tore through his chest as his mended heart shattered for the second time. He reminded himself he was tough and had survived worse.

It took three medics to hold him down after the grenade exploded in his face. He remembered how the antiseptic burned his open flesh, and how he screamed in agony as they dug the shrapnel from his skin. He begged them to leave it, opting to die from infection rather than endure the agony of having the shrapnel wrenched out.

Now he felt the same pain.

Tory was that deeply embedded in him.

Leaving his truck, he stumbled blindly through the trees. The forest reached out to him, trying to draw him to itself to comfort its wounded son, but there was no comforting him.

He walked until he could not go another step, then sank to his knees on a carpet of pine needles. Kneeling under the trees with his face lifted to the sky, he felt his last ounce of hope fade into the darkness and raised his voice to the heavens, screaming like a wounded animal.

Chapter Three

She had to tell him the truth or something close to it.

She couldn't talk to him that morning, when they were face-to-face. That afternoon, away from him, Tory found she couldn't stop. She conversed with him in her mind as she rang up sales, restocked shelves and counted change. She shared with him her every thought, hope and fear. She loved him desperately, which was why she had to leave him.

She was impatient with the customers who thronged into the store and the seeming endlessness of the day. She also dreaded the thought of going home and facing him. She had to let him down gently, because she owed him that, but how?

It was after four o'clock when Penny finally locked the door. "Enough is enough. Gracious! I'll be late for my bingo."

Tory was still mulling over the possibilities as she deposited the day's earnings into the night-deposit box. By the time she reached home, though, she was still at a loss. If only she could make Jake see her in a bad light, it would make things easier. She could tell him she was a villainess on the lam who had killed someone.

He'd never believe it.

She coasted past his house, saw his truck in the driveway and veered down the path leading to her cabin. She'd go home first to freshen up. Maybe the right words would come to her.

She took a quick bath, dressed in clean clothes and then toweled her hair. She'd make dinner first. Maybe cooking would help her to think.

In the kitchen, she turned on the radio and hummed along with Frank Sinatra as she tore into a head of lettuce for a salad. She was slicing the last of the tomatoes when a shadow fell across the sink.

Tory turned. Jake stood in the doorway, watching her. She smiled.

"I thought I told you not to sneak up on me like that."

Her smile faded when she saw his dark expression. It suggested he'd had another run-in with Pierce Matthews. He shoved away from the doorjamb and crossed the room, his eyes never leaving her face. It was definitely anger she saw, and she had the uneasy feeling it was directed at her.

"Jake? Is something wrong?"

"I know who you are."

She gripped the back of a chair. "What?"

"Good news. It turns out you're a star."

The rush of air that escaped her was one part surprise, two parts relief. He clearly mistook it for laughter, because a muscle twitched under his jaw.

"Don't be silly," she stammered. "I'm not a star."

"No?" His scars deepened to crimson, showing the tethered fury under his calm exterior. "Who are you, then?"

Something was coming. A way out was being offered. Suddenly, she wasn't sure she wanted it.

"You know I don't have an answer for that."

"I think you do." He reached for a strand of her hair and wound it through his fingers like he did the previous night but not, though, in a tender gesture. "I think you know a lot more than you let on, don't you?"

She took a slow breath. *Relax*, she thought.

"What happened in town this morning, Jake?"

"Had it all thought out, didn't you?"

"I don't know what you're talking—"

"You were an equation that added up to nothing," he said harshly.

She'd never heard him like that before.

"You didn't know who you were. You came from a town that didn't exist, so there was no way to check. You were smooth, Darlin'. Your only mistake was the car."

"What are you talking about?"

"I searched these woods at least a hundred times. There's no car. Why do you think that is, Victoria?" he spat, his scars pulsing with anger.

She felt her own anger rising, too. "I don't know, and I resent—"

"Maybe it was because someone dropped you off!" he shouted.

"Like who?"

He seized her wrists. "You've been playing me for a fool, both of you. I'm wise to your act, Little Sister."

"You're crazy! Let me go!" She struggled to free herself, but he was too strong and angry.

"You could have won a damn Academy Award!" he shouted. "You honestly had me believing you—" His voice cracked.

Abruptly, he released her and turned away. His pain instantly erased her anger.

"Jake, please listen to me. I don't know what you've been told, but it's a lie." She placed her hand on his shoulder.

He shrugged it off. "Prove it."

"I wish I could."

He crossed the room and paused at the chair, then grabbed her purse. "The proof must be in here."

"I don't have any identification," she stammered, keeping her eyes on his hands and praying he wouldn't open the clasp. "Remember? I dumped my purse that night in the woods."

He held it out to her. "I'd like to see it for myself."

She took the purse and held it for a moment, indecision fogging her mind. Refusing would be an outright admission of guilt, but what could she do? Show him a driver's license showing a date of birth twenty-three years in the future?

"Show me, Tory." His eyes pleaded with her. "Show me I'm wrong."

Time seemed to stop.

"I can't."

The coldness that crept into his eyes told her his love was withdrawn. "I didn't think so."

She felt something break inside her, as if every one of her organs were being wrenched from her.

"Jake, I—"

He walked toward the door. "Save it, Sister. You've got nothing to say I want to hear."

It was ending and she didn't want it to, especially not like that. She'd never pleaded with a man before, but she would've thrown herself prostrate before him had she been able to move.

"Please don't leave like this," she said. "Where are you going?"

He stopped in the doorway, his back to her. "Out. When I get back, I'd appreciate it if you're gone."

"You can't mean that. Please, Jake. You've got to trust me!"

He faced her one last time. "That was my first mistake, Victoria. I'm not fool enough to make it again."

The last trace of love drained from his eyes. He shoved his way out the doorway and disappeared.

•

It isn't turning out like it was supposed to. What did I do wrong?

As the freshly waxed Frazier glided through the square, Louise glanced down at her new outfit, a white pique evening gown with sequined bodice. She was the best-dressed woman in town for all the good it did her. That afternoon, she had her nails manicured, and her hair freshly bobbed, imagining how it would turn out.

Jake would come for her, sweep her off her feet and they'd confront her bastard of a husband. How she'd looked forward to wiping that pompous grin off his face! Somehow, though, none of those things ever happened.

She checked her watch. It was nearly seven. By then, she and Jake should've been tucked away at a table-for-two in some intimate little bistro in the city, planning their beautiful future. Why was she there? Her eyes slid toward her husband.

Pierce turned and saw her watching him. He smiled. "Everything all right, Darling?"

Something in his manner made her uneasy. He was a bit too happy. His eyes were a bit too bright.

She forced a smile. "Will we have to stay awfully long, Lover?"

He turned his gaze back on the road and smoothly steered the Frazier onto Main Street. "Just long enough to be seen."

She pulled out her compact and frowned at her reflection. They'd be seen all right, but by the wrong people. She snapped shut the compact case and dropped it into her purse, knowing how it would all be. The dingy hall would be decorated with those dreadful crepe paper lanterns in a sorry attempt at elegance. Coarse men would dance with their cheaply dressed wives, a brat planted on each hip.

What was Pierce thinking? What could he possibly hope to gain by dragging her out to the American Legion to rub elbows with the hoi polloi? She eyed him angrily, the question burning on her lips, but something in his manner told her to hold her tongue.

"The place will be a diamond mine of potential clients," he said, as if hearing her thoughts. "Try and be nice, won't you?"

"Clients?" She turned in surprise, ignoring the subtle threat behind his words. "You mean the housing project is back on track?"

He nodded. "A new development has arisen. The possibilities are quite pleasant. Actually, I have a feeling we'll be back in business very soon."

The words struck like an elbow in the stomach. Blood rushed to her head. "Why, that's wonderful news, Darling," she managed. "How'd you finally persuade him to part with his land?"

Pierce reached across the seat and patted her knee. It was all she could do not to recoil at his touch.

"It's business, Dearest. Nothing to worry your pretty little head about." His hand, cold as an iceberg, hovered on her thigh. "I've taken care of everything just like I always do."

•

Tom Hopewell hadn't worn a matching pair of socks since 1946.

That was the year Jimmy was born, and diapers were king. Tired and irritable, Nancy hadn't the time nor inclination to worry about the state of her husband's underwear.

Jonas arrived in 1947. In '48, the twins were born. By then, Tom had taken matters into his own hands and no longer fretted over things like wrinkled trousers or spit-up on his ties. In fact he'd become uncomfortable in their absence.

He contemplated that as he stood before the half-length mirror above his bureau, dressed in his seersucker suit for the second night in a row. He sucked in his paunch and slowly closed his zipper. It immediately sprung open in protest. He gritted his teeth and tried again.

The previous night, it was the foolishness at Penny Candy's. That evening, Nancy insisted he take her to the dinner dance at the Legion Hall. He sighed. Pregnancy was hell.

"Tommy?" Nancy's reflection appeared behind him in the mirror, wearing a slip and clutching a dress in each hand. "Which of these dresses do you think looks best on me, the red or the blue?"

"Ah ..." He contemplated the question, seeking land mines. "I like the red."

"Really?" Her brow wrinkled. "I'd half decided on the blue."

"The blue's pretty, too," he said quickly.

She held up the blue gown and scrutinized her reflection. "I was going to wear it last night to the poetry readings, but I thought it looked a bit tight around the middle."

A light bulb went off in Tom's mind. He understood what it was about. It was the "am I too fat?" discussion. He went to her, wrapping her in a bear hug.

"I don't care how big you are, Sugar Plum," he said in his most jocular voice. "You'll always be the prettiest girl on the block to me."

He puckered his lips, waiting for her kiss. Instead, she burst into tears and ran from the room. Seconds later, he heard the bathroom door slam shut and sighed, thinking of twenty-eight weeks to go, God help him.

It was a quarter past seven before he heard the bathroom door open, and another ten minutes before he plucked up his courage to go downstairs.

Nancy's mother bustled in the kitchen, banging pots and pans as she prepared a dinner of macaroni and cheese for the children. Nancy sat at the table, wearing a pale-yellow gown, a baby on each of her knees. A few strands escaped her bun and hung in silky wisps around her flushed cheeks. She glanced up and smiled at him in the doorway.

His heart overflowed. Lord, how he loved her.

He held her hand all the way to the Legion Hall, listening attentively, answering carefully, determined not to trip himself up again. He made it all the way through town.

While he was stuck at a red light, a dark shadow caught his eye and his hackles rose. He frowned, unconsciously reaching for his notepad until he remembered he was off duty. It was probably nothing.

"… just impossible lately. Dearest, are you listening?"

He squeezed her hand. "I couldn't agree with you more, Sugar Plum."

She smiled, and he congratulated himself for not missing a beat. As he steered his Willey's toward the American Legion Hall, he gave his ear to his wife but his eyes were on the taillights of the dark sedan that slowly snaked up the mountain road.

•

Tory sat on the porch of her cabin, watching the last trace of daylight melt into dusk as she waited for Jake to return. Heat lightning raged in the sky above the mountain, strangely impotent without its partner, thunder. They belonged together. It was as simple as that. She had to tell him the truth—all of it.

When she heard the rumble of his Model A coming down the old logging road, she gathered her purse and nerve, and picked her way down the path leading to his house. The night was absolutely still, pregnant with foreboding despite the festive music that drifted up the hillside from somewhere in town. It was going to be the most difficult thing she'd ever done.

As she neared his property, preparing for every possible scenario, a dark sedan rolled into Jake's driveway. It looked like the one she saw before and she froze.

That was one scene she hadn't anticipated. Though it was nearly dark outside, the car's headlights were off as if the driver wished to arrive surreptitiously. Tory fled back to the shelter of the trees, paralyzed by a fear she couldn't name. A cool breeze lifted her hair and whispered urgently in her ear.

Be careful.

A lamp glowed softly on Jake's porch, shedding just enough light to show two men get out of the sedan. They were dressed in black raincoats, black shoes and wide-rimmed black hats. They were definitely the two men she'd seen before.

They crept toward the house with their hands beneath their coats. With her fingers pressed against her lips, she watched the two men duck under the picture window, steal onto the porch and enter the house without knocking. Raucous music rose up the hillside like the soundtrack to a bad movie.

Once again, the wind whispered, *be careful.*

Seconds later, she heard a crash inside the house. It wasn't a gunshot. It was more like breaking glass. The noise catapulted her into action. She sprinted across the yard, ducked under the picture window and slipped in the back door.

Raised voices came from the living room, followed by silence. Breathing hard, she fumbled her Derringer from her purse, pressed her back against the wall and eased soundlessly toward the doorway. When she peeked into the living room, her heart almost stopped.

The room was in chaos. A creeping Charlie sprawled from its broken pot, its roots exposed like spidery fingers reaching for nothing. Books lay scattered across the floor. Fibber McGee and Molly traded banter from the splintered radio. A table lamp was upset in the center of the room, shining on the scene like a spotlight.

Jake stood in the corner, his shirt torn, his hands tied behind his back. Two gangsters flanked him on either side. The one with the sandpaper voice held his arms. The other held a gun.

"One more time, Mac," the gunman said. "Where is she?"

"She's gone," Jake said.

The other man shoved Jake's face into the wall. "Gone where?"

"Ask your boss."

The gunman nodded, and his partner spun Jake around and punched his face. Jake staggered.

"The boss hired us to find out. He wants two bodies, see? Yours and the blonde doll."

"Why should he kill her?" Jake asked. "She's done what he asked. Just kill me. He'll get my land either way."

The gunman mumbled something Tory couldn't hear.

"Come on, Old Boy." The other man pulled Jake to his feet and shoved him roughly toward the front door. "You're about to have a hunting accident."

Tory stifled a cry. Adrenaline coursed through her veins. There was no time to spare, no time to plan. She clamped the gun tightly in both hands and burst through the doorway, fully prepared to shoot.

A quick assessment of the situation told her there was no clear shot. She couldn't hit the gunman without hitting Jake. She aimed the Derringer at them and barked the first words that came to her mind.

"FBI! Drop the gun!"

Startled, the gunman hesitated long enough to give Tory confidence.

"Drop it!"

Jake stared at her in disbelief. The gangsters looked at each other, then her. The gunman smiled.

"You drop the gun," he said.

Lakes of sweat formed under her arms. She kept her hands steady, praying no one would see them shaking, and forced a sneer into her voice.

"Don't be a fool. We've got the house surrounded." She nodded at Jake. "Shoot him, and you'll never get out the front door."

The gunman's smile wavered. Sensing his hesitation, Tory said, "Don't make it tough on yourself. It's not you we want. It's the boss man. We've had our eyes on him for months."

The gunman nodded to his friend. He shoved Jake in front of him as he crossed to the window and peered out. He turned back shaking his head.

The gunman's smile returned. "Got us surrounded, eh?"

"That's right."

"My partner says you don't. I say you don't. I say there's nobody out there. Nobody at all."

"You think we're stupid enough to stand in plain sight?" she scoffed. "This ain't no baby-face operation, Mister. You're playing with the big boys now."

The gunman smiled at his friend, then Tory. "You don't look so big to me."

The other man stepped toward her. "Let's have the gun, Sweet Cakes."

She moistened her lips with her tongue. She had two bullets. If she were careful, that was all she would need.

"Don't come any closer," she warned.

He took another step.

"Give it up, Sis. We'll let you go. We'll tell him we couldn't find you."

"Last chance," she told the gunman. "Lay it down now, or I'll shoot."

It happened quickly.

The other man sprang at her. She whirled toward him, squeezed shut her eyes and fired. The room erupted in confusion. The man she fired at shoved Jake toward her, knocking her down.

As she and Jake toppled to the floor, the Derringer flew from her hands and skidded across the room. Her ears rang with the blast of gunfire.

She opened her eyes to see the gunman standing over her, his gun aimed at her face.

He sneered. "You'll want to say your prayers now, Sissy."

"I'm sorry, Tory," Jake said, his face inches from hers.

She stared into his eyes and saw only sorrow, not fear. It was over and they both knew it. She cradled his head to her breast, saying the only thing that mattered.

"I love you."

She closed her eyes and waited for the crash that would end her existence. It came within seconds.

"Hold it right there!"

Tom Hopewell burst through the door, wearing a rumpled seersucker suit with a cocktail napkin shoved down the front of his open shirt. Two uniformed officers followed him, their guns drawn and aimed at the gangsters.

"It's all over, Boys," Tom said. "Turn around with your hands on your heads and don't try anything cute."

Suddenly, everything blurred in Tory's sight. She didn't move or breathe until the gangsters were in handcuffs. Through a shock-induced haze, she saw Tom drop to his knees beside her.

Pulling out a pocketknife, Tom cut Jake free.

"Mother of God." Tom mopped his brow on his coat sleeve. "We heard the shot clear across the yard. I prayed we weren't too late." He glanced at Tory. "You all right, Miss?"

She nodded slowly. "I think so."

Tom glanced around the room. "What the Sam Hill happened here?"

"A couple of hired guns," Jake said. "Evidently, someone wanted us dead."

"Any idea who?"

Jake shrugged. "Nothing I can prove."

Tom scowled at the two glowering criminals and then nodded to his deputy. "Run 'em in, Charlie."

As the officers led the men from the house, Tom pulled off his cocktail napkin and scribbled notes on it. Tory's eyes went across the room to where her Derringer's shiny barrel poked from under the couch.

Tom picked up the gun and studied it curiously, turning it over in his palm. "I've never seen one like this before. Where'd you get it?"

Jake watched for Tory's reaction, but she didn't reply.

"War souvenir," Jake said quickly. "I picked it up in the Solomons."

Tom handed the gun to Jake. "Try not to touch anything. I'll be back in the morning, then we'll talk."

Jake clapped a hand on Tom's shoulder. "I never saw it coming. I'm glad as hell you showed up tonight."

"Lucky hunch. We'll grill them hard and try to get them to talk, but I doubt it."

Jake nodded.

"I'll get out of here now so you can get this young lady into bed." Tom's face colored at his faux pas.

When the door closed behind him, Tory collapsed into Jake's arms.

"It's all right," he said. "Everything's all right."

She felt the warmth in his eyes and knew his love had returned. "Is it, Jake?"

He stroked her hair. "I thought you were working for Pierce Matthews."

"I'm not."

"You're not a policewoman, either, are you?"

She lowered her eyes and shook her head.

He snorted softly. "You'd have made a hell of a Marine."

She crumbled into tears. "Oh, Jake. I was so scared."

"Me, too." He was silent for a moment. "I love you."

"Still?"

"More than ever. I'm sorry I doubted you, Tory."

"I'm sorry I gave you a reason."

It was time to set him straight. She took a deep breath and said, "There are things I need to tell you, things you need to know."

He pressed a finger to her lips. "Do you love me?"

"Yes," she whispered, "I do. So much."

He pulled her deeper into the circle of his love, kissing her tenderly. "That's all I need to know."

Chapter Four

The following morning when Pierce opened the Sunday paper, the front-page headline knocked the smile of anticipation from his face.

Local Police Foil Attempted Homicide:
Two Unnamed gunmen Arrested

He stared at the headline in disbelief, read the story twice and slammed his fist against the table. How could they have botched it? By the time Louise came into the kitchen, he was near violence.

"Good morning, Darling," she said cheerfully.

He glared at her.

She gave him a cautious glance as she poured his coffee. "Didn't you sleep well, Lover?"

"Like a baby," he growled.

Taking her place at the stove, she began preparing his breakfast. His eyes slid back to the newspaper. As he perused the sports section, Louise turned up the volume on the radio. She rattled pots and pans as if deliberately trying to set his nerves on edge.

"Must you make all that racket, Louise?" he snarled.

She turned from the stove, an expression of hurt innocence on her face. "I was only trying to—"

"Don't bother with the bacon," he snapped. "I'm not at all hungry this morning." He folded the newspaper, tossed it aside, and reached for his coffee.

Louise set a plate of scrambled eggs before him, sat across the table and reached for the newspaper. A moment later, she gasped.

"Good heavens! Did you see this?"

"Of course I saw it. It's all over the damned front page."

She read the story aloud. The words of failure, coupled with the nails-scraping-slate sound of her voice, were more than he could bear. He clenched his hands into tight fists, fighting the urge to lace his fingers around her neck and choke the life out of her.

"Enough!" he thundered.

The hurt expression returned to her face, but her veiled amusement showed she knew. Everyone knew, or soon would. A wave of bile rushed up the back of his throat. For the first time in his life, Pierce Matthews, the tower of strength, the man with the iron nerves, felt the faint stirring of panic. It was only a matter of time before the bastards ratted on him. That was rule number one in the bastard's code of conduct—save your own ass first.

What should he do?

He pushed back his chair and walked unsteadily to the window. Staring at the cloudy sky, he fervently sought guidance from a silent disapproving God.

An hour later, he sat in his pew at Heatherfield First Presbyterian, fidgeting and trying to act natural. The pastor's voice grated in his ears, and set his already taut nerves dangerously near the breaking point.

"And so, dear Brethren, let us learn to forgive, as we have been forgiven."

The church was half-empty, thank God. Most of Heatherfield was still in bed, drunk or hung over from the previous night's party at the American Legion Hall. His eyes slid across the room, studying the faces the parishioners in turn. There were no accusing glances or stares of retribution. No one was watching him.

His panic ebbed. He chuckled. No one could possibly link him to the crime. Everyone in town saw him out the previous night. He made sure of that. He left no evidence or uncovered tracks—or had he?

He tried to retrace his movements but found he couldn't concentrate. The pastor's voice droned on, reciting drivel about love and forgiveness. Once again, Pierce's hands tightened into fists. Wait until he got his hands on that pair of incompetent bastards. He'd kill both of them.

As he drove home, an eerie calm settled over him. Louise's screech-owl voice couldn't spoil it. Even the threat of his empire crumbling around him no longer seemed to matter. Only one thing did, and that was settling the score.

Fingering the bruise on the back of his neck, he felt his sense of calm deepen. It wasn't just business anymore. Jake Benjamin had crossed the line, daring to put his hands on him. That made it more than business. That made it personal.

•

High up on her mountain, Tory didn't know the town below buzzed with excitement and wouldn't have cared if she had. She was never more at peace. Overnight, she and Jake seemed to have evolved to a new level of closeness. She awoke with a sense of optimism and belonging, her newfound joy marred only by the nagging feeling there were things she'd been going to tell him.

Unfortunately, she couldn't remember what they were.

Late in the afternoon, while Jake worked to repair the furniture broken in the previous night's scuffle, Tory stole away to the river. Standing at the river's edge, she pulled the Derringer from her purse, running her fingertips across the smooth, cool barrel.

Memories of the previous night crashed into her newfound tranquility and she shuddered. How had she come into possession of such an ugly instrument? She drew back her arm and threw it into the water, smiling as it sank from view.

She leafed through the contents of her wallet, fingering the identification badge, photos and credit cards. Her brow furrowed. It was as if those things belonged to someone else.

The river babbled its encouragement as, one-by-one, she skipped the items across the water like stones. She watched, feeling lighter than air as the water swirled around the hated burdens and carried them away.

"Here you are." Jake's arms encircled her from behind. Though she hadn't heard him approach, she somehow knew he was there.

She nestled against him.

"I looked for you in the house and couldn't find you," he said. "It made me nervous."

She smiled. "You didn't have to be nervous. I'm perfectly safe. See?"

"I like you where I can keep an eye on you." He turned her to face him, planting gentle kisses on her forehead, nose and lips. "Don't ever leave me, Tory."

Her arms tightened around his neck. "Where would I go?"

He stroked her hair. "We'll have a beautiful life together, Darlin'. I promise."

•

Lord have mercy, but it was hot for May. As daylight fell from the sky, Penny Candy hobbled to the coolness of her front porch. One gnarled hand clutched her cane as she walked. The other held a tattered newspaper, filled with frightful news.

She hauled herself into her rocking chair, adjusted her spectacles and glanced at the headline again, shaking her head. Lord have mercy. The story set the whole town on edge.

Her lips formed a thin line as she reread the account. Everyone had a theory. Her good, God-fearing brothers and sisters at the First Presbyterian Church blamed it on secular music. The right-wing Conservatives who drank their morning coffee at the Stardust Diner linked the incident to Communism. A handful of irate parents even said the Lone Ranger was to blame.

Penny blamed herself. Tossing the paper aside, she pulled out her handkerchief and mopped beads of perspiration from her brow. If only she'd— The clamor of chiming baubles came to her on the evening air, diverting her attention. She peered into the twilit street. A figure bobbed perkily down the sidewalk, arms swinging, skirt swaying. Within moments, the figure turned up the walk that led to Penny's store, preceded by an invisible cloud of Tabu.

Penny smiled. "Why, good evening, Child. I didn't expect to see you until morning."

"I've been out at my auntie's in the country all day," Millie said breathlessly. "I just now got home. Have you heard the news?"

Penny tapped the newspaper. "Frightful."

"Isn't it just not to be believed? Gangsters in Heatherfield!" Millie shivered with excitement. "My ma says we're getting as bad as the city."

Penny sighed. "It's my fault, I suppose."

The girl gaped. "Your fault?"

Penny sighed again, thought for a moment, then gratefully laid down the burden she carried since morning. "We've taken in a good bit of cash recently. There's not a soul in town who doesn't know it. Maybe word got out and those dreadful creatures thought it was stashed at Jake's house, Tory being a partner and all. Jake says not, but still—"

"You talked to him?" Millie broke in.

"I phoned first thing this morning as soon as I heard the news. Tory was resting, the poor lamb."

Millie leaned in eagerly. "How did he seem?"

"Just fine, Child. Why?"

Millie shivered again, briskly rubbing the gooseflesh on her arms. "Ma heard tell in the Stardust how he fended off those goons single-handed. He had them both hog-tied before the police even got there." She lowered her voice. "They say he's awfully strong. They say he never lifted his rifle all through the war. He just killed enemy soldiers with his bare hands."

Millie's voice dropped to a whisper. Penny leaned close to hear. "They say he hasn't got a conscience."

"Nonsense, Child!" Penny said sharply. "Jake Benjamin's a fine, decent man, as decent a man as you'll find."

Millie lowered her eyes guiltily. "Sure, Mrs. Candy. I know that. I'm just telling you what they said. Myself, I think he's dreamy even with, you know—" She daintily brushed her hand across her cheek.

"War is hell, Child, and don't ever forget it. It left a lot of good men with rough edges." Penny's eyes grew moist. "Love has a way of softening folks."

Millie was still thinking about that statement a week later. Spring hung heavily in the air and her thoughts turned to love. She hummed as she swept and mopped the floor, watching carefully as Tory made notes in the ledger. Love had changed her, all right. It made her dull.

Millie felt a surge of disappointment, followed by guilt. She was still as classy a dame as any Millie had known, but somehow, Tory seemed more ordinary.

As if feeling the weight of Millie's stare, Tory glanced up and smiled. Millie smiled back and resumed mopping.

The hubbub surrounding the gangsters began to die off. Tory wasn't a celebrity anymore. It was more than that, though. Millie peered at her covertly from over her mop. Her high-gloss lips turned down in a pout. Tory was dressed in a plain white blouse and A-line skirt, her gorgeous hair trapped in a schoolmarmish bun.

She looked just like everyone else.

Millie's disappointment returned. Mrs. Candy was right. Love softened people. The edge that made Tory seem larger than life, one that Millie strove so hard to duplicate, was gone.

Tory glanced up from her ledger again, regarding her employee thoughtfully. "Anything wrong, Millie? You look as if you're a million miles away."

Millie chewed her lip in thought and set down the mop. "May I ask you a question, Tory?"

"Of course."

"How'd you know you were in love with Mr. Benjamin? I mean, really, truly in love?"

When Tory hesitated, Millie blurted, "I only ask on account of there's this certain fellow I sort of like, but everyone says I could do better."

Tory thought for a moment, trying to remember what it was like to be eighteen and unsure of herself. She found she couldn't remember being Millie's age at all.

"How do you feel when you're with him?" Tory asked.

Millie shrugged. "I don't know. He's got a really great sense of humor, and he's really smart. He wants to be an accountant."

"That's not what I asked, Millie. How does he make you feel about you?"

"Good, I guess." She smiled shyly. "Well, real good."

"Then what's the problem?"

"Well, it's just that he's sort of, well, short."

"Ah."

"But he's sweet, and he's got his own money," she blurted. "He's saving to buy a car. He wants to take me to the movies on Saturday night. Think I should go?"

Tory folded her hands in front of her. "Aside from the maybe car, you like him for who he is?"

"Sure, I do."

"Then I say go for it."

"Go for it." Millie pondered the words, her expression softening as she gazed across the street toward Grimley's Market.

Tory immediately remembered the shy boy with the blond crew cut stocking shelves on Saturday morning. He was short—five feet tall at most.

"Is it me or is it hotter than the devil in here?" Millie asked.

Tory hid a smile. "It's not you. How about running to Grimley's and getting us a couple of cream sodas?" She opened the register and pulled out a crisp one-dollar bill. Handing it to the awkward girl, she winked. "Take your time."

When Millie left, Tory turned her attention back to the ledger. The figures looked good. If nothing else, the previous week's debacle had boosted sales. If only they could keep that going. Her brow wrinkled. She needed to look into hiring another part-time girl. The strain was too much for Penny, who'd recently started napping in the afternoon.

She heard the bell and glanced up as a woman in a tweed skirt and matching jacket entered the store. Her brown hair was swept into a beehive without a bobby pin out of place.

Tory smiled. She was the type they liked to encourage, well dressed in the kind of clothes that said their owner had money and wasn't afraid to spend it.

"Is there something I can help you find?" she asked brightly.

The woman gave Tory an odd smile. Saying nothing, she turned and sauntered down the aisle labeled *Romance*.

Tory shrugged and turned her attention back to the ledger. When she glanced up again, the woman stood in front of the counter. As she stared at Tory, her strange smile seemed painted on her lips.

Tory shivered unaccountably. The woman's eyes seemed to look inside her.

"Something I can help you find?" she repeated.

"I'm looking for a story, a certain story."

"Yes?"

"Yes."

"If you'll tell me the name, or something about it," Tory said, mildly irritated, "I'll be glad to help you look."

The woman hesitated and gave Tory a piercing stare. "It's about a girl who finds herself trapped in a storybook. Would you know anything about that?"

Tory shivered again. The woman made her uncomfortable. Why was she staring at her like that? "I'm sorry. I don't think we have anything on that order."

"She's involved in a dreadful automobile accident and awakens to find herself in a strange new world. You wouldn't know anything about that?"

The statement struck a chord. The flesh on Tory's arms prickled. "Who are you?" she whispered.

The woman smiled again. "You might say she's a captive of destiny."

A thousand fragmented images exploded in Tory's mind—a rainy night, a car accident, a drunken poet. She began shaking. "Destiny?"

"Exactly."

"Th—this girl," she stammered. "Does she ever find her way out?"

The woman laughed. "She could, if she really wanted to."

Tory swallowed. "What's the way out?"

"The same way any character leaves any story. It's quite simple, really. The way out's the same as the way in."

"What does that mean?"

She laughed again. "The way in is the way out."

"Please. I don't understand."

The woman cocked her head to one side as if listening intently. Her smile vanished. "I must go now."

"Wait!" Tory scrambled around the corner after the fleeing woman. She raced to the porch. "Please, wait!"

The woman continued down the sidewalk without looking back. A sudden blinding light split the sky. Tory stared in disbelief, as the woman disappeared as if she'd been erased.

Moments later, Millie bounded onto the porch bearing two bottles of cream soda. "Some crazy weather," she chirped. "Did you hear that thunder just now?"

Tory whirled to face her. "Millie, I have to go."

Millie's grin faded. She set down the bottles. "Say, you don't look so good. You sick or something?"

Tory took both Millie's hands in hers and squeezed them. "Say good-bye to Penny for me, will you?"

"Sure, Tory."

"Take care of her, will you?"

"Aren't you coming in tomorrow?"

"No." She choked back tears. "Be good to yourself, Millie."

Millie clutched Tory's hands, her impish face etched with concern. "You're scaring me, Tory. You make it sound like you aren't ever coming back."

Tory shook her head and hurried from the porch, racing to Penny's car and pretending not to hear Millie calling after her.

She drove up the mountain road, her foot heavy on the gas pedal. Scenery rushed past her window, surreal in its beauty, as if she'd stepped into a painting. A sense of *déjà vu* overcame her. She'd felt that way before, but when?

Concentrate, she told herself.

The memory returned in pieces. There was a dream, a car wreck and an image of herself wandering in the forest, cold and frightened.

A chill went down her spine as realization dawned.

This was where she came in.

The way in is the way out.

She pondered the words. That was the road that brought her into the fairytale. If the woman was speaking literally, the road should take her out, right?

"How, Destiny? How?"

"Victoria!"

Tory cried out in alarm as Destiny's voice came through the car radio.

"It's the same way any character leaves any story."

Tory's hands trembled on the wheel. Most characters left the way Destiny Paige had, through death.

"Victoria!"

"Stop talking in riddles," she shouted. "Say what you mean!"

"The way in is the way out."

"It was a dream, damn you, a dream!"

"Exactly."

The radio crackled violently and shorted out. Tory pressed a trembling hand to her lips, thinking about the dream.

She realized there were two, the one that plagued her for her entire life, and the new one. They were similar but not the same. What made them different?

Concentrate!

There was the forest, the rain, the old men and the voices. Something wasn't right. Her heart beat furiously as she forced the image into focus, then she gasped.

It wasn't old men. It was tombstones.

She thundered up the hill, suddenly driven by a demonic fear that she was running out of time. Her foot went down harder on the accelerator. The way in was the way out. There were two dreams, two answers to the riddle. Both seemed to lay in the graveyard.

Chapter Five

He had to wait until the conditions were optimum. The ground had to be dry, while the wind, gusting, shouldn't be too strong. He had to wait until the confusion died down and forgot about him. Waiting was the hard part. After that, it was easy.

The Frazier wound its way up the mountain road, gliding over the crest of the hill and down the other side with the radio playing softly. Pierce hummed along, not really hearing.

He had to start at the bottom of the hill, not too far down, and not on the side that faced the city. Too many people would see, and then he might not get a chance to finish. Finishing was important, especially when there was a score to settle.

Three-quarters of the way down the hill, the Frazier pulled off the road and into a grove of trees. Pierce got out, retrieved the cans of gasoline from the trunk, and continued on foot. Dry leaves crunched underfoot as he walked, making him smile.

He had to start on the opposite side of the hill, about half a mile up. Fire moved like a hungry demon up a steep, wooded hillside, especially when the wind was right. The demon raged as it grew hotter until the whole forest became its feast.

He shaded his eyes with his hand as he regarded the landscape. If he started halfway up, he could cover a lot of territory quickly, but not too quickly. He needed to reach the top of the hill before the demon did, so he could finish the job. He needed to settle the score.

•

Something was happening. Jake set down his axe and raised questioning eyes to the sky. The mountain was eerily still. There was no bird song, chatter or animal scuffle in the trees—nothing at all.

He closed his eyes, listening, clearing his mind and slowing his breathing until he reached a state of oneness with the forest. A muffled sound came to him. It was mournful, like a hundred women weeping.

The weeping grew to a moan. He took a lung full of air and slowly released it. The mountain's heartbeat pulsed at his feet. It skipped a beat, and icy fear crept into Jake's chest. An enemy was in the forest.

"Shake a leg, Soldier!"

He turned. An apparition appeared in the trees. A daytime nightmare, it played out like a dance macabre before his eyes. He stood, rooted to the ground, eyes wide with terror, watching ghosts.

"Shake a leg, Soldier! We've got work to do."

The South Pacific sun glared down around him. The air was wet, perspiring with disease.

"You take his feet, Private. I'll take his head, what's left of it."

He fought a wave of nausea as together, he and the corporal loaded the blackened, bloated bodies into the waiting ship. Burial at sea was kinder than leaving his comrades here for the enemy to find and mutilate. He tried not to look at their faces or listen to the dull clink as he clipped their dog tags from around their necks, dropping them into his canvas bag to identify the men later. Despite his efforts, their faces rose up, grotesque and accusing, shouting, "It should've been you!"

He shook his head. "No," he whispered.

Immobilized by fear, he stood as the earth convulsed under his feet. All around him, tall, proud trees wailed in pain. He opened his mouth to scream but managed only a hoarse whisper.

The enemy closed in, filling his nostrils with its stench. It was an enemy he knew well. Its chief weapon was terror, and its spoils were sorrow and despair. Its name was Death.

•

Tory pulled off onto the side of the road and scrambled down the steep embankment. She stumbled over a tree root, regained her footing and raced on.

She reached the graveyard within moments. Breathlessly, her lungs grabbed for air. She cast frantic glances left and right. Something was wrong.

Though it was barely noon, the sky had grown dark. The air had a hazy, dreamlike quality. Her eyes swept over the moss-covered headstones that jutted from the ground at crooked angles, shoulder-to-shoulder, as if conferring like attorneys—or like wise old men.

The good-earth scent of burning twigs and the undertone of voices came to her as if someone were having a campfire nearby. In the trees on the other side of the graveyard she saw a faint, red glow. Inclining her head, she listened carefully.

The voices reached her again, low and murmuring. She followed them to the edge of the clearing. With trembling hands, she parted the branches and peered through.

She didn't notice the men at first. Her eyes were drawn to the throbbing, red light. It swept across the hillside, cutting like a beacon through the hazy air. She stepped closer, drawn by its hypnotic pulsing, and saw it was connected to an ambulance.

She gasped.

The light reached down from the road above, painting everything it touched with an eerie red glow. It lingered for a moment on a pile of wreckage in the trees before retreating back up the hillside. Tory squinted at the twisted mass of metal, her eyes flying wide with horror.

"No." She took a step back. "Oh, please, Destiny. There's got to be another way."

Feet away from the wreckage, two men knelt over a woman's body, their faces glowing red in the steady strobe of light. One man pounded on the woman's chest while the other breathed into her mouth. The woman's hand bent at an awkward angle as if beckoning. Light reflected off a silver band on her finger, identical to the one Tory wore.

"Who are you?" she screamed.

The men didn't acknowledge her. They continued their work, their devil-faces etched with determination, their movements as rhythmical as the light pulsing around them, red, red, silver and red.

Suddenly, one of the men sat back on his heels. Glancing around, he shivered. "Let's call it a night, Don. I got a real bad feeling about this."

"Keep trying!" the other man barked.

"Who are you?" Tory shouted.

"Keep trying!" The man pounded fiercely on the woman's chest. "We're losing her!"

As Tory drew nearer to the men, a sense of exhaustion overcame her. She stumbled, grabbing onto a nearby tree to steady herself. She was dizzy and tired all at once, barely able to keep her eyes open.

She tried in vain to get the man's attention. Why wouldn't he answer or look at her?

"Who are you?" she murmured.

Her head spun. Lord, she was tired. If only she could lie down a moment.

Trance-like, she walked toward the men, stumbling and falling again. The ground was soft and cool under her feverish brow. She closed her eyes.

"Wait a minute. I'm getting a pulse."

Her eyes fluttered open. The man discovered her at last. He knelt above her, his eyes filled with concern, speaking in a soothing, kind voice.

•

"Stay with me, Darlin." He took her hand. "Just stay with me now."

At the sound of his voice, terrifying blackness engulfed her. She spun head over heels as if falling upward through a tunnel. The man's voice faded and other voices vied for her attention, echoing around her in the tunnel, screaming, *Jake! Jake! Jake!*

"Jake?" she asked groggily.

A furious wind lifted her, propelling her back through the tunnel. Insistent shouting broke through her lethargy, and she struggled to her feet.

The smoky smell was stronger, almost acrid. She'd been wrong about the campfire. Where was that awful odor coming from? She gazed around, confused and disoriented.

Then she let out a blood-curdling scream—the entire hillside was swallowed in flames.

The men didn't seem to care and resumed work on the woman.

"Damn it! We're losing her again."

Tory turned and fled through the trees, one thought dominating her senses. Jake was in danger.

She stumbled through the woods in panic, trying to remember where he'd be working that day. She choked on a sob, remembering how he kissed her that morning before she left, telling her to be careful.

Oh, Jake. Oh, God. Oh, God, she thought.

Smoke enveloped her as she tore through the hillside. The trees reached toward her, seeking comfort. She heard the terrible sound of timber exploding around her.

In the midst of her nightmare, she heard someone call her name. Turning for a backward glance, she ran headlong into a tree. The collision threw her off balance and sent her sprawling.

She sat for a moment, dazed. Then two strong arms encircled her waist and lifted her to her feet. She collapsed against his rock-hard chest.

"Jake. Thank God. I thought you'd—"

She raised her eyes, the words dying on her lips as she stared into the face of Pierce Matthews.

He smiled. "What's your hurry?"

His demeanor was cool, strangely calm, but his grip on her waist was vise-like. She struggled to free herself.

"Let me go, you fool! Can't you see the forest is on fire?"

•

He threw back his head, wicked laughter ringing from his lips. When he turned his eyes on her again, she saw they burned with a mixture of excitement, cruelty and something else, something inhuman.

"Let go of me!" she shrieked.

"Never," he hissed.

The coldness in his eyes made her shiver despite the heat raging around her. She clawed at his arms as he dragged her down the path. The effort was too much for her. She went limp, then was spinning again.

When he saw the fight go out of her, Pierce hoisted her over his shoulder and carried her. The smoke was viscid as they ascended the mountain path. It burned Tory's eyes and choked the breath from her lungs.

She took a desperate gulp of oxygen and shouted Jake's name.

Pierce laughed, slapping her rump. "Don't worry. You'll be together soon enough."

That reawoke her rage. She focused on the taut muscle inches from her face, changed position and sank her teeth into it.

Pierce howled and threw her to the ground. "Witch! You little witch!"

He drew back his fist and hit her. Pain exploded in her head. He tore a strip of cloth from his shirt and tied it snugly around her mouth, then they were moving again. She faded in and out of consciousness, lulled by the swaying motion of his body.

When it stopped, she forced her eyes open. "No," she moaned.

Her cabin was on fire. Wisps of smoke curled from the rooftop, floating to the sky like dark angels. All around the cabin, angry red flames raged in the trees. She began her futile struggle again, but Pierce held her fast.

He hauled her across the yard and up the front steps. The rocking chairs tossed crazily on the porch as they passed. She tried to grab a porch post but couldn't control her hands.

Pierce, kicking open the door, carried her inside the house. Panting, he laid her on the floor and laced his fingers around her neck.

His smile was dazzling white in contrast to the grayish air. She heard the sound of wicked laughter and labored breathing, followed by a strangled scream.

Everything went black.

•

Jake drove until the road was impassable, then got out of the truck, dropped to his knees and crawled. Clawing his way through the inferno, he felt his eyes burning and his lungs screaming for air.

He heard a thunderous explosion as his truck ignited and blew up. Instinctively, he shielded his head against flying debris. All around him, apocalypse raged. The sky was dark as pitch. The forest was an angry ball of flames.

He battled his way through the destruction, propelled onward by fear and the undeniable feeling Tory was in danger. He stopped intermittently. His battered lungs were torn by violent fits of coughing. His teeth felt gritty and his throat was coated with soot.

He tore a sleeve from his shirt, tied it around his mouth and nose, and forged ahead. Terrorized animals skittered over his hands and feet in their frenzied attempts at escape.

He followed their lead to the end of the footpath, and then became disoriented. He glanced around in panic. There were no familiar landmarks to guide his way. He choked back a scream. For the first time in his life, Jake Benjamin was out of synch with the land. He was lost and out of control.

For the first time, the forest couldn't help him.

Fighting a rising tide of hysteria, he drew a ragged lung full of air and screamed Tory's name.

Far above the roar of burning timber, he heard an answering cry. Shading his burning eyes, he peered that way. In the distance was a faint outline against the smoke-filled sky.

He squinted, unable to believe what he saw. A murder of shrieking crows circled in the distance, showing him the way.

•

The ceiling was giving way. Pierce Matthews was a madman.

Those two things Tory knew for certain. Everything else was hazy. Her fevered brain registered smoke and flames. Pierce stood in the center of the room, dousing the walls with gasoline, his face demonic in the light of the rising flames.

He stood transfixed, chanting nonsense as the flames raced across the walls. His chanting was broken by intermittent, maniacal laughter. Fire licked greedily at the seasoned pine, its insatiable hunger fueled by gasoline.

Do something! a voice shrieked in her head. *Do something now!*

All she could do was watch, numb with horror and disbelief, as Pierce bowed low to worship the fire.

Flames raced upward and ignited the weakened ceiling joists, but Pierce didn't seem to notice. Tory fought to drag herself from the burning house but found she couldn't move her legs. Her hoarse screams were interrupted by a fit of coughing.

The sound pulled Pierce from his trance. He whirled to face her, his expression of worship turned to one of rage.

"Interferer!" Spittle flew from his mouth. "Frustrator of the holy ordinance! Hindrance to all that must be!" He lifted the can of gasoline and shook it at her. "We'll defeat you! That which must be, shall be!"

As he advanced toward her, the ceiling beam above his head gave way. He tumbled backward and disappeared beneath the burning debris. A high-pitched wail shook the house. Flames danced across his body, flaring upward as if growing from his chest until the whole room was bathed in their violent orange glow.

Demonic faces tormented Tory from the flames. She screamed in terror, then mercifully fell into darkness.

•

Jake fought his way through the burning forest, his eyes focused on the dark figures circling in the distance. He was almost there.

He broke into a trot when the cabin came into view. Just as he reached the porch, a large portion of the roof collapsed. An animal scream rose from his chest. The crows picked it up, formed a black arrow in the sky and carried it to the heavens.

Jake hurled himself through the open door. The inferno's heat shoved him back. He clawed his way inside, casting panicked glances through the smoke-filled air. Fear slashed at his insides repeatedly as he shouted Tory's name. She had to be there.

Faintly, above the roar of burning timber, he heard his name come back to him. Squinting in that direction, his watering eyes could barely see. Through the smoke, he saw a body huddled in a corner. He dropped to his hands and knees to crawl toward it, his heart thudding in his chest. As he drew closer, he saw a beautiful, angelic face framed by a halo of spun gold.

"Tory!" He lunged and pulled her limp body close to his. Shielding her face in the crook of his arm, he carried her from the conflagration.

He was almost outside when again someone called his name. He carried Tory a safe distance from the cabin and gently set her down. His work-roughened hands searched frantically for a pulse. Satisfied she was still alive, he turned and fought his way back inside.

"Jake, help me!"

The voice was strange, neither male nor female. He cast a quick glance outside. The smoke was dangerously thick, as the fire closed in around the cabin.

"Where are you?"

"Over here. Hurry!"

He battled his way across the room until he found a body buried in the wreckage of the collapsed ceiling. Jake stared in revulsion at the figure. As near as he could tell, it was a man. A smoldering shirt was open in the front, revealing raw patches of skin pulling away from a pulpy mass that had once been a chest. The man's face was charred beyond recognition.

Jake choked back a wave of nausea. He'd seen worse, but not by much.

"Help me, Jake. Please." The man extended a blackened hand.

Gritting his teeth, Jake grasped the hand, finding the burned flesh strangely cool to his touch. Instinct made him jerk his hand away, but the skeletal fingers tightened their grip. The sound of maniacal laughter filled the air.

Jake watched in horror as new flesh grew on the man's hands. It crawled up the ruined chest and the sinewy neck, creeping across the cheekbones until it formed a face.

Seconds later, he stared into Pierce Matthew's eyes, dark and burning with hatred. Evil laughter rang through the house as Pierce slowly pulled Jake into the flames.

With the strength born of fury, Jake grasped Pierce's hand and gave it a violent backward twist. As the hand broke off at the wrist, Pierce's laughter turned into an anguished scream.

A pool of thick, black blood flowed from the stump.

The stench of death filled Jake's nostrils.

Pierce's eyes fluttered closed, as his head dropped to his shoulder. The evil smile on his lips widened until it formed a grotesque O.

While Jake watched, a black dove emerged from the opening. It ascended upward into the flames with a blood-chilling shriek. Jake turned and fled in terror. Racing across the yard to where Tory lay, he gathered her hastily in his arms and stumbled across the clearing.

Fire raging across the mountain began its ascent down the other side. He was racing against time. Within moments, the entire forest would be sealed off by a wall of flame. He fought his way back down the path, desperate to reach the one place that offered shelter.

The river.

•

She was dreaming again.

A dozen sensations crowded her senses. She floated downstream, water lapping at her thighs. She was safe, cradled by strong arms, her head resting against a man's chest. She heard his ragged breathing, and his heart pounded furiously in her ear. She wasn't certain who he was, only that he loved her very much.

They were like driftwood, she thought groggily, she and the man, two branches intertwined, carried along or set adrift at the river's whim. She tried to open her eyes but found she couldn't.

She drifted deeper into the dream, lulled by the rocking motion of the man's body and the river's voice whispering in her ear a truth as old as time. The secret to life's journey lay not in struggling to reverse the tide but in not traveling it alone.

She wanted to tell that to the man, but she couldn't seem to speak. Abruptly, the river disappeared from underneath her. She felt a steady clip-clop rhythm as the man's feet pounded the dry earth.

When she forced her eyes open, fear tore through her. Her arms tightened around the man's neck. He was taking her to the graveyard.

"No," she moaned. "I don't want to go back there. Please. Don't take me back there."

The man didn't seem to hear. He raced across the clearing and set her down gently. Placing his fingers on her neck, he moved them from place to place, searching for a pulse. His anguished eyes searched her face and looked right through her.

Tear tracks glistened on his soot-stained cheeks.

"Jake," she whispered.

He lowered his mouth to hers like Prince Charming offering Sleeping Beauty the kiss of life. His breath was warm and his tears hot on her neck.

"Please, Tory," he whispered, "please don't leave me."

She tried to reassure him but couldn't speak, tried to hold him but couldn't control her hands. She felt herself slipping away, spiraling upward into the tunnel.

•

"She's back."

She opened her eyes again. A man knelt above her, light strobing across his face. "Good girl. Just stay with me, Darlin'. We're doing fine."

"Where's Jake?"

"She's responsive now. I think we're good to transport."

The man strapped her into a stretcher and lifted her into the air. A sense of vertigo overcame her. She closed her eyes, wishing she could sleep.

•

"Tory!"

Jake's hazy face was etched with despair. He took her shoulders and shook her roughly.

"You can't do this! You can't! You promised!"

Her tongue was thick and heavy in her mouth. "Who was that man?"

Sobs wracked his body as if he hadn't heard. "I can't make it without you, Tory. If I don't have you, I don't have anything."

His fingers lifted her hair again, searching frantically. He threw back his head and howled. She reached for his hand, desperate to offer comfort, but she couldn't find it. She couldn't seem to see anything at all. She was spinning wildly, shaken to the core of her being.

"Please," she murmured. "Make it stop."

Mercifully, it did.

•

When she opened her eyes again, she was in some sort of tomb that smelled strongly of antiseptic. Cool, white sheets shrouded her body, and her arms were bound at her sides. She heard two men speaking softly and looked around wildly for Jake.

He was gone.

All light disappeared from her life in the overwhelming emptiness of his absence. She thrashed wildly but couldn't move.

Terrified, she screamed. "Jake! Jake! Jake!"

The world spun out of control. Other voices joined hers, screaming his name—and once more, she plunged into the tunnel.

·

"Jake!"

"I've got you, Tory. I'm right here."

Strong arms lifted her from the tunnel. She spun violently as lights exploded in her head. A light rain misted her face. She laid her head against his chest, concentrated on the steady pounding of his heart and knew that it beat for her.

A siren wailed in the distance, and she clung to him in terror.

"They're coming for me. They're trying to take me away. Oh, Jake, don't let them take me from you."

"They're only fire trucks, Darlin." He smoothed her hair. "No one will ever take you away from me. I won't let them."

The heavens opened and drenched her in purifying rain, washing away all doubts. This was where she belonged.

"Hold me, Jake," she whispered. "I'm falling."

The wind whispered a gentle lullaby as the ravaged forest sizzled under the healing rain. Fire trucks screeched to a stop on the mountain road, and men shouted directions. A white dove circled in the sky overhead. Jake wrapped his arms around Tory and kept her from spinning off the edge of the world.

Epilogue
Beautiful Haven
May, 2005

The problem with Beautiful Haven was that it wasn't. Mark Lange shook his head. It's a misnomer, he thought, a sin to even call it that.

A haven was a place of safety and tranquility. A New England lighthouse was a beautiful haven. The thing he saw was a decrepit leftover from World War II, a cold, whitewashed building that squatted in the weeds on Mosely Street between a crack house and a burned-out laundromat. Outside were a lot of gray stone benches nobody used, while inside, a lot of used-up people nobody wanted.

Mark sighed. Next week, it would all be his. He wasn't complaining. Les Weatherby's cancer was a godsend.

Admittedly, geriatrics wasn't a likely first choice for a young, ambitious, top-of-his-class graduate of the University of Rochester. When Mark enrolled in pre-med, he dreamed of internal medicine or brain surgery. Then he met Mary Weatherby.

Six years later with a child and a quarter-of-a-million-dollar house in progress, Mark scrambled for the chance to take over his father-in-law's position as head physician in hell. Physician, heal thyself, he thought.

All things considered, the morning went better than expected. Steeling himself against the foul-food smell and lunatic shrieks of dementia, he trailed behind Les Weatherby, smiled reassuringly and looked at corns and pitting edema as he listened to bowel sounds and found pulses in people he wouldn't have believed were still alive.

By noon, they covered the entire first floor with only one room to go. Mark moved impatiently toward the door at the end of the corridor, wondering if the old man was up for eighteen holes.

Outside the door, Les placed a restraining hand on the young man's shoulder. "This one will bother you," he said.

Curiously, Mark followed the older man into the room.

It was markedly different from the others. Instead of the standard white, the walls were washed in soft adobe tones. Gargantuan bouquets adorned the tables and windowsills while candles flickered in glass cups.

A pretty young Latina sat opposite a wheelchair, visiting with the patient. She broke off her conversation when they entered, smiling at Dr. Weatherby.

"How are we doing today, Frankie?" Dr. Weatherby asked amiably.

The girl stood. "Her color's real good, Doctor."

"This is my son-in-law, Dr. Lange." He nodded to Mark. "I believe I mentioned he'd be taking over for me soon."

The girl's eyes went to Mark with unmistakable hostility. She squeezed the patient's shoulder in a protective gesture. "Nice to meet you," she mumbled.

As Frankie left the room, Mark circled in front of the patient. When he glanced at her, he did a double take. Sitting quietly beneath a lap robe, her sky-blue eyes staring at nothing, sat damned near the most beautiful woman he ever saw. He shot the older man a questioning glance, but Les was intent on the girl.

He dropped to a squat beside the chair, speaking soothingly. "Good morning, Victoria. Mind if we take your blood pressure today?"

She gave no indication she heard. Les fit the cuff around her upper arm, patting her shoulder with one hand while he pumped and released the rubber ball. After scribbling a note on her chart, he shone a scope into her eyes.

She didn't flinch.

Mark tore his eyes from her to give his father-in-law another questioning look. Les slowly stood.

"Victoria Sasser," he said, "thirty-three years old. The most baffling case in the history of this institution. You'll undoubtedly want to spend some time reviewing her file."

Mark waved a hand before the woman's eyes. "What happened to her?"

"She can't see or hear you. She's in a complete state of suspended animation."

"Fill me in."

Les made a final note to the chart and tucked it under his arm. "She received a blow to the head in an automobile accident six years ago. She lay in the rain for nearly an hour before she was discovered."

"Oxygen deprivation?"

Les shook his head. "She was breathing when the paramedics found her. Her heart stopped when they tried to transport, but they were able to resuscitate within seconds."

"Major cerebral trauma?"

"The air bag took the brunt of the hit. Scans revealed only slight trauma. Brain wave activity continues to be normal."

"There's got to be something, Les."

"Nothing medical. Regional gave up on her a year ago. That's why she's here." He patted the girl's shoulder. "There's simply no medical reason for her trance-like state."

"There must be," Mark insisted.

The other man regarded him carefully. "Spiritualists believe under extreme duress, the soul withdraws from the body and finds a kinder place to inhabit. I believe that's what happened to her. It's as if she hovers on the brink of consciousness. For reasons of her own, she refuses to return. In the six years since the accident, she spoke only one word—Jake."

Mark shook his head. "What can we do?"

"As medical doctors, absolutely nothing. As human beings, we make her comfortable and be here for her in the event she someday breaks through. The rest is up to her." He stroked her hair and let his hand fall away. "Ready for lunch?"

"Give me ten minutes. I'd like to speak with her friend."

Moments later, the young Latina returned.

"Doctor Weatherby said you wanted to speak with me?"

Mark caught the resentment in her tone and donned his best bedside manner. "I'd like to talk to you about Victoria. Do you know her well?"

Frankie shrugged. "I used to."

Mark leaned against the wall. "What can you tell me about her?"

The girl's tone softened. "She's a beautiful person, inside and out. Classy, but not arrogant, you know? She'll come out of this. She's tougher than she looks."

Mark gestured toward the silver band on the woman's finger. "Is she married?"

"No. That was her mother's. She loves that ring. She wore it since the day her mother died."

"Who's Jake?"

Frankie shrugged again. "Couldn't be anyone important. Nobody comes around anymore. Nobody does, except me. I'll never give up on her."

"She's fortunate to have such a devoted friend."

"I didn't do her no favors coming into her life. If it wasn't for me, she wouldn't be like this."

"Why do you say that?"

"Tory helped me put my life together. I messed it up again. She wouldn't have been out in that storm, except she was coming to help me." She blinked back tears. "I owe her. I'll never give up on her. Ever."

Mark squatted beside the chair and took the patient's hand in his. Her skin was pale and as soft as an infant's. He'd always loved puzzles, and that case was a damned good one.

He glanced at Frankie and smiled. "Neither will I." Mark turned back to the China-doll face and stared into her bottomless blue eyes. "What goes on behind those pretty blue eyes, eh?" He clasped her hand. "Where are you, Victoria?"

• • •

M. Jean Pike

Photo Credit: Sharon Burr

Abandoned buildings. Restless spirits. Love that lasts forever. These are a few of M. Jean Pike's favorite things. A professional writer since 1996, Ms. Pike combines a passion for romance with a keen interest in the supernatural to bring readers unforgettable stories of life, love and the inner workings of the human heart. She writes from her home on a quiet country road in upstate New York.

CAST IN STONE

BY KERRY A. JONES
ISBN: 978-0-9793252-2-9

He had waited seven hundred years to love her.
She was sworn to destroy him.

"Do I have a great book for you to read! ...a dazzling paranormal romance that will grab your attention from the first chapter straight through to the last... It's gothic and sexy! "

Romance Reader at Heart

"If the following books [in the Quinguard Immortals Series] are as good as the first, it will be an excellent series and a must-have for those who believe in soulmates. I for one will never look at gargoyles in quite the same way again."

Once Upon a Romance

"An extraordinary tale with memorable characters, a fresh premise and solid writing. Ms. Jones crafted a winner."

Paranormal Romance Reviews

"A riveting tale of love, lust, hate and magic... a must-buy!"

Romance at Heart Magazine

"...everything one could ask for in a paranormal romance - evil curses, ageless villains and compelling heroes - without falling back on the cliches that so many others rely upon."

Digigirl's Library of Paranormal Romance

"...a wonderful combination of fairytale archetypes, complete with a brave, beautiful heroine, strong, immortal hero, dark evil that must be stopped, and puzzles that must be solved. This paranormal romance is a wonderful story about the power of soul mates, and I give it the highest rating, a Best Book."

Long & Short Reviews

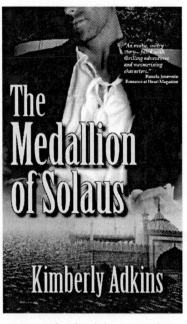

A lush, exotic
paranormal romance
by Kimberly Adkins
ISBN: 978-0-9793252-3-6

A Darkly Enchanted Artifact.

A Passion to Outlast the Centuries.

Solaus had but one wish of the medallion: to save his dying bride. But when he placed the pendant around his neck, his wish was changed by a malevolent twist of magic that made him Djinn, but also took away the knowledge of what he is and who he used to be. Flung from Ancient Persia into immortality, Solaus has only the memory that he did not save his true love—and nothing more as time begins to pass.

Eager for a fresh start, New York City photographer, Kaitlin Sommers accepts a rare assignment on a deserted island fortress off the coast of Alexandria, Egypt. Surrounded by the shadowy underworld of illegal treasure smuggling, Kaitlin finds herself in the arms of man who seems to spring directly from dreams of her past—a man Fate threatens to tear her away from a second time.

The Medallion of Solaus

"With the penning of this novel, Ms. Adkins is definitely on her way to being the ultimate paranormal princess... THE MEDALLION OF SOLAUS is the type of tale true love and legends are spun from—timeless and magically beautiful."
Paranormal Romance Reviews

Printed in the United States
219734BV00001B/12/A